GODZILLA™

BOOKS BY STEPHEN MOLSTAD

Independence Day
(with Dean Devlin and Roland Emmerich)

ID4: Silent Zone

Godzilla

Published by HarperPrism

ATTENTION: ORGANIZATIONS AND CORPORATIONS

Most HarperPrism books are available at special quantity discounts
for bulk purchases for sales promotions, premiums, or fund-raising.
For information, please call or write:
Special Markets Department, HarperCollins*Publishers,*
10 East 53rd Street, New York, NY 10022
Telephone: (212) 207-7528 Fax: (212) 207-7222

NOVELIZATION BY
STEPHEN MOLSTAD

BASED ON THE SCREENPLAY WRITTEN BY
DEAN DEVLIN
AND
ROLAND EMMERICH

HarperPrism
A Division of HarperCollinsPublishers

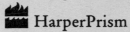

HarperPrism

A Division of HarperCollins*Publishers*
10 East 53rd Street, New York, NY 10022-5299

If you purchased this book without a cover, you should be aware that this book is stolen property. It was reported as "unsold and destroyed" to the publisher and neither the author nor the publisher has received any payment for this "stripped book."

This is a work of fiction. The characters, incidents, and dialogues are products of the author's imagination and are not to be construed as real. Any resemblance to actual events or persons, living or dead, is entirely coincidental.

Copyright © 1998 by TriStar Pictures, Inc.
All rights reserved.
No part of this book may be used or reproduced
in any manner whatsoever without written permission
of the publisher, except in the case of brief quotations
embodied in critical articles and reviews.
For information address HarperCollins*Publishers*,
10 East 53rd Street, New York, NY 10022-5299.

GODZILLA, BABY GODZILLA, and the GODZILLA
character design TM & © 1998 Toho Co., Ltd.

ISBN 0-06-105915-3

HarperCollins®, 🔥®, and HarperPrism®
are trademarks of HarperCollins*Publishers,* Inc.

Cover illustration and insert photos courtesy of
and © 1998 by TriStar Pictures, Inc.

First paperback edition: June 1998

Printed in the United States of America

For more information about GODZILLA, log onto the World
Wide Web at http://www.GODZILLA.com or at www.sony.com

Visit HarperPrism on the World Wide Web at
http://www.harperprism.com

❖ 10 9 8 7 6 5 4 3 2 1

For Little Bit

"It may be doubted whether there are many other animals in the world which have played so important a part in the history of the world."

—Charles Darwin

He was large.

He was huge, enormous, gigantic in a way that defied everything we thought we knew about the natural sciences. He was also the most terrifying thing I'd ever seen: a powerful and cunning predator who had grown to such a staggering size that even when I was directly between his feet, I could barely believe he existed. It's like that old saying: "Truth is stranger than fiction" (to which I would add "and science is stranger than truth"). When he emerged, so suddenly and without any warning, to take center stage in the world's imagination, it seemed as though one of humankind's most enduring and horrible nightmares had come to life. Ever since the biblical serpent caused our expulsion from the Garden of Eden, we've held a special type of fear and hatred in our hearts for all things reptilian. Prior to his appearance, we in the scientific community were absolutely convinced that no animal could grow so large. It was an accepted fact that the dinosaurs had pushed the envelope in terms of size and body weight. Any land animal that grew larger, our theory said, would collapse under its own weight, breaking its own spine, and be unable to do anything except lie on the ground and pant for air. Obviously, our theory was wrong.

I'm not a writer, but a scientist. I'm writing this book because, as far as I know, no one spent more time being "up close and personal" with the creature than I did. During the hectic days when this story was taking place, circumstance thrust me into a front-row seat. Some people think I was crazy for getting as close as I did; others consider me lucky to have seen all that I saw. Since I'm not sure which opinion is closer to the truth, I'll let you decide for yourself. If you're like most people in the world, you've already learned a great deal about the story by looking at newspapers, magazines, and television. Images of the monster are everywhere. (The other day I even saw a set of fuzzy children's slippers in the shape of the big lizard's clawed feet.) But I will try to take you beyond the images and headlines to offer you new information and an insider's perspective. Mainly I'll try to communicate a sense of what it was like to be there.

There's one other reason I'm writing this book before returning to my own research—and this one is more important. I want people to have a better understanding of the terrible danger we were in. Even though the situation looked spectacularly bad, it was actually much worse than it seemed. Humans found ourselves locked in a struggle for our very existence, the likes of which my hero, Charles Darwin, could never have imagined. Never before in the history of the earth has there been such a clear-cut case of two species fighting each other for their very lives. And what a battle it turned out to be.

And there's a good chance it's not over. If, as I believe, the creature was the result of exposure to high levels of nuclear radiation in and around the Tuamotu Island group, then his arrival in the world was not a freak accident. It was the logical consequence of our continued pollution of the earth's environment. If we continue with our present behavior (eating away at the ozone layer, overpopulating the planet, conducting nuclear test explosions, and so on), there is not just a chance, but a statistical probability we will face similar—or even worse—dangers in the near future. An ever-growing body of evidence suggests that we humans are paving the way to our own extinction by altering the ecosphere around us.

But I promised my editors I wouldn't turn this book into a pulpit from which to preach about environmentalism—something I'm prone to do at times. Instead I'm going to do my best to stick to the facts and tell you the story of what happened during that rain-drenched week in early summer when I went nose to nose with a five-hundred-ton lizard who stood taller than the Statue of Liberty.

This book is dedicated to all those poor souls who got even closer to Gojira than I did, and lost their lives in the process.

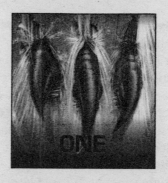

ONE

The precise origins of the creature are still a mystery and a source of heated debate among natural scientists. I recently drove down to Washington, D.C., and visited the National Historic Films Archive. The chief librarian there, Mr. Eric Johnson, led me to a series of short films that I believe give us important clues as to the creature's genesis. These films, shot on 16mm color film back in 1963, were made by a group of French nuclear scientists who had invaded a remote corner of paradise. They were conducting nuclear test explosions in Polynesia and had set up shop on the thirty-kilometer-long Moruroa Atoll. Moruroa is part of the Tuamotu group, a twelve-hundred-kilometer-long chain of low-lying coral atolls that looks like a long, rocky necklace half submerged in sparkling turquoise waters. For hundreds of thousands of years this archipelago was the undisturbed home to abundant populations of green sea turtles, banded iguanas, and exotic species of birds such as the cagou. Its crystal-clear lagoons teemed with brightly colored pelagic fish. Many of these species are now endangered thanks to the reckless antics of our French friends.

The grainy Kodak color films the scientists took have a home-movie feel to them. As the camera pans unevenly across the landscape one sees flocks of *Acridotheres tristis* perched in the pandanus trees. The birds look uneasy, on edge, as if they know what's coming. Then we see a tranquil, empty beach bathed in bright sunlight. It could be a scene from a travelogue or some footage distributed by the local chamber of commerce to promote tourism, except for the sinister sound of a man counting down in French.

"Quinze . . . quatorze . . . treize . . . douze . . ." An abrupt new camera angle puts us twenty-five thousand feet above sea level, looking down on the chain of islands stretching out seemingly to infinity, brilliant white specks shimmering between the blue of the ocean and the blue of the sky. *"Quatre . . . trois . . . deux . . . un . . . zéro!"*

The film jumps once and then the center of the screen burns to white as the atomic bomb detonates and spreads a massive, ring-shaped concussion across the area known as the Centre d'Expérimentation du Pacifique. A mushroom cloud slowly boils skyward as the men behind the camera casually discuss what they are witnessing. Everything is in French, but of course they must be saying things like *"Ooh-la-la, très bon"* and *"Sacrebleu"* and *"Quelle grande explosion!"*

One particular incident serves as an example of

the lax safety standards governing these tests. In September 1966 President Charles de Gaulle came to watch the explosion of an atomic bomb suspended in the air by a balloon. Weather conditions caused the test to be postponed, and on the next day conditions were still unsuitable. The winds were blowing straight toward Tahiti. With typical French arrogance, de Gaulle complained that he was a very busy man and ordered the engineers to proceed with the test. Radioactive fallout from the blast spread across the entire area, hitting populated areas, a fact the French deny to this day. Over the years these ecobarbarians conducted more than 175 such tests with varying degrees of disregard for the consequences of their actions.

Of course, I had known about Moruroa and its sister islands long before watching these old films—something I did only recently. The area is one of the must-see research destinations for people in my line of work, an environmental madhouse where imported species are quickly decimating the fragile native populations and radiation is affecting all forms of life. I'd been writing grant proposals and wheedling my bosses at the commission for several years to send me there so I could investigate the effects of all this atomic mayhem. Given what we now know, they should have sent me. Who knows, I might even have been able to stop this story before it ever got started. (Then again, I might have been gobbled up and disappeared without a trace.)

By themselves the films prove nothing. I haven't been able to find any direct evidence linking the creature to these radioactive islands. But ever since I watched those films I've been having this recurring vision, the same disturbing daydream. In it I find myself standing on a neighboring atoll in the moments before one of the explosions. I'm wearing a heavy, lead-lined suit to protect me from the fallout I know is coming. The suit is made of rubber and forces me to walk around clumsily, like the villain in some old-time horror movie. All around me life on the island innocently continues: graceful *Phaëton rubricaudas* return to shore with small fish in their beaks; marine iguanas splash out of the water and congregate on the sun-drenched rocks, staring out to sea with the patience of baking statues. Turtles crawl up the beach looking for snacks. I plod among them awkwardly, invisible in my heavy gray suit, watching the scene through the small rectangular frame of glass built into my helmet. When the explosion comes, all the animals dart into hiding places or take to the sky. When the blinding light is over and the delicate flakes of radioactive ash begin sifting down like a gray, desiccated snowstorm, I wander further inland until I find something hidden in the tall grass. It is a nest filled with lizard eggs. I bend down for a closer look and, as gingerly as possible, use the suit's bulky glove to uncover a few of them, clearing away the moist impasto of ferns and regurgitated insects left by the parent. I imagine that one of the eggs moves slightly, as if struggling to flee from the skin-burning poison raining down on it.

In the daydream I wish that I could protect this defenseless little creature, a simple animal with no expectations for his life beyond scampering around in search of food and, eventually, leaving behind some offspring of his own. "Poor little lizard," I say to myself, realizing the animal inside the egg will probably die or come out deformed.

Because I was conscripted by the U.S. Army to help in the hunt for the animal, I was given access to several hours of videotape footage that document his first, disastrous encounter with humans. These videotapes were recovered from the *Kobayashi Maru* by the U.S. Navy's Deep-Sea Salvage Unit.

At shortly after 11 P.M. the *Kobayashi Maru* was in international waters in the Pacific Ocean, between the Tuamotu Archipelago and the Marquesas Islands. It was floating peacefully despite the fact that there was a giant typhoon raging outside. The ship's instrumentation recorded ninety-mile-per-hour winds that were shredding the twelve-foot waves outside into so much spindrift. But the *Kobayashi* was large—one of those floating fish factories where the bounty of the sea is caught, cleaned, and "quick-frozen for freshness." If you've never been aboard or at least seen one of these vessels, it's hard to fathom just how very immense they are. Think of a three-story factory building that takes up an entire city block. These ships are ten times longer, ten times wider, and ten times as tall. Big and heavy enough, at any rate, that the four hundred crew members felt next to nothing of a tropical storm that was wreaking havoc on large parts of the hemisphere.

Although it's not really part of the story, I'd like to add a quick note here. Of course I feel terrible about what happened to the *Kobayashi* that dark and stormy night. But I'm not sorry Japan is minus one of her supertrawlers. These monster-sized boats gobble up and deplete the globe's fish populations at a frightening rate with their vast nets, often also killing whole colonies of dolphins, which swim along with the tuna schools. The endless container rooms of these vessels can hold up to *ten million tons* of fish—a good place to work, I suppose, if you enjoy sushi.

The *Kobayashi*'s skipper was on the bridge when the trouble started. He had his feet up on the million-dollar instrument console that was actually steering the ship and he was watching a snowy broadcast of *Sumo Digest* on the television. If you've never watched sumo yourself, you should. It's more than just a couple of fat men in diapers battering each other with their stomachs. It's actually a very graceful and exciting sport.

Like many of the sailors belowdecks, the skipper was glued to his television set. The most anticipated bout of the evening pitted crafty little Tanaka against the unbelievably huge, towering figure of

Akebono. When the smaller, underdog wrestler tossed the blubbery giant out of the ring with an armlock throw, the skipper shot out of his seat, threw his arms in the air, and cheered. He was so excited he reached for the handset of the intercom and was about to make a general announcement to the rest of the ship when his eyes fell on the main sonar screen.

His smile changed to a concerned frown. What he saw on the electronic display was impossible. He quickly made a series of adjustments to the equipment but failed to make the problem go away. His eyes narrowed as something abnormally large blipped under the sweeping arm of the sonar. Something enormous was in the water, and it was headed straight for the *Kobayashi Maru*. Before the skipper could move, a loud automatic warning buzzer sounded, filling the bridge with a harsh honking noise. He punched one of the buttons on the console and spoke into the microphone.

"*Sencho, hijojitai desu*—Captain, there's an emergency!"

Alarms erupted through the entire ship. Sailors poured into the narrow hallways and raced toward their stations. In the kitchen, the ship's chief cook stepped through a bulkhead holding a butcher knife. He was an older, heavyset man with a long, scraggly mustache and fresh blood on the front of his apron.

"*Nani goto da?*" he demanded. But the members of the crew knew better than to stop and chat during an emergency call. The omnipresent video cameras were rolling, and the company was always ready to dock an undisciplined sailor's pay. The videotapes, since recovered from the *Kobayashi*'s black box, show the cook shouting angrily at the men, waving his knife over their heads and threatening them with inedible food for the rest of the voyage if they wouldn't stop and tell an old man what was happening. A second later his question was answered.

An enormous thud slammed through the ship, jolting the entire vessel. Everything—crew members, cook, every pot and pan in the kitchen—crashed to the floor at once. Then the sirens suddenly shut down, leaving the men in an eerie silence. The loudest sound was the breathing of the seamen. The overhead lights flickered, died, then came on again. Although it was impossible, it seemed as if they could hear the deep, dark water of the Pacific sloshing against the sides of the ship

"Nan da are wa?" someone asked.

"Hoka no hune ni sesshoku shitanoka—maybe we rammed into another ship?" another one asked.

"Let's *hope* that's all it is," the cook said. He had an ugly feeling in the pit of his stomach, a feeling that the ship would not survive this strange encounter (at least this is what he would claim later). As the sailors hurried away, he retreated to the imaginary safety of his kitchen and began absentmindedly gathering whatever food was closest at hand. He was stuffing onions into the pockets of his apron when there came another huge thud.

Once again the old man was knocked to the floor by the sudden, terrifying impact. It was no ship that was battering them, he knew. He stumbled out of the kitchen and was trotting down the passageway when the ship was hit for a third time. Instead of a dull thud, this time there was a quick explosionlike noise followed by an earsplitting squeal that was worse than fingernails dragging across a chalkboard. When he looked behind him he saw exactly how much worse.

Three curved spikes had penetrated the *Kobayashi*'s hull and were shredding the steel walls as though they were made of balsa wood. Each one was over six feet long, and there was no mistaking them for anything except what they were: the talons of an enormous, incredibly powerful animal. Water gushed in through the holes left by the claws, creating a flash flood in the hallway.

As the panic-crazed cook reached the stairway, the water was already surging up to his knees and rising at a foot per second. Though old and out of shape, the cook had enough adrenaline pumping through his system that he should have been able to reach the top of the stairs and close the hatch behind him—if only the ship hadn't started rolling onto its side. He was near the top of the stairs when his feet slipped out from under him and he crashed against the iron side rails.

Hanging on for dear life, he looked back and saw the claws still moving toward him, sailing like three peaked ships through the gray metal. Before they reached him, the rising water level shorted out the lights.

By that time the *Kobayashi*'s captain had come upstairs to take command of the bridge. But there wasn't much he could do. The sonar display showed him that an unidentified swimming object had struck them on their starboard flank. *"Sensuikan ni chigainai,"* he said to his skipper, who shook his head in disagreement. *"Sensuikan ni chigainai*—it must be a submarine," he said again and again, trying to convince himself despite the evidence in front of his eyes. The object on the screen was as large as a skyscraper, but it seemed to be thrashing!

With the boat listing dangerously to one side, the captain ordered his skipper to override the computer system and throw the ship into full reverse. A moment later the engines growled and the boat jerked backward. Both men were thrown toward the front wall of the bridge, and the attack—by that point they knew it was an attack—came to a temporary halt.

A check of the sonar screen showed that the shape in the water was gone, suddenly vanished. Moving to the controls, the captain scanned the ocean in all directions. Whatever had torn open the side of the *Kobayashi* had disappeared as mysteriously as it had appeared. The big ship righted itself in the water and everything became quiet again. There was the sound of the rain hitting the front windows, the squeak of the wiper blades, and a calm, cool, computerized voice telling them in

Japanese that water was continuing to flood into certain sectors of the ship. The craft had sustained extensive damage but was still a long way from sinking.

Then, through the noise of the storm raging beyond the plate-glass windows, the captain heard a telltale sound, a plaintive, screeching wail that sounded at once both otherworldly and distinctly familiar. *"Sensuikan ni chigainai,"* he pleaded, although by then he'd given up any real hope the crisis could be explained away so easily. Besides, submarines don't howl. He moved to the front of the cabin, pressed his nose to the window, and cupped his hands around his eyes to block the light behind him. Each time the wipers stroked by, he caught a split-second glimpse of the foredeck. Sky and sea were a uniform black mass under the sheeting, wind-whipped rain. Nevertheless, the captain thought he saw something moving in the distance. He was about to mention this fact to his skipper when they both heard the same forlorn wail again. This time it was loud, close by. They looked at each other, alarmed, almost as if they recognized the sound. The captain turned back to the window just in time to see something huge moving toward them. By the time he recognized what it was, it was too late—it had smashed down through the roof of the bridge, killing them both instantly.

● ● ●

That's where I came into the picture. My own windshield wipers were squeaking back and forth across the window of the van I was driving, but they were so old they merely rearranged the water streaming down outside. The engine kept stalling out, and of course neither the radio nor the cassette player worked at all. I was driving along a rutted road through a gray, highly polluted landscape that was desolate even at the height of summer. Ah, the splendors of Ukraine, heartland of the former Soviet Union!

I swerved just in time to avoid a roadblock marked with various international warning signs: NUCLEAR RADIATION and NO TRESPASSING. Squinting through the blurred window, I could see the rusting hulk of the damaged Chernobyl nuclear power plant looming straight ahead. I was driving to the very center of the worst *accidentally* radiation-contaminated site on earth. I pulled off the utility road into a muddy field of dead crabgrass and stepped out into the elements.

One look at the withered, diseased landscape surrounding the Chernobyl site is enough to convince any sane, impartial observer that radiation is some seriously nasty stuff. Only a few stunted trees punctuated the dreary, lifeless valley. Clearly, we are not ready, technologically or intellectually, to be using this method of power generation. This holds especially true in a place such as the former Soviet Union, where quality workmanship went out of style with the tsars.

Nevertheless I was in high spirits. Splashing to the rear of the van, I began hauling out my equipment, all of it clearly labeled with big yellow stickers that identified my employer: NUCLEAR REGULATORY COMMISSION. The sight of those stickers on my belongings never failed to give me a jolt, a reality check. I'm not going to bore you with my whole life story, but every time I saw those boldly printed words I had to shake my head in disbelief. How did a campus crusader for environmental issues like myself end up working for the biggest, baddest wolf in the ecological forest? Most NRC employees, people who have the facts and should know better, actually believe that nuclear energy is a *good* thing, in spite of the fact that we still haven't figured out what to do with the spent plutonium. Little did my coworkers suspect that it was my ultimate goal to bring the entire nuclear industry to its knees. And that is why I was out there on that intemperate afternoon. I was hunting for the evidence I needed.

I grabbed my conducting rods and speared them into the earth in a big circle, then popped open the hood of the van and hooked them up to the van's battery. *Bzzt!* I made a face and shook the electric tingle-burn out of my right hand. I'd been so busy singing, I'd forgotten I was standing in a puddle. Working more carefully, I attached the cable to the positive terminal, then jogged back to the circle of rods and dropped to my knees to watch the magic happen.

Almost immediately they came wriggling up to

the surface: earthworms, terrestrial annelids of the class Oligochaeta and the family Lumbricidae. They were the reason I had endured three years of struggle with the post-Soviet bureaucracy. I was there to collect specimens of these creatures living at the epicenter of the contamination caused by the Chernobyl accident back in '86. They came to the surface by the handful, racing to escape the electrical charge of the conducting rods. I watched their segmented bodies squirming like so many hermaphroditic Gene Kellys—minus raincoats and umbrellas—and felt compelled to sing.

With a terpsichorean grace of my own, I waltzed to my kit box and lifted the lid. As I fell to one knee and reached dramatically for a glass specimen jar, I saw something that yanked most of the sunshine out of my heart: Audrey. Beautiful Audrey, my darling earthbound angel, staring up at me with that impish grin of hers. She'd been my college sweetheart and—I might as well admit it— the only woman I'd ever truly loved. It had been a long time, eight years, since I'd seen her in person, and I wondered about keeping those photos of her taped to the inside of the kit. At what point does enduring love turn into an inability to let go of the past?

Oh, Audrey! I bit my lip the way she was doing in one of the photos and wished she could have been there with me at that moment. I sensed that I was on the verge of making a breakthrough discovery and would have liked very much for her to witness my moment of personal triumph. But then I remembered why we'd gone our separate ways. Or perhaps I should say why I *thought* we'd gone our separate ways, since I never actually got the chance to ask her. Unlike me, she found no particular fascination in things that slithered, crawled, and carried their sex organs in their heads. *Groady, repulsive,* and *icky* were all words she'd used at one time or another to describe my research. I glanced up at the dirty, wet landscape and the oppressive dome of the rusting reactor. *Nope,* I told myself, *Audrey definitely wouldn't like it here.* I took a deep breath and forced myself to sing. I wasn't going to let anything ruin this day for me. Turning my attention back to the dancing worms, I started depositing them one by one into my sample jars.

> *I'm singin' in the mud,*
> *just scooping up my worms,*
> *You'll be sliced up in the lab,*
> *not eaten by birds.*

They were huge, positively titanic. Some stretched out to an awe-inspiring thirteen inches. Can you imagine that? Earthworms twelve and thirteen inches long? This highly abnormal finding, I was convinced, was the smoking gun, the piece of evidence I needed to stop the worldwide madness of the nuclear power industry. I held one of my foot-long champions in the air between my fingers, allowing him/her to dance to the last bars of the song. Sotto voce I improvised some more new lyrics:

> *You're very, very large,*
> *Gonna have to name ya Marge.*
> *You're proof of what I been statin',*
> *You worms are all mutatin'!*

Or something like that. Somehow I failed to notice the dark shape looming over my shoulder until it was almost directly on top of me.

A large, drab Russian helicopter set down next to my van, and several military men, Russian or Ukrainian soldiers—I couldn't tell the difference— hurried toward me. I was sure they were going to tell me the facility was off-limits and try to kick me out. Like a kid caught with his hand in the cookie jar, I hid some of the evidence, stashing a fistful of worms into the pocket of my raincoat. It took me a second to remember that I was there with official permission. I stood up and pulled out my wallet.

"Dobryi den!" I called out. I'd picked up a few words of Russian during my travels, but not enough. I did my best to tell them I was engaged in legal, government-authorized research. *"Ia dzes . . .* uh, *razresheniem. U menia . . .* permit. How do you say *permit?"*

To my horror, they ignored my feeble attempts to speak their language, marched right past me, and began gathering up my equipment.

"Hey, what's going on?" I stepped right in front

of one of them, momentarily blocking his path. The muscular, square-jawed man stared down at me with expressionless eyes. Only then did I realize how large he and his trench-coat-clad, jackbooted comrades were. I grinned and let him pass. As he began pulling up my conducting rods I sloshed over to the officer who seemed to be in charge and explained, "*U menia* . . . permitski! Understand? Documenti okayski!"

I held my papers up for his inspection. He gave me a superior grin and ignored my papers. Another man came trotting from the helicopter wearing civilian clothes. He flashed me a fast, fake smile and asked me if I was Dr. Nick Topapopolosis, which sounded like some kind of communicable disease.

"It's Tatopoulos," I corrected him.

"Right, I know all about you. You're the worm guy, aren't you?" He had an American accent and a dismissive edge to his manner. At that point my hand was still hiding in my coat pocket. I could feel my little friends squirming between my muddy fingers. "The name's Terrington," he said gruffly, offering to shake my hand as if he were doing me some kind of favor. "I'm with the U.S. State Department. Glad to meet you, worm guy."

I couldn't help it. All smiles, I reached out and firmly gripped his hand. "Glad to meet you, too, state department guy."

The soldiers were packing up my equipment and loading most of it into the helicopter. As one of them marched past me with my toolbox I yanked it out of his hands. "What's going on here?" I yelled at the American guy. "What are you guys doing? I'm working here with permission!"

Terrington was wiping his hand clean with a handkerchief. The way he looked up at me told me I hadn't made a new friend. "You've been reassigned."

"What? That's impossible! On whose orders?" He didn't answer. He and the Russian officer walked back to the helicopter, leaving me standing there in the downpour.

A chill rose up my spine, literally raising my hackles. I knew in a flash that this was the beginning of one of those byzantine government cover-ups. Someone somewhere had reviewed my experiments and figured out the staggering logical consequences of my research. The Chernobyl earthworms were a full 17 percent too large. Because they reproduce asexually, they are the ideal species with which to measure the gene-altering effects of exposure to radiation. Once the scientific community got a whiff of my findings, their heads would clear as though they'd been given a stiff dose of smelling salts. They would rouse from their collective slumber and demand an end to the madness of the current nuclear power industry. And so these menacing soldiers had been sent to keep me from completing my work.

Wanting no part of their conspiracy, I stood my ground and called after the retreating officials that I wasn't going to be a pawn in their ugly little game, that under no circumstances was I coming with them. But when a couple of the soldiers drove away with my van, I was forced to change my tactics. I marched angrily toward the helicopter, shouting something about how they wouldn't be able to stop science and the great march of knowledge.

Just about the time I was in Kiev boarding a jet that would take me seven thousand miles to the south-west, events important to this story were taking place in a small hospital six thousand miles to the southeast.

Dusk had settled like a golden glass bowl over Papeete, Tahiti, the end of another balmy, eighty-degree day in Polynesia, when a herd of black Lexus SUVs hissed up and left unsightly skid marks outside the main entrance to Papeete Municipal Hospital, the island's most modern health facility. A slew of Caucasian men who looked like they probably worked for a government threw open the doors and prepared to enter the building. But they lingered, waiting for their leader, who stepped, at some leisure, from the back of his Lexus and lit a cigarette. Smoking is a disgusting habit to begin with, but to light up as you're preparing to enter a *hospital* betrays a monumental arrogance, a disdain for the conventions of common decency. It announces you as someone who is mad, bad, and dangerous to know.

Such a man was Phillipe Roache. He was in his

forties, with a salt-and-pepper grizzle of beard and dark, heavy eyes that made him look droll in a continental sort of way. He was intense and alert. He was clever and unpredictable. And, suspiciously, he was French. He sucked hard at his filterless Gauloise, then led his henchmen inside, where they fanned out and quickly located the French doctor who had called the case in to Paris. Of course, their whole conversation would have been *en français,* a language everyone says is beautiful to the ears but which has always sounded to me like someone trying to speak through a mouthful of yogurt. I will translate what I imagine they must have said to one another.

The young doctor (we'll call him Jean-Jacques): "Finally, you have arrived! The Americans have exerted much pressure upon us to tell them if there were any survivors."

Phillipe Roache: "What have you told them so far?"

Jean-Jacques: "Nothing as of yet."

Roache: "Very good. Where is this survivor, the fisherman?"

Jean-Jacques: "Here, sir. Directly behind this door. He is indeed very lucky to be alive!"

At that point the young doctor would have pushed open the door to reveal, in the corner of the darkened room, an elderly Japanese curled into the fetal position on his bed. A couple of nurses puttered nearby, offering whatever mercies they could to their traumatized patient, the sole survivor of the *Kobayashi Maru.* Before leading the way into the room, the doctor, Jean-Jacques, would have glanced down at the burning cigarette and reminded the visitor, "Of course, smoking is not allowed."

"Get them out of here," Roache growled, probably waving his cancer stick in the air for dramatic effect as he shooed the medical staff away like so many houseflies. Once they were gone, he signaled his men to set up the video camera they would use to record the interview.

Moving to the side of the bed, Roache squatted down and examined the sailor through the metal side rails. It was the same man, the *Kobayashi*'s cook. The old man's eyes were open but stared straight ahead vacantly. He appeared to be lost inside some private nightmare only he could see as he rocked himself back and forth, arms locked tight around his knees, whimpering softly.

"Get over here and ask him what happened," Roache demanded brusquely of one of his agents. "We need to know if he saw anything." And another Frenchman, let's call him Jean-Luc, approached the bed and spoke in passable Japanese to the shell-shocked mariner, asking him several questions. He received no reply.

"It's no use. Whatever happened to him on that ship, it put him into a complete state of shock. I don't think he knows we are here."

Roache, resourceful to a fault, rummaged through his pockets and found his platinum lighter. He ignited it at its highest setting, then brought it dangerously close to the patient's face. "What did

you see, old man?" he asked in a throaty whisper.
"What did you see out there?"

The old cook began to tremble slightly. The far-
away look of shock that had frozen itself on his face
changed to one of all-too-present horror. The flame
of the lighter was melting his calm, transporting him
back to the frigid sea and the terror he'd experienced there.

"Gojira," he mumbled. *"Gojira."*

Roache glanced up for a translation, but Jean-
Luc only shrugged to show he didn't understand.

"Gojira . . . Gojira!" The old man began repeating the sound over and over, each time with increas-
ing power, until he was screaming at the top of his
lungs and had to be restrained. *"Go-ji-ra!"*

I catnapped most of the way between Kiev and our
destination, which was good because I was going to
need the rest. It's never a pleasant experience being
kidnapped and dragged halfway around the world
by people you believe to be part of a multinational
paramilitary quasi-governmental conspiracy bent
on suppressing your research. It was a long flight,
and each time I woke up I argued with Terrington,
demanding to be told why I was being abducted and
where we were going. The only information I could
wring from him was that there was some sort of
emergency that required my attention. I was really
upset and didn't care who knew it. My mood light-

ened somewhat when I realized where we were headed. They were taking me to Panama, one of my favorite places on earth. I'd been there twice before, mixing scientific business with vacation pleasure. The people are friendly, the scenery is breathtaking, and the dollar goes a long way. This trip, however, was going to be all work and no play.

By the way, the name Panamá, in the language of the indigenous people, means "an abundance of fish." Think about it.

We landed in the capital, Panama City, then transferred to an amphibious seaplane and headed north toward the Golfo de San Miguel. I'd never been to this area, a part of the country I'd been wanting to visit for years. The view from the open doors of our plane was magnificent. We scared up huge flocks of birds as we skimmed over the treetops of the endless green jungle, the northernmost reaches of the great tropical rain forest that extends down into South America. Did you know that the biological diversity of this primeval jungle is unmatched on the planet? Or that the forest's lush plant life is responsible for filtering and generating a vast quantity of the fresh air we breath? I'm very tempted to interrupt the story again and explain all the horrors being wrought by the logging industry down there, but I'll save that for another book.

We landed on the water near a small, very remote fishing village. I noticed electricity and telephone lines connected to the quaint row of waterfront buildings with their picturesque palm frond roofs. On a normal day the population of this village couldn't have been more than a couple of hundred souls. It looked like any number of peaceful little towns I'd visited in other parts of the country. But the morning I arrived was no normal day. Row after row of military vehicles, some Panamanian and some U.S., were parked along the shore, and as we taxied up to a flimsy wooden pier extending out into the water, we were greeted by a horde of news crews. The army had forbidden them from setting up onshore, so they'd rented the local fishing boats and were floating out in the little bay. It was comical watching these citified reporters with their expensive camera equipment trying to keep their balance in the overcrowded boats. They shouted questions to us as we came to the pier, but I couldn't hear them over the noise of the engines.

We were met by a contingent of Panamanian policemen and U.S. Army officers. The one who seemed to be in charge came forward and introduced himself. He was in his early fifties and had the gruff, sobering look of a human bulldog.

"Dr. Niko Topodopeless?" he asked.

What is so difficult about my name? Why am I constantly having to correct people's pronunciation? I could understand if it were something exotic like Schweitzerlangen or Capaccione or Xiaoching or Tsiblisian. But it's not. "Tatopoulos," I corrected him a little testily, "just like it's spelled: T-a-t-o-p-o-u-l-o-s."

"Sorry 'bout that," he said without really mean-

ing it. "I'm Colonel Alexander Hicks." The power of
his grip when we shook hands threatened to dislocate
my second and fifth metacarpal bones. It wasn't a
display of machismo; I think he was simply distracted by all the pressure of the situation. He turned
around and barked orders at his men to clear the pier.
Some of the more aggressive reporters were clam-
bering off their boats and snapping photos.

"Excuse me," I said, shaking the numbness out
of my right hand, "would you mind explaining to
me what the hell I'm doing here? I was in the middle of some very important research work when—"

"Watch your step!" he warned, seizing me by
the arm and "facilitating" my passage toward the
shore. We hustled past the bobbing boatloads of
reporters, who shouted questions at us in Spanish
and English. As we bullied our way between them
Colonel Hicks smiled. It was one of those frozen,
stonewalling smiles that government officials learn
to wear when they are under fire.

Once we were on solid ground, we came to a
military cordon beyond which policemen were not
allowed to pass. We marched up a hill toward a line
of trees. At the top of the slope, where he finally
relinquished control of my arm, I was treated to a
painful sight. From the air, I hadn't realized that
most of the village was built up here, away from the
beach. Perhaps the reason I hadn't noticed was
because the entire village was wrecked.

Actually, *wrecked* isn't a strong enough word.
Obliterated or *flattened* is probably a more accurate

term for what I saw. The houses were broken off cleanly at their foundations, as if a giant wrecking ball had swept past low to the ground. Fragmented walls and the shattered remnants of a water truck lay in pieces at the edge of the clearing. Articles of clothing and most of a canoe hung in branches of the surrounding trees.

"Yowza!" I said, reacting to the devastation. "Looks like there was a pretty powerful explosion here."

"Something like that," was all Hicks would say.

I immediately realized I'd been wrong about their reasons for taking me away from my earthworm work. They were bringing me in on some kind of disaster investigation. I was carrying my equipment box, which was rather heavy. Doing my best to keep up, I jog-walked after the colonel, always half a step behind. We continued moving uphill until we came to a plateau. We passed a temporary field headquarters, which had been established under a camouflage fabric roof. It looked as though they had quite a lot of equipment in there, but we weren't headed in that direction. Our destination seemed to be a ruined church that stood at the crest of the hill. Hicks stopped briefly to growl some orders to a couple of photographers who were snapping off picture after picture of the wreckage. As he spoke to them I realized there were no signs of a fire. It couldn't have been an explosion.

"What happened here, Colonel? Some kind of spill?"

"Something like that," he said, taking off again.

Huffing and puffing, I lugged my load up the hill. Behind us there was a spectacular view of the ocean. "Look," I said hotly, determined to make him listen to me, "if you guys had a spill, that's terrible. Sorry to hear it. But I can't help you with that, because I'm just a biologist."

Hicks turned his rugged, no-nonsense face toward me and looked me over carefully, as if seeing me for the first time. Worry lines wrinkled his forehead. His jaw pulsed as he gnashed his teeth. After briefly sizing me up, he sniffed and turned away as if taking the time to explain would be a waste of his time. He had bigger fish to fry. "A biologist, huh?" He resumed walking, leading us past some freshly broken trees. Soldiers interrupted their work to salute him as he marched doggedly forward.

"That's correct. I'm a biologist who happens to be working for the Nuclear Regulatory Commission," I told him, "but accidents and spills aren't my thing. If that's what happened here, I'm afraid you've got the wrong guy."

As we walked, a new conspiracy theory began to unfold in my mind. It went like this: The army, having caused some horrible ecological disaster, was intent on sweeping the whole matter under the rug. But since there were already reporters sniffing around the area, they couldn't simply deny that anything at all had happened. They needed a halfway plausible cover story. Furthermore, in order to sell this story to the press, they needed a so-called expert, some stooge with scientific credentials who would stand before the press and tell them the problem wasn't as severe as early reports seemed to indicate. To this end, they had called upon *moi,* low man on the NRC totem pole. I suspected that after a quick "tour" of the area, they would present me with some bogus "scientific" report and lean on me to give it my rubber-stamp approval.

But as we came into an open field where soldiers were working in a series of pits, I remembered an important rule of thumb: Never attribute to deviousness that which can be explained by incompetence. Maybe they really *had* grabbed the wrong guy. It was time for me to put my foot down.

"Do you guys have any idea who I am? Do you understand that I'm an environmental researcher, with a degree in ecological medicine, conducting research for the Nuclear Regulatory Commission? Do you realize you just interrupted a three-year study of the Chernobyl earthworm?"

"You implying we picked up the wrong Dr. Nicholas Topopoloss?"

"Tatopoulos!" I steamed. "Niko Tatopoulos."

He stopped at the top of a makeshift wooden ramp. There were four or five men working in the ditch at the bottom of this ramp. They stopped working to listen to our conversation. "We know who you are. You're the worm guy."

I was taken aback. For the second time in as many days someone had called me "the worm guy."

I wasn't comfortable with that description and hoped it wasn't going to stick.

"Why not *Homo sapiens vermiculum?*" I suggested. Of course, he didn't get it. I realized I was going to have to explain myself in layman's terms. I followed him down the ramp into the muddy earth of the pit, where one of his lieutenants handed him a clipboard. "Look, Colonel, the radioactive residue around the Chernobyl contamination area has caused this 'worm guy's' worms to undergo genetic mutation, a significant restructuring of their DNA." I asked him if he had any idea what that meant, and before he could answer I told him. "It means that due to man-made changes in environmental conditions, the course of nature has been radically altered! The Chernobyl earthworms are now over seventeen percent larger than they were before!"

"Seventeen percent larger, huh? Sounds big." He whistled through his teeth. The lieutenant next to him cracked a smirking smile.

I had never dealt with the U.S. Army before. The stereotype I had of them was that they were a bunch of testosterone-heavy dimwits. I thought they weren't understanding a word I was saying, so I waved my arms in the air to encompass the entire plateau around us, "They're *enormous!* But look, Colonel, sir, what I'm telling you is this: I'm a biologist. I take radioactive samples and I study them."

"Fine," Hicks said. He pointed to the ground. "Here's your sample. Study it." Then he turned and walked away. I had the distinct feeling that, in spite of his serious-as-a-brick way of speaking, he was somehow making a fool of me. A couple of soldiers at the side of the pit snickered before turning back to their work. Something was definitely going on, I decided.

I looked down at the ground, then yelled after the colonel, "What sample?" Hicks didn't turn back, but the lieutenant he'd left in charge was grinning from ear to ear. *Either this man is a simpering idiot,* I told myself, *or I'm missing something here.*

"You're standing in it."

I still didn't see anything. I took a step back. I checked the bottoms of my shoes. And then, slowly, it dawned on me. For the first time I noticed that the pit I was standing in was freshly made. And it wasn't the only one. A series of identical pits formed a path that ran from the beach through the village and disappeared over the crest of the hills. Some of the trees and buildings around me had been utterly destroyed while others remained undamaged. I realized that something had climbed out of the Pacific and walked—*stomped*—away over the hills toward the Atlantic.

I was standing inside of a footprint! It was impossibly large—forty feet wide and six feet deep! Once I knew what I was looking for, it all became so clear: The muddy earth of the plateau had been squashed down by a three-toed creature with pointed, recurving claws and a vestigial hallux (a stubby, rather useless fourth toe like the one found at the back of a chicken's foot). A chill sense of dread spread over my skin as I tried to imagine what kind of beast had made these mind-boggling tracks. Obviously, it had to be unbelievably large and heavy to leave such deep impressions in the ground. I climbed out of the pit and ran along the trail until I came to the next one. It was the mirror image of the first, made with a left foot. I was in a mild state of shock and stood there for a long time with my mouth hanging open, watching a pair of soldiers using a Geiger counter. They were finding trace amounts of radiation.

This is impossible, I told myself. And although I didn't want to admit it, I recognized the print at once. Based on the splay of the toes and the distinctive shape of the claws, I knew what kind of animal must have walked past. It was a reptile, but more than 17 percent larger than normal. Suddenly my worms didn't seem so massive.

After taking a look around, I went off in search of Colonel Hicks. He'd gone back to the camouflage tent pitched alongside the debris of the village. Inside there was all manner of high-tech machinery: computers, radar screens, a videotape setup, a scanner-fax, and a bank of cell phones. I remember thinking that this branch of the army really traveled in style. I found the colonel standing next to that most basic piece of military hardware, the coffee urn. I marched up to him and prepared to make an announcement.

His eyebrows arched under the brim of his field cap. He was waiting for me to speak. I tried. But I was so flabbergasted by what I'd seen, the words wouldn't come. All I could manage to do was point toward the tracks. "Footprint," I blurted. "Footprint. That was a footprint!"

Hicks nodded.

"I was standing *inside* a footprint," I repeated, hammering on the obvious.

"That's correct."

"But there's no animal in the world that can make a footprint like that," I declared. "Is there?"

A woman's sultry voice interrupted. "I told them this isn't your field, but they never listen to genius." She was about my age, dressed in a set of tight-fitting camouflage fatigues, with a pair of bifocal glasses perched on the end of her nose, and she had her long red hair pulled back into a loose ponytail. My first thought was that she looked like a sexy jungle librarian.

Hicks did the honors. "Dr. Ta . . ."

"Tatopoulos," I coached him.

". . . Tatopoulos, this is Dr. Elsie Chapman, chief researcher at the National Institute of Paleontology. She's your boss."

She was going to ignore me, but then suddenly she changed her mind and gave me a very warm greeting. Maybe a little too warm. Her firm hand-shake let me know that Dr. Chapman was a self-assured, professional academic who had risen to the top of her specialty. But her smile suggested that, under the right circumstances, she could be one very naughty kitten. She looked me over carefully from head to toe and seemed pleased with what she saw. "Call me Elsie."

"Those *are* footprints, right? Did anyone see what made them?"

"No such luck," Elsie explained, finally releasing my hand. "Whatever it was, it came through here fast. No one knew what hit them till it was too late. We're finding signs of radiation, which is why you got picked up." As she talked she laced her fingers behind her back to stretch out her shoulders. I couldn't help admiring the way her uniform snugged to her curves. Was she flirting with me?

For several moments no one said a word— although I was trying. I kept looking off in the direction of the footprints, thinking of logical explanations for what could have made them. But each time I turned to the others and went to speak, my mind went blank. I might still be standing there fumbling for words if the Jeep carrying Dr. Craven hadn't pulled up.

Like most people in the scientific community, I'd known about Mendel Craven for years. I recognized him from the dust jackets of his several books and appearances on shows like *Good Morning America.* He was a chubby, charming, enthusiastic man who had an endearing way of explaining to television cameras all the frightening ways humanity could be wiped away into extinction. I'd only picked up one of his books, *The Ebola Virus and You: Ten Easy Steps to Prevention,* but never finished reading it. After a brief struggle to extricate himself from the seat belt on the passenger seat of the Jeep, he came racing toward the tent waving a videocassette in the air.

"Tape's in! The Fr—*ah-choo,*" he sneezed. "The French finally released it."

Both Hicks and Chapman reached for the tape, but Craven tucked it under his arm like a fullback and straight-armed his way past them until he arrived at the VCR and slammed the cassette into the machine.

"The French? The tape?" I was confused.

Hicks thought he was filling me in when he said, "A Japanese cannery ship was attacked and sunk last night in the South Pacific, near French Polynesia." But I didn't see any immediate connection between a set of oversized animal tracks in Central America and some fishing boat being torpedoed near Tahiti. Then I heard Elsie's voice in my right ear. She'd come up behind me and practically set her chin down on my shoulder. I could feel her uniform brushing against my back.

"We're pretty sure there's a connection," she whispered before stepping around me. "Dr. Craven, have you met Nick? He's our worm guy." The way she said those words, "worm guy," seemed to suggest a double entendre.

Craven covered his mouth and sneezed again.

The handshake would have to wait. "Sorry. Summer cold. Weird, huh?" After flashing me a so-very-glad-to-meet-you smile, he whipped back around and hit play. On the television monitor we saw men moving around a hospital bed speaking in French. One of them leaned down and began speaking French-accented Japanese to the patient.

"Why is that man smoking in a hospital room?" I asked. Everyone shushed me. Then we watched as the man with the cigarette leaned in and worked his sinister magic with his lighter. We heard the old sailor chant the mysterious word *Gojira,* then we heard him scream it over and over until orderlies rushed in and held him down.

We all turned and looked at one another, wondering the same thing: *What the hell is a* Gojira? But there wasn't much time to contemplate this issue, because a few minutes later news arrived of another encounter several hundred miles to the northwest.

As we left Panama and headed for the Caribbean, it began raining in New York City. An early summer storm had gathered in the Gulf of Mexico before pushing north toward New England. I checked the National Weather Service's user-friendly Web page and learned that the average precipitation in the New York metropolitan region for a seven-day period in early summer is a scant 0.7 inches. The all-time record had been 11.98 inches of rain, set way back in 1889. And that was for an entire month. We surpassed that mark in one week, suffering through an astounding 23.78 inches of rain.

Understandably, people became suspicious. Could it be a mere coincidence, they asked, that the creature arrived during a period of freakish, unprecedented weather? Were the two somehow connected?

My answer is yes, they were. But not in the way many nonscientists are currently claiming they were. In the rush to find comforting explanations, many people have retreated from rational explanations and fallen back on superstitious mumbo-jumbo. This rash of irrationality has been fueled by those unscrupulous snake-oil salesmen known as local TV weatherpersons. Willing to say or do just about anything to improve ratings, these pseudo-scientists have invented a voodoo meteorology claiming either that the great quantity of rain *caused* the creature to erupt out of the bowels of the earth or, just as preposterously, that the creature somehow conjured the rainstorms. Both ideas are ridiculous.

Nevertheless, I believe there is a connection: Our own rampant pollution of the earth caused both the creature and the rain.

Allow me to elaborate. The first law of environmental science is that all parts of an ecosystem, in this case the global biosphere, are interconnected. Changes in one part of the system can trigger unforeseen consequences in another. I have already explained my belief that exposure to the radiation spread by the atomic testing in French Polynesia gave rise to the creature. Likewise, I think a different sort of pollution is responsible for the unseasonable weather that gripped the Northeast. Two little words: global warming. In our lust for burning fossil fuels, those syrupy remains of dinosaurs and ancient plants, we are also burning away the earth's protective ozone layer and making the planet a hotter place to live. My tour of the National Weather Service's Web page turned up another startling piece of information: Over the last forty years, the average global temperature has increased from 76 to 76.7 degrees! That might not seem very dramatic, but it means that more and more of the world is becoming tropical. Consequently, weather patterns are changing. If we don't begin taking action soon, we might be looking at the end of seasonal patterns altogether!

With that said, let's get back to the story.

It was raining cats and dogs in New York City when a cab dropped Audrey Timmonds off in front of the WIDF-TV building with two armfuls of groceries. Yes, the same delightful Audrey whose photos adorn the inside of my equipment box, the same small-town girl I fell in love with when were in college. After leaving me in the lurch, she'd gotten out of Ohio and headed for the bright lights of Manhattan. She was determined to launch a career in journalism, and WIDF-TV was where she'd landed a job. It wasn't exactly the prestigious *NBC Nightly News with Tom Brokaw.* In fact, it wasn't even a network affiliate—just a funky little station with a double-digit channel number that specialized in covering lurid crimes and local politics. The important thing was, she'd gotten a foot in the door. From there, she was sure, her hard work and talent would carry her to the top.

She rode the elevators up to the nineteenth floor, then hurried through the busy office trying not to break open the soggy bags and spill the groceries on the floor. She succeeded in reaching Lucy's desk, where she gingerly set down her load. "Can you believe this weather? They're saying it's going to rain like this all week!"

Lucy leaned back in her chair and turned an eye toward the wet bags on her always-organized desk. "What's all this?"

"Groceries."

"I can see that, can't I?" Lucy, the station's receptionist, was from Patchogue, Long Island, and had the accent to prove it. She was also something of a fashion plate who had become Audrey's unofficial wardrobe consultant. "And why, may I ask, are you bringing groceries with you to work?"

Audrey lowered her eyes in shame and admitted the truth. "They're not mine. They're Caiman's groceries."

Lucy clapped her hands over her face and shook her head in disappointment. She peeked out from between her long green fingernails and moaned. "Oh, girl, now he's got you doin' his *shopping*? Tsk, tsk, tsk." Audrey said she could explain, that it wasn't as bad as it looked, but when she tried to talk, Lucy interrupted her, saying loudly, "Speak of the devil."

Just then the dapper if little figure of Charles H. Caiman, WIDF's lead anchorman for the past two decades, was moving past them, the top of his head being the only part of him that was visible. It bobbed past the partition that defined Lucy's workspace, his transplanted hairs covering most of his bald spot. People were always telling him he didn't look a day over forty, and the fifty-eight-year-old anchor paid a staff of cosmetologists to keep it that way. Like many men who are under 5'4", Caiman had a Napoleon complex. But unlike many of his pusillanimous peers, he didn't *suffer* from the syndrome, he *cultivated* it. Sometimes he went so far as to tuck his hand into the gaps between his shirt buttons.

The mere sight of him—or part of him—threw Audrey into a dither. "Think I should ask him?"

"No!" Lucy said.

"I'm going to ask him. You think I should? I will." And as Lucy rolled her eyes and shook her head, Audrey took off.

Caiman was walking fast. He was headed for the broadcast studio at the far end of the office and seemed to be preoccupied with other thoughts. When he noticed Audrey chasing after him, he walked faster still. But it was no use. She caught up to him and peppered him with questions as they walked.

"Did you talk to Humphries?" she asked, biting her lip.

"Ms. Timmonds, this is neither the time nor the place—"

"Oh, come on, just tell me. Did you talk to him?"

The anchorman kept moving. "He said he'd consider it. It's between you and Rodriguez." The expression on his face was calculated to dampen her hopes, but Audrey took the news as though she'd just won the lottery and did that cute little clappy-jumpy thing she does whenever she gets really excited.

"Are you serious? That's great. You're serious, right? He's going to consider me for the job? That's terrific. What else did he say?"

They came to the door of the soundproof broadcast studio. A large-as-life cardboard cutout of Caiman stood beside the entrance. With one Caiman standing there beside another Caiman, it was impossible not to notice that he was much taller in cardboard than he was in real life. He turned to Audrey and ran his tongue once around the inside of his mouth.

"Why don't I tell you all about it over dinner tonight? Say, your place? Say, eight o'clock?" His collagen-enhanced lips stretched into a lascivious, Cheshire-cat grin as his eyes hungrily examined the parts of Audrey between her neck and her knees.

"Mr. Caiman," Audrey gasped, "you're married!"

He already knew that, and he leaned in far

closer than he should have. "And you're very beautiful. Have I ever told you that before?"

"Mr. Caiman!"

"Call me Charlie."

Audrey was stunned. Angry and hurt, she
wanted to burst into tears, but she knew she couldn't
because Caiman would just dismiss it as a "female"
reaction. "Mr. Caiman! I've been doing extra
research and tracking down leads for you after hours
and on weekends for three years now. This job—the
one from Humphries—is really important to me.
I'm too old to be your assistant anymore. I need to
know this position is leading someplace."

Most men would have been fazed, taken aback.
Not Caiman. He glanced over his shoulder to make
sure no one was listening before making the price of
his help explicit. "Look, Miss Timmonds, I *want*
you to get the job. So, let's have—you know—'dinner' together. I'd really, really like to have 'dinner'
with you."

Is this the price of getting ahead? Audrey asked
herself, repulsed by the idea. She watched a fast-
forward nightmare flash through her mind—the last
three years and all the hard work she had done were
a path leading up to this supremely ugly conversation. Now her promotion had boiled down to a sex-
ual thing. She took a breath and looked him squarely
in the eyes. "Mr. Caiman, I can't do that."

"It's your choice," he said softly. Then, with a
wistful oh-what-could-have-been smile, he pulled
open the door and marched into the studio.

Through the soundproof glass Audrey watched him hurry past the cameras to the news desk. There was a new co-anchor, Desirée Pawn, and the two of them quickly shook hands. When Caiman settled into his chair, he looked across and noticed, much to his consternation, that Pawn was a full head taller than him. He looked like a child sitting at a dinner table. In a panic he called for the stagehands to bring him something to sit on: a cushion, a phone book, anything.

But there wasn't time. They were going on the air any moment. "Five, four, three . . ."

"No, hold on!" Caiman said. But Murray the station manager flashed him the signal that announced they were live. Caiman reacted by lifting himself out of his chair and saying to the cameras, "We've got news and sports just ahead. Now here's Fat Pat with the weather."

Audrey stood on the far side of the glass staring daggers at her libidinous boss. She was so angry, she wanted to kick something or somebody. Instead she took out the wad of gum she was chewing and smeared it across the cardboard nose of the smiling Caiman cutout.

My kidnapping at the hands of the American military was beginning to feel like a cut-rate vacation in the hold of a cargo plane. From Panama we flew to Jamaica. We landed on solid ground this time, not far from Great Pedro Bluff. The Jamaican authorities were waiting for us with ground transportation. We three scientists climbed into a Jeep and met our driver, Peter, a tall, severe man in mirrored sunglasses. He wasn't exactly a talkative fellow. Mendel and I rode in back, while Elsie rode up front. Before we started out, Peter took care to strap down the equipment we'd brought out of the plane. It's a good thing he did, because the unpaved road we took was extremely bumpy.

Once we got up to speed, Elsie turned around and lifted her sunglasses so she could take a good long look at me. Her eyes traveled slowly from my hiking boots up to the beret I was wearing on my head, scrutinizing every inch of me, sizing me up. I'd never met a woman who flirted so aggressively. When she opened her mouth to speak, the bumps in the road distorted her voice.

"Three yeaEars out in the booOOndocks digging up worms? How did Mrs. Tatopoulos haAAndle that?" she asked as we bounced along. When I explained that I wasn't married, she made no effort to disguise her delight. "ReaLLy? A girlfriend, then? Or are youOU the kind of guyEYE who has a woman in EHevery port?" She sounded like she had the hiccups, but they were sexy hiccups. Although I didn't want to, I started thinking about Audrey and tried to change the subject.

"No. EYEI'm the kind of guy who woERks too much." I glanced over at Mendel, who, it seemed to me, was fuming with jealousy. Although he would never cop to it, I think he was madly in lust with Elsie Chapman.

She wasn't going to let me off the hook easily. "Are youOO telling meEE there's no one who holds a speEHcial place in your heart?" she asked. In fact, there *was* someone who held a special place in my heart. Audrey had an entire wing dedicated to her, but I didn't want to talk about it. Elsie was playing pretty hard, unaware that she was opening up an old wound.

"Not for a long time noOW," I said.

"Well, I think you're cute," she announced, leaning back and taking a quick bite out of the airspace in front of my nose. With a broad, satisfied grin, she turned away to enjoy some of the passing scenery. I leaned toward Mendel and whispered, "Is shEE always like this?"

Masking his heartbreak, he whispered back conspiratorially, "I've had to BEeat her off with a stiIIck."

"I heard that," Elsie said.

Our convoy of Jeeps brought us to the edge of a beautiful white beach and parked at the tree line. We unlashed our equipment and carried it toward the water, where we beheld an alarming sight.

The entire beach was occupied by an enormous Liberian cargo ship lying on its side in the sand. It must have been left there by the receding tide. Two spectacular holes had been torn into the vessel's hull, one at the front and the other at the rear. The smaller opening, the one at the front, was approximately twenty-five feet across. The opening at the rear of the ship pierced all the way through to the opposite wall. In addition, there were fifty-foot gashes torn down the side.

"Curiouser and curiouser," quoth Mendel as we made our way down the sandy slope toward the shoreline.

A fair number of local people had come out to gawk at the mangled metallic corpse of the ship. Most of them were gathered up on the dunes, talking among themselves, exchanging ideas about what in the world could have opened the ragged wounds in the ship's flanks. A conspicuous group of Caucasian men in fashionable clothing was busily investigating the wreck. They were no tourists. In addition to their cameras and tape measures, they seemed to be using Geiger counters and ultrasound equipment. Something about them was vaguely familiar.

"Who the hell are those guys?" Hicks wanted to know. He ordered his soldiers to establish a cordon around the wreck. He wanted the local civilians to be kept off the beach, and he wanted to know who the nattily dressed white men were. He didn't have to wait long for an answer.

"They are with me," someone answered in a French accent. A man with a salt-and-pepper beard and secret-agent sunglasses was puffing on an unfiltered cigarette. With a friendly smile he tossed his cigarette into the sand and approached us with a confidence that looked almost like boredom.

"And who might you be?" Hicks asked in a way that suggested no matter what answer the man gave, he and his men were going to be booted out of the area with the others.

"Hey, you're the guy from the hospital we saw on the videotape," Mendel said. "The guy with the lighter, right?"

The Frenchman answered with an enigmatic smile. He reached into his breast pocket and pulled out a business card. With a magician's manual dexterity, he twirled it around a couple of times between his fingers before extending it to Colonel Hicks.

Cie. de La Rochelle Internationaux
Property and Casualty Insurance
Paris, France

There was no address, no phone number, and none of us could begin to pronounce the name of the company.

"My name is Phillipe Roache, and my company represents the registered owners of this ship. We are preparing a report on the damage," Roache said.

"You sure got down here awful fast," Hicks observed, openly skeptical of the man and his story.

The Frenchman shrugged. "That is our job."

Elsie must have smelled a rat. Or perhaps she was flirting again. She stepped up close to the stranger and narrowed her eyes. "And I suppose you also insure whichever Japanese company owns the ship that went down in Tahiti."

"We're not discussing that subject," Hicks reminded her.

The insurance agent offered the barest shadow of a smile to the paleontologist. "Our great size," he explained, "allows us to offer very attractive rates."

Hicks wasn't prepared to let himself be sidetracked by a bunch of insurance peddlers, especially French ones. "I apologize to you and your company, sir. But right now your people are getting in the way of my job and I want them cleared out of here."

"Colonel, let me ask you a question. What in the world do you think could have done this?" There was a dollop of mockery in his voice, a light challenge that did not go unnoticed by Hicks.

"Get your people out of the way," Hicks said between clenched teeth, "or I'll move them myself."

"Very well," Roache replied, moving jauntily down shore to begin collecting his men.

"And from now on put your butts in a trash can!" I added. When he spun around to face me, I made sure he knew what I meant. "Your cigarette butts shouldn't be thrown on the beach." He thought for a moment before offering me a sturdy thumbs-up.

"Another battle won in the war to save Mother Earth," Mendel said sardonically, picking up his gear and walking toward the water.

For the next hour or so we conducted a close-up investigation of the wrecked ship while Hicks's soldiers combed the beach in search of additional clues. What we found was significantly more frightening than an oversized paw print. Mendel and I waded out knee deep into the water to get a closer look at the far side of the ship, which towered above us.

He went into one of his sneezing fits, nearly dropping the Geiger counter he was carrying into the water. "It's hot," he told me. "I'm picking up the same levels of radiation we found in Panama. Why would it be radioactive?"

While he worked and sneezed, I took several steps back, moving deeper into the water so that I could get a better view of the damage. "Am I imagining this," I called, "or does it look like something punctured the walls before prying them back?" I gulped. "It almost looks like this hole was *clawed* open."

Mendel looked up and studied the damage. "Like opening a can of sardines," he agreed.

And that comment turned out to be closer to the truth than either of us expected. I felt something under my foot, something that didn't feel right, so I reached my hand into the water and grabbed it. I pulled up a six-ounce can of tuna fish, one of hundreds I noticed scattered around me. An unformed idea started worming around in my brain: *fishing boat, fishing village, cans of fish.*

But the pieces of the puzzle didn't fit themselves together in my mind until about five minutes later, when I noticed something dangling from one of the razor-sharp edges of the torn hull. Opening

my tool kit and avoiding eye contact with the photographs of Audrey inside, I took out a specimen jar
and a pair of tweezers. Then I collected my first tissue sample.

It was a five-inch-long strip of meat. It was covered on one side with a protective layer of scales,
each one the size of a thumbnail. These scales were
keeled instead of being flat, so I knew for sure it
hadn't come from a fish. It had come from a reptile.

I dropped the sample into the jar and looked
around for Mendel, anxious to tell him about this
latest discovery. But he had wandered deeper into
the cargo area, which contained hundreds of thousands of boxes of tuna. The gaping hole around me
made it feel as though I were standing inside the
giant jaws of some sharp-toothed sea creature. For
some reason I became uneasy. I felt like I was being
watched. And when I looked out into the sunlight, I
realized I was. The Frenchman, Roache, was standing on the beach staring straight at me. Although he
was quite a distance away, I sensed that he knew
what I knew.

TWO

An hour and a half later we were back on the plane, headed for Washington, D.C., and the National Institute of Paleontology, where we could do further analysis of the data we'd gathered. But none of us was really expecting to get there. The mysterious creature was on the move and we were expecting another sighting to be reported at any moment. In fact, we were anxiously hoping there would be one. At that point we still had no idea what we were up against. We were eager to catch up with the animal and find out what it was.

From comments Elsie made as we boarded the plane, it was clear she thought the beast must be a dinosaur of some kind, a refugee from a lost world, flushed out into the open after sixty-five million years of hiding. Mendel, smitten with the shapely paleontologist, wanted desperately to agree with her dino theory but found he couldn't. Too many things didn't fit. When he began pointing out the inconsistencies to her, she angrily challenged him to come up with a better theory.

We were riding in some sort of smallish military cargo plane, empty inside except for a few odd-sized crates and the antislide webbing that hung from the walls. We had the belly of the plane to ourselves and spread out as far as possible from one another in order to engage in solitary work. I pushed one of the larger crates against the back wall and began setting up my field microscope. Elsie turned a crate on its side and used it as a table for the impressive library of reference books she'd carted along with her. She obviously knew the books well. She riffled through them expertly, checking facts against a long sheet of data on a computer printout. Dr. Craven, meanwhile, paced the length of the floor dramatically, lost in an unending brainstorm, which he snapped out of now and again to record an idea into his handheld tape recorder. I think he was dictating notes for the book he was planning to write. For all his show of intense concentration, I could see he was, in fact, keeping one adoring eye on the boss, Dr. Chapman. She was in the habit of mumbling to her books, and nearly every time she did so, Mendel looked up, thinking she might be talking to him.

Colonel Hicks walked back from the cockpit holding a computer printout of some kind. He didn't say a word, but sat down on a supply crate and began to review the pages. Soon he was lost in thought and staring out the window. I couldn't blame him for having a lot on his mind.

I hand-sliced a razor-thin, fairly uniform section of reptile flesh off the sample I'd collected and treated it with a wash of iodine. Within twenty minutes I had prepared a decent slide and put it under the microscope. Although the lens vibrated and jumped with the plane, I quickly noted the sample's most remarkable quality.

It was perfectly normal!

This was odd. Typically, creatures presenting even the slightest of outwardly visible mutations show a whole host of concomitant abnormalities at the cell and tissue levels. I should have found irregularities of cell composition, chemical balance, and muscle construction. The two-headed lambs I've examined around the Chernobyl area, for example, look just as strange under the microscope as they do with the naked eye.

At lower levels of magnification, I saw that I was looking at superficial epidermis with a layer of subcutaneous fat and a very small section of muscle. A certain amount of decay had already begun to corrupt the sample. I noticed a high density of chromatophores, or pigment-bearing cells. The ratio of melanophores to allophores was typically reptilian and suggested the creature might be able to change color, chameleonlike. A large, flat oval with a hollow at the center was a femoral scent-gland pore. Only males have these pores.

At a higher level of magnification, the arrangement of blood vessels and striations of the muscles told me Elsie's dino theory was probably wrong—

although this animal was definitely reptilian, it was also cold-blooded, something dinosaurs were not.

I was on the verge of announcing these discoveries when one of the soldiers walked back from the cockpit holding another sheaf of printouts for Hicks's inspection. The way the soldier moved told us something new had happened. He stepped up to the colonel and yelled over the noise of the engines, "Sir, we just got a report of three fishing trawlers going down."

Hicks yelled back at him, "So what? What makes you think it's related?"

"The trawlers were *pulled* under, sir."

Pulled under? That got everyone's attention. Hicks snatched the report out of the soldier's hand and scanned it. It was bad news, and as he read down the page his shoulders fell forward under the mounting weight of the situation.

According to the Coast Guard's report, a trio of fishing boats—the *Harpo,* the *Chico,* and the *Groucho*—had been trawling the waters a few miles off the New England coast. It was raining steadily, but the sea was relatively calm. As the first light of day began to leak through the clouds, the skippers of the three boats had reported to each other that their engines were beginning to drag. At first they'd thought they were "heavy in the bunt" (the bagging portion of a fishing net). But that theory was abandoned when the ships lurched to a sudden halt. Something had them by the nets they were trailing behind them. It was at this point the first call went out to the Coast Guard.

Orders were given to haul in the nets, but the lines wouldn't budge. Then the three trawlers found themselves moving backward through the water, slowly at first but then faster and faster. The crew must have been terrified, wondering, *What in the hell did we catch?* Deckhands used axes to try to cut themselves free of the nets, but the steel cables were too strong and the sterns of the vessels were dipping low to the waterline, being pulled not only backward but down. A moment after everyone bailed out over the sides, the three ships disappeared completely under the surface.

For the next few minutes the petrified sailors were left to bob in the frigid water. They had seen nothing and didn't have the faintest idea what was happening to them. Then, with a great hiss of air pressure, the surface of the water erupted and the *Groucho* burst up out of the water and flew into the air. The other two vessels shot up seconds later. All three ships keeled over or capsized. Miraculously, no one drowned. A Coast Guard helicopter found the men clinging to the sides of the boats and airlifted them safely back to shore.

"That's the most ridiculous thing I've ever heard," Mendel informed Elsie, tapping the ashes from an imaginary cigar and wiggling his eyebrows like Groucho Marx. She turned away from him with a sharp, withering glance.

"Sixty-seven degrees longitude, forty-seventh parallel," Hicks read from the report. He moved to the low table Elsie had been using as a desk and pushed her books aside. Unfolding a large map of the world and smoothing it out, he used his index finger to find the coordinates. "Oh, for crying out loud!" he cried out loud when he saw where the pulling-under incident had taken place. "This damn thing is only two hundred miles off the eastern seaboard, and we still don't even know what it is!"

The colonel looked for a moment as though he would slam his fist through the tabletop. Instead he reached up and massaged his temples. The orders he had been given from his commanding officer, General Anderson, sounded simple enough: Find the thing causing all the property damage in the ocean and destroy it. As he would explain to me later, several maritime merchants had suspended operations in the wake of the *Kobayashi* incident, preferring to wait until the danger had passed—a move that was costing the United States $450 million per day in lost revenue. After a moment of internal agonizing, he snapped out of it and got back to work.

"All right," he yelled, in a dangerous mood, "I want to know what you brainiacs have come up with so far."

Elsie, unaffected by the colonel's apoplexy, pursed her lips and clucked her tongue. "Alex, Alex, Alex. Is that the only thing you men want from a woman—brains? I'm tired of being treated like a slab of gray matter. There's more to me than just a cerebellum, you know."

Hicks smiled tightly, tolerating her shtick,

waiting for her to get down to business, which she quickly did. She and Mendel took places at the low makeshift table in the center of the space. She reached into the pile of books she had scattered around and thumbed through a large text until she found the page she wanted. She spun it around to face Hicks and shoved it across the table. As she did so she pronounced the very same name that had come to my mind back in Panama, when I had been standing in that swimming-pool-sized footprint.

"Theropoda Allosaurus."

Hicks looked down at the page, then up at Elsie. "It's a goddamn dinosaur?"

"Allosaurus?" Mendel rolled his eyes. "You have got to be kidding."

"No, Dr. Craven, I'm afraid I'm perfectly serious," she announced, reaching across the table and squeezing her colleague's chin. "It all fits," she continued. "Bipedal locomotion exclusively on the hind legs, the vertebrae horizontally balanced over the pelvis, the recurving razor claw on the flanged fingers . . . and when you add that to the evidence of the serrated tooth marks left in the side of that boat, it all points in the same direction—Theropoda Allosaurus."

"Perhaps," Craven shouted with the exuberance of a sword fighter, "but there are *at least* three problems with your theory! Number one: The only known remains of Theropoda Allosaurus were found in Utah and Wyoming—meaning, I suppose, that the creature we are pursuing is just now returning to his home on the range after a vacation in the South Pacific. Number two: While members of Theropoda can certainly run and fly with great dexterity, I've never heard of one *swimming*. And number three: If this is supposed to be a dinosaur, where do you propose it's been hiding for the last, oh, sixty million years or so?" He smiled smugly, savagely, confident in his debunking prowess.

Hicks blinked at both of them, on the verge of losing his patience. "What in the hell are you two talking about?" he demanded.

Elsie came around the table and draped herself over the soldier's shoulder, a move she knew would cause Mendel to seethe with jealousy. She called Hicks's attention to the textbook and the artist's sketch of her prime suspect. The drawing showed a lateral view of the skull and skeleton of a forty-foot-long dinosaur. She explained: "Theropoda is a suborder of enormous reptiles, the same group that gives us the tyrannosaurus and the velociraptor. It is probably the ancestor of many modern-day species, such as the fighting gamecock. All of these creatures are extremely powerful, agile, and fast. The fellow you see pictured here, Allosaurus, has been thought to be extinct since the late Cretaceous period."

"Did I forget to mention problem number four," Mendel interjected, "that Allosaurus would fit inside any one of those footprints we found in Panama?" As enamored as he was with our red-headed coworker, Mendel Craven relished a sharp debate, a trait that made him an excellent guest on the talk shows he visited while promoting his books.

Hicks stared at the picture, shaking his head. He almost looked as if he was going to be airsick. Obviously, the idea that we were poised for an encounter with a powerful, overlarge dinosaur didn't agree with him. He blinked down at the page and seemed startled each time he reopened his eyes.

I stepped away from my microscope and gave him even worse news

"I think we're missing something here," I said, joining them around the table. "What about the radiation? I don't think the radiation is an anomaly. I think it's the clue. Elsie, you're right: Those prints are very similar to Allosaurus, but they're far too large. And Mendel, you're right: A land creature like Allosaurus wouldn't have been able to tear up those boats so far out to sea."

"Don't tell me what it isn't," Hicks snapped. "Tell me what the hell it is!"

I would have liked to give him an answer. But the trouble was, I still wasn't sure exactly what this thing was. I sat down at the table and looked at the map. "Okay, let's look at what we know so far. The first sighting was made in French Polynesia, an area that has been exposed to over a hundred nuclear tests over the last thirty years."

"That would explain the traces of radiation we've been finding. The thing must be contaminated."

"I think it's more than contamination. I believe that what we're dealing with here is a mutated aberration, the result of a severe disruption in genetic coding material. It's the only way to explain the remarkable size."

"I see." Mendel stroked his goatee in amused contemplation. "It's sort of similar to your earthworms: Radiation makes them large."

"Exactly. Only the worms I've been studying at Chernobyl are recognizable as the offspring of their parents. But this thing, this reptile, this whatever-it-is, seems to be different from any creature we've seen before. It's possible that the instructions encoded in the DNA structure have been so radically altered that we might never be able to identify this animal's parents."

"Strange."

"But possible," Craven the debunker allowed.

I went on. "With DNA samples and a year or two of research, we might be able to determine its genetic heritage. But based on the evidence we've gathered so far, I think it's safe to say we're looking at a brand-new life form. I believe we're witnessing the dawn of a new species. The very first of its kind."

I would have gone on, but the look on Hicks's face told me he'd had enough paleontology and mutation biology for the moment. He took a long, deep breath, then exhaled even more slowly.

"In other words, it's impossible to say for sure what this thing is."

I nodded. He nodded. Elsie and Mendel nodded. We were in agreement.

I remember feeling a twinge of pity for the bulldoggish army colonel. After all, the three of us were only scientists, people who labored in relative safety far from the front lines. But Hicks, I sensed, would have to face this thing sooner or later while the rest of us watched from a distance. I could see he was anticipating such a showdown, and I tried to imagine what it would be like having a responsibility such as that weighing on my shoulders.

"My life sucks."

Animal and Lucy looked up from their sandwich plates with sympathetic smiles. Their friend and coworker, Audrey, was standing in the aisle dripping water on the restaurant floor. The diner across the street from WIDF was as busy as they'd ever seen it, packed with office workers and businesspeople escaping the deluge. When neither of them said anything, she felt compelled to reiterate and elaborate. "My life sucks rotten donkey eggs."

"Oh, sweetie, please," Lucy consoled her, "your life doesn't suck. Him"—she pointed across the table at Animal—"now, *his* life sucks."

Animal's mouth happened to be stuffed full of hamburger at that moment, but it didn't stop him from firing back, "That's 'cause I'm married to you."

"Shut up."

"You shut up."

"No, I will not shut up, because I'm talking to my friend Audrey." And as her husband chomped once more into his sandwich, Lucy's face quickly registered her disgust at his bad table manners. "How can you eat like that?"

"Iig igh."

"What? I can't understand a single word." As Lucy shook her head, Audrey slid into the booth. Animal chewed through his mouthful well enough to repeat himself.

"Big bites," he said. Animal and Lucy had spent the last five years bantering insults back and forth, mutual incredulity at the lunacy of the other being the foundation upon which their marriage was built. Despite the nonstop bickering, they remained very much in love. Animal was about to jump back into the fray when he noticed that Audrey was wearing a long face.

"I can't believe it," she moped, wringing drops of water from her blond curls into little pools on the tabletop. "For three years I've worked like a slave for him and then—tell me it's just a bad dream—he actually puts the moves on me. After all I've done for him!"

"Exactly." Animal grinned. He was a cameraman at the station, an Italian boy from Bensonhurst, a gonzo hipster who fashioned himself as a young Sinatra. The smirk on his face told his wife that he was about to enlighten their tender-hearted friend on some of the darker, seamier aspects of male psychology. A sharp look from her made him think better of it. Lucy was only a couple of years older than Audrey, and pretty under all her makeup. She had a very highly developed maternal instinct and a pair of shoulders custom-designed to be cried on. She threw a consoling arm around Audrey and squeezed. "I know, I know, I know—that man is scum! You're a bright, talented girl, but as far as he's concerned, you're just a pair of breasts that talk."

"Oh, there's an image." Animal chewed.

"You know how I spent last weekend?" Audrey asked. "Walking his stupid dog!"

"What kind of dog has he got?" Animal asked. "Something huge?"

"A Great Dane. How'd you know?"

"He's compensating," was all Animal would say.

"He's the worst!" Lucy decided. "He's dirt. He's nothing but a douche bag, gutter slime, dog crap, puke chunk!"

"Hey, hey! I'm trying to eat here!"

"Aud, sweetie," Lucy said sympathetically, "you're just too damned nice, that's your problem. I've worked at WIDF long enough to see who gets ahead and who gets left behind as roadkill. It's not just how hard you work, it's whether you've got that me-first attitude. It's whether you're willing to step on a few necks on your way up the ladder. It's rough out there. You gotta be a killer to get ahead, know what I'm saying? And I'm sorry, baby, but you just don't got what it takes."

Audrey gasped and pulled away, not quite sure if she ought to be angry. She stared at Lucy, then at Lucy's husband. "Animal, you don't think that's true! Do you?"

The man behind the triple-decker burger shrugged. "Nice guys finish last. First rule of the jungle."

Once again Audrey gasped. She stared at Animal, then at his wife. She realized the truth of what they were saying: She wasn't tough enough. Caiman wasn't the only one at the station who had walked all over her. She'd been working extra hard, coming in early, leaving late, volunteering to do the dirty work whenever something out of the ordinary needed doing. But three years later, she realized, she was spinning her wheels. Instead of making her more respected, her double dutifulness had only turned her into a doormat. After thinking it over for a moment, she crossed her arms and composed herself behind a cruel, chilly smile. "Well, I can be tough if I need to be."

Lucy and Animal saw what she was doing and couldn't completely suppress a sudden case of the giggles. "Yeah, we know. No, yeah, no. Sure you can."

"I can! I can be very, very, very tough." Audrey skewered them with what she imagined was a piercing, laser-beam stare. That only made things worse. Animal almost had an up-the-nosey, and Lucy slapped her hand over her mouth trying not to burst out laughing.

Audrey went on protesting her fierceness until she saw something that lifted her out of her seat. "Oh, my God." She was looking at the television set hanging on the wall above the bar. "Oh, my God," she said again. Her companions looked at the television and saw the image of a man walking down a wooden pier in Panama. Audrey shouted over the noise of the busy lunchroom to the bartender. "Turn it up! Turn up the television!" Whoever the dashing, handsome fellow being escorted down the pier by a contingent of soldiers was, he was obviously making quite an impression on her. "It's Nick! Oh, my God, it's Nick!"

Lucy thought her friend might be having an episode. "Who's he? Who's Nick?"

Audrey gazed dreamily up at the set. "My college sweetie! Look at him. He looks so handsome on TV." Then her expression corkscrewed into a natural-born reporter's look of curiosity. "I wonder what he's doing in Panama."

The answer to her question was about to arrive in Manhattan.

Everyone who laid eyes on the creature has a story to tell. In the short time since these events transpired, a million anecdotes, stories, and jokes have been told and passed along. As they circulate, each storyteller adds his or her own touches, gently reshaping the tale and turning it into a legend. A whole new urban folklore is emerging based on the creature's visit. The following section is based on one such story I heard the other day. I have no idea how much of it is true, but like many of the lizard tales I've listened to recently, it captures something of the heart-stopping shock of seeing the beast for the first time. It goes like this.

A group of bums was hanging around under the FDR Drive down by the South Street piers. Another bum, about sixty years old and known to the others as Shaky Joe, came walking from the direction of the Fulton Fish Market with a fishing pole he'd found. Tucked under one arm was a loaf of rye bread he intended to use as bait.

The minute they saw him, the other bums broke out laughing. "Hey, Joe, you gonna catch one of them delicious East River fishies?"

The old guy turned and waved to his friends. "You never know," he said. "Sometimes you get lucky." And off he shambled down to the end of the pier, where he baited his hook with a piece of the bread. He cast his line into the water and not ten seconds later got his first nibble. "What do you know," he said to himself. "Today must be my lucky day after all."

But then the line yanked hard and his reel started spinning madly as the line paid out into the river. The thing was rotating so fast, Shaky Joe didn't dare reach down and try to stop it. Though alarmed, he managed to turn and wave to his friends again. "I think I got one!"

When the fishing line ran out, the pole snapped out of his hands and disappeared into the brown-green-gray water. "What the hell kind of fish takes a man's fishing pole away from him?" he wondered.

Then something started coming toward him. It was under the water and Shaky Joe couldn't tell what it was. But it was big and fast enough to create a five-foot-tall bulge in the water. It looked like a submarine, except that it had a big pair of fins sticking twenty feet out of the water.

When he saw this, Joe turned tail and started running back toward shore. He ran down the wooden pier as fast as his shaky old legs would take him. When they saw what was happening, his drinking companions yelled at him to hurry. He pushed himself to the limit of his speed, afraid to look back. Behind him he knew the fish, or whatever it was, had reached the end of the pier, because he could hear it shattering, plank by plank, behind him. Whatever was chasing him was beginning to force its way under the pier with incredible strength. It gained on him, moving supernaturally fast. It looked as though Shaky Joe was a goner, but he jumped ashore just in time. He dove head-first behind a concrete piling and trembled in his hiding place as he listened to the giant thing lifting out of the water. Joe was afraid to look, but he had to. When he finally did take a peek, he was sorry he had. He saw a giant eyeball staring down at him. It was honey yellow and had a dead white pupil. The creature stooped down for an even closer look and brought its eye right up to the terrified old man.

"I am very sorry," Shaky Joe supposedly told the giant animal. "I was only trying to catch something small."

The scale-covered leviathan turned back to the river and lifted a couple of fishing boats out of the water, anchors and all. Then, without another thought about Joe, he stepped up onto the FDR Drive, where he proceeded to cause one monster of a traffic jam on the expressway before stepping down on the other side and following the smells to the Fulton Fish Market.

"Four more years! Four more years! Four more years!"

Inspired by thundering applause, the portly mayor of the world's most glamorous, most dangerous city—New York, New York—sidestepped away from the microphone and fell into a dramatic, nearly Shakespearean bow, as though he were some chubby Hamlet being slain by the adulation of the crowd.

It was the kind of thing reporters ate up like popcorn. The kind of thing the dailies liked to carry on the front page. The kind of thing his strategists said he would need to do a lot more of if he was going to have a snowball's chance in hell of winning reelection after four years of pissing off every single person in the five boroughs at least once. Mayor Ebert, justifiably famous for being the loudest man in New York, came back to the microphone and started to speak—which is where his troubles usually began.

"I'd like to thank you all for coming out on this beautiful New York City day!" he shouted into the sea of black umbrellas. Only a few people chuckled, so candidate Ebert felt it necessary to explain that his previous comment had been a sort of joke, what with the weather being what it was. The same people chuckled again. He turned around to consult with his chief advisor, Gene.

"Gene, don't we have some of our own people in the audience?"

"Well, yes, I thought we—"

"Because that was not unfunny, what I just said."

"I don't know what to tell you. I—"

Ebert turned back and pounded his fist hard on the podium. "When I came to office four years ago, people didn't think we could reduce crime. *But I did!*" The crowd broke into roaring applause, strong enough to let Ebert ignore the first rumblings. "When I came to office four years ago, people didn't think we could improve city services without raising taxes. *But I did!*" The second time the ground shook, a woman in the crowd came unglued. She screamed, and everything came to a stop.

"Gene, what the hell is that noise?"

The aide was befuddled and could only shrug. He didn't know that the city's fish market had just been gutted of most of its merchandise. Semitrailers had been lifted high into the air, emptied out, and then tossed aside. Two-story buildings had been stepped on and crushed flat.

The next time they heard it, the sound was more distinct: a ground-rattling thud accompanied by the sharp crack of concrete breaking apart under five hundred tons of weight. At an intersection a few blocks away, terrified pedestrians ran screaming into the street as if something was chasing them.

Everyone at the rally sensed something large and frightening was about to appear around the corner. But they didn't have to wait for it to arrive at the end of the street because they could see its head moving past the tops of the buildings. It was brownish gray and the size of a railroad car. Behind the blunt snout, a bright honey-yellow eye was set deep between ridges of armoring scales that seemed to glisten with an opalescent blue sheen in the rain.

The moment they saw it, everyone who had come to hear the mayor's speech took off running for cover.

In the dry, temperature-controlled comfort of WIDF, Charles Caiman strode the decks of the newsroom like a pint-sized Captain Bligh speaking on a cordless phone. He was complaining to one of his field reporters about how bad weather inevitably kills news. Light news days always made Caiman nervous and irritable. It wasn't just that he would have to stretch out the transitions between segments with lots of small talk during that evening's broadcast. It went deeper than that—some people said he was a news vampire who would begin to starve unless he got his daily quota of juicy stories. But the truth was that even though he had been a fixture at the station for almost two decades, he was terrified of losing his job. His reason for living was to be in front of the cameras every night. He loved being a celebrity—especially in New York. It gave him the sense of making history instead of merely talking about it all the time. Earlier in his career, he'd entertained hopes of jumping up to one of the network stations and becoming a national figure. But now he was hanging on to the Big Apple by his fingernails, realizing that in a year or two he could be shipped off to an affiliate in Boise or Milwaukee or Pittsburgh.

"That's not a story," his secretary remembers him complaining into the phone. "Why should I give a rat's stinky ass about a war in a country whose name I can't even pronounce? We're going live at five with nothing to goddamn talk about! Now give me something we can use on the air. We need a story!"

The reason the secretary remembers this exchange so clearly is because of what was happening through the windows of the nineteenth-floor office, just behind Caiman's back. First an enormous mass of wrinkled flesh came into view. It was the creature's snout. The jaws were closed, but the teeth protruded like jagged pieces of broken yellow glass. The entire street quaked as the enormous animal stomped past the windows. Somehow the self-described "Sherlock Holmes of News" managed to remain focused on his phone call, missing this phenomenal occurrence completely.

"Mr. Caiman," the secretary sputtered, "I think your story just walked past."

Sherlock spun around and studied the windows carefully for a second or two before deciding the woman was either crazy or stupid or both. He turned away from the windows and gave her a dirty look before returning once more to his phone conversation.

A second later a muscular tail, gray-brown with a luminous blue sheen, whipped silently past the windows, but Caiman didn't see.

Near the front doors of the crowded diner, Lucy pulled on her coat while Animal stood in line at the cash register waiting to pay the bill. "So, Audrey, this Romeo of yours, did he have a name?" Lucy asked.

"Nick," she replied. "Nick Tatopoulos."

"That why you dumped him?" Lucy sniggered, even though there's nothing especially funny about my name.

"No, Lucy, I just couldn't look five, ten, maybe twenty years down the road and see myself with some scientific egghead who spends his life picking apart cockroaches."

"What, is he in the pest control business? Those guys make a pretty decent living. Anyhow, you must be ecstatic that you dumped him so you could move up to the exciting and glamorous life of being Caiman's assistant."

"Very funny."

Through the soles of their shoes they felt a pounding rumble. The sound was distant and they ignored it, assuming it was one of those giant pneumatic jackhammers used so often at construction sites around the city.

"How long were you and this Nick guy going around, going steady, or whatever?"

"Four years. Well, three years and nine and a half months, to be exact. And everything was going along great and then, kaboom, it all just fell apart in a couple of days. I think I got a little nervous."

"Four years is a long time, girl." *Kaboom.* "I'm surprised he didn't ask you to marry him."

"Actually, that's what makes it so sad. He did."

Kaboom. Lucy and Audrey looked at each other. *Kaboom* again. The windows of the restaurant began to rattle. The demolition machine was moving closer. Lucy was saying how she hoped it wasn't another one of those damned parades when she looked outside just in time to see another *kaboom* move the whole street. Taxicabs and delivery trucks shook and swayed from the shock waves.

"That ain't no parade," Animal said, listening for the next rumble. Sensing something camera-worthy was about to happen, he started moving toward the door. Through the plate-glass windows he saw a giant foot smash down on the street and, *kaboom,* flatten a parked car like a pancake. It was long and sinuous and three-toed like a chicken's foot. But the skin covering it was a drab gray-brown and covered with scales like a snake's. The restaurant shook so hard, pictures fell from the walls and plates skittered across the lunch counter.

Lucy gaped at Audrey, who gaped at Animal, who gaped at the size of the foot. Everyone in the restaurant was stunned by what they saw. As the crowd backed away from the windows Animal bolted toward them. He hurried toward the door, wanting to get a look at this thing. Before he made it outside, Lucy yelled at him, "Victor, don't do anything stupid!"

"I don't think it's dangerous," he called back to her, trying to ignore the obvious danger the huge animal presented. He stopped in the doorway and watched a slab of limestone crash to the ground just outside. Looking up, he saw the beast's hindquarters and tail soar by overhead. Held parallel to the ground, the tail was two hundred feet long and armored with rows of serrated bone along the top or dorsal edge. It glided past the front of the restaurant like a thick flying eel. As the very tip moved past, it twitched involuntarily to the side and ripped through the diner's big plate-glass windows, shattering them onto the screaming patrons.

So much for not being dangerous. A creature that size could kill you without even noticing. But Animal Palotti had never backed away from a news story before and he didn't intend to start now. He pushed through the doors and ran into the street in time to watch the reptile, as tall as the buildings around him, walk around the nearest corner. There were a few people in the street. They had ducked into doorways or pressed themselves against the walls of the buildings as the titanic lizard had marched past. They stood and gaped in silent amazement. They must have been almost equally amazed by Animal's reaction. He yelled after the beast, "Hey, wait up!"

By the time Lucy came outside to talk some sense into him, Animal was already rummaging through the WIDF news van he was driving that day. He wanted to find his video camera and capture the phenomenon on film. The van was thirty feet from where he'd parked it. It was on the sidewalk, lying on its side. Luckily, it hadn't been crushed flat like a lot of cars on the street. He heard Lucy running up behind him and knew he should protect himself against The Purse. But he was in a hurry and, instead of shielding himself, he grabbed the last of his equipment. He turned in time to feel his wife's handbag come crashing down on his shoulder. *"Ouch!"*

"Victor, you retard, don't you go chasin' that thing!"

"I gotta, honey, I'm back on the clock." And then, before she could tell him how ridiculous he sounded, he was gone. He sprinted down the block, weaving his way between wrecked cars, fallen chunks of building debris, and terrorized people running in the opposite direction. As he ran, he struggled to load a fresh videotape into the camera. When he came to the end of the block and looked in the direction the creature had gone, he saw Grand Central Station straight ahead. The beast had turned again and the only part of him that was visible was his tail.

Still fumbling with the videocassette, Animal continued to chase after the towering reptilian life form. All around him, hordes of terrified pedestrians were running in the opposite direction. Although frightened out of their minds, these people showed strong instincts for self-preservation. Victor "Animal" Palotti, on the other hand, was answering to a very different instinct, one that told him to shoot some tape of this bizarre event before some shmuck from a competing station got it first. *Oof!* He collided headfirst with a man large enough to play linebacker for the Jets. Both men went sprawling to the ground. Unfazed, Animal sprang back up and ran to the next corner. Smashed and overturned cars littered the sidewalks. Where a fire hydrant had been shorn away, a column of water spouted high into the rainy afternoon sky. Rubble, shattered glass, and pieces of the facades from the surrounding buildings covered the street.

At the front doors of Grand Central Station, he got some good news and some bad news. The good news was that his camera finally accepted the videocassette. He pushed the record button and saw the little red light pop on. Hoisting the camera onto his shoulder, he pointed it down the street and shot the first images of the gargantuan reptile. It was walking away from him. Jagged scales, like the protective dorsal shields of a stegosaurus, ran up the creature's back. The two that erupted from behind the shoulder blades were especially large, over twenty feet each. They looked like a pair of bony blades that had tried to grow into wings. They waved back and forth heavily as the beast marched methodically forward, its wide body filling the street from sidewalk to sidewalk.

"It's a goddamn lizard," Animal said.

Walking exclusively on its hind legs, the lizard covered about a hundred feet with each stride. When it came into a large intersection it stopped and looked all around, trying to decide which way to go next. And that's when Animal got the bad news.

The creature decided it didn't want to go uptown after all, so it began to turn around. Although Madison Avenue is a large street, the lizard was larger. Including his tail, he stretched out to well over three hundred feet. A U-turn seemed out of the question. But despite its great size, the creature's movements were well coordinated, even graceful. The tail curled tight against the body and, with snakelike flexibility, the creature wrapped his head past his hips, executing the turn with a minimum of damage to the surrounding buildings. Only the tail, as it unfolded behind, caused any damage at all—it ripped a series of lamp posts out of the ground in a single swipe.

With his head hung menacingly low to the ground and swinging side to side, the scaly brown dragon came prowling back the same way he'd come. The rain brought out a blue tint in the creature's skin, a shimmering opalescent hue. Craggy, misshapen teeth protruded from the jaw like shards of broken glass. Animal should have made himself scarce. He should have dropped the camera and run screaming into the lobby of the closest building. But he was a man possessed.

"Oh, that's beautiful. A little closer, baby," he whispered to the gigantic reptile, coaxing him closer. Like many professional cameramen, he suffered from a delusion that once he started filming, he was invisible and protected by some sort of benign magic. Whether it was a wild gun battle between cops and bank robbers or a twenty-story-tall creature marching directly toward him, Animal felt safe as long as the camera was rolling. Confronting dangerous situations through a viewfinder gave the feeling of watching it all transpire on television.

But he was not safe, and by the time he realized the danger he was in, it was too late. The big feet were swiftly closing in on him. *Just another second or two,* Animal kept telling himself, *then I'll get out of the way.* He felt his heart rate shoot up as the dragon's angular head came swinging directly toward him, but he continued to stand in the middle of the street and film until the last possible moment. The viewfinder in his camera began to overflow with leathery, scale-covered flesh. Then one of the razor-clawed feet lifted and blotted out most of the frame. Too late Animal realized it was going to come down directly on top of him. There was nothing to do but film all the way to the bitter end.

He screamed. And then *kaboom*—the foot crushed down on the pavement and everything went dark and quiet for a second. Animal opened one eye and looked around. In terrified amazement, he saw that he was standing *between two of the beast's toes*! He was surrounded on three sides by walls of metacarpal flesh as tall as he was.

The foot lifted and sailed overhead as the creature continued marching.

The camera kept rolling, but Animal wasn't looking through it any longer. He had gone into a sort of catatonic shock. His feet felt nailed to the pavement and, under his jacket, he could feel the sweat running down his body. He followed the creature with his eyes, craning his neck backward to stare into the sky as the towering animal cruised away. "This is not a good thing," he mumbled to himself, barely aware that the powerful tail was swishing by only an arm's length above his head.

As it stalked deeper into the heart of midtown, the beast paused several times and stretched its long crocodilian neck to one side or the other. It was making a careful inspection of the area, totally unconcerned with the panic of the tiny humans below. Animal could tell it was looking for something.

Our plane landed at Newark International Airport and headed away from the passenger terminals. Out on an isolated patch of tarmac was a convoy of white army vehicles and police cars waiting to take us to our next destination. A man in civilian clothes holding a walkie-talkie rushed out through the rain to meet us. Even before the door of the cargo bay swung open, we could see by the expression on his face that the creature had been sighted again. As soon as we stepped outside he delivered the bad news.

"Colonel Hicks, it's here, sir. Came ashore in Manhattan a few minutes ago, down around the Fulton Fish Market."

Hicks cursed under his breath, then asked, "What's it doing?"

"The situation is pretty chaotic, but from what we can gather, it's stomping through town like it owns the place."

Hicks cursed again. As we piled into the waiting vehicles he turned to Elsie, Mendel, and me, saying, "It won't be long now." We knew he meant it wouldn't be long until the creature was killed. As soon as our gear was loaded up, we took off. We raced toward the city behind the wailing sirens of our police escort. As we drove we listened to the police radio and heard the panicked, scattered reports coming out of Manhattan. There were so many people shouting over the airwaves at the same time, it was impossible to get a clear picture of what was going on. But three things became clear: It was huge, it was frightening, and it was on the move. Even though the creature was causing an enormous amount of mayhem and damage, I couldn't help but harbor a secret, selfish hope that the army wouldn't be able to kill it until we got a chance to see it with our own eyes. After all, this was a remarkable, never-before-seen species, and I wanted the chance to study its movements and behavior before it was gunned down.

It didn't take long to reach our destination, a fenced-in parking lot on the Jersey riverfront just across the river from New York City. The army had commandeered the site and was in the process of transforming it from a lonely patch of asphalt into a fully functioning military base. They called it the command center.

By the time we got there, a dozen large tents— larger than ordinary houses—had been pitched. Soldiers were off-loading scores of supply trucks and hauling crates of sophisticated electronic equipment into the tents. In less than an hour the army had set up barracks for hundreds of soldiers, a mess tent, portable toilets, and a mobile chemical analysis laboratory, and had moved in enough weaponry to fight a war against a medium-sized country. Besides the Humvees and armored personnel carriers, there were M1-A1 tanks, mobile rocket launcher trucks, and tall, long-barreled cannons. Parked along the riverfront was a squadron of Apache helicopters, fearsome, heavily armored flying machines that looked as if they could sink a battleship all by themselves. And, of course, there were soldiers. Everywhere we looked, soldiers were running from place to place, helping to set up the encampment. Those that weren't involved in the construction effort patrolled the surrounding rooftops in their black rain ponchos, machine guns in hand.

As we pulled up to the main gate we were confronted by a different army, an army of reporters. Standing under a forest of umbrellas, they shouted questions to us as we drove past them and entered the compound. Once we were inside, we rolled up to the largest of the tents, the war room, where we were greeted by a tense soldier dressed in a combat helmet and full camouflage jumpsuit. He introduced himself as we stepped out into the rain.

"Sergeant Oliver O'Neal reporting, sir!" he shouted to Hicks, snapping into a rigid salute. He motioned to a few of his men, who were standing by with large black umbrellas to protect us from the rain.

Hicks looked at the man as though he were crazy and began marching past him into the tent. This wasn't the time to worry about formal greetings and military protocol. "Any word from the mayor's office?"

O'Neal broke out of his salute and jogged along behind the fast-marching colonel. "Yes, good news. Good news on that front, sir."

"Well, what the hell is it?" Hicks demanded. He'd only known O'Neal for ten seconds and was already annoyed with him.

"I just spoke to city hall and they've agreed to the evacuation order, sir. The mayor is calling in the National Guard."

Elsie interrupted. "Are you talking about evacuating Manhattan? That's over three million people!" She looked at me. "Has that ever been done before?"

"I don't know. I don't think so," I told her.

As we climbed a set of stairs to enter the command center's main tent, Mendel started sneezing. "This weather cannot be good for my nasal passages."

Hicks continued moving down a long hallway. On all sides of us, soldiers were hooking up equipment and finishing the construction of the temporary headquarters. He yelled over his shoulder at O'Neal, "Where is it now?"

All at once it became apparent why Sergeant O'Neal was so nervous. "We lost sight of him, sir."

The colonel stopped dead in his tracks and turned around. He cocked his head to one side and said, "You wanna run that by me one more time? I don't think I heard you right."

"After the initial, um, attack, he . . . well, he can move around pretty quickly, sir, and he just, um, disappeared."

Colonel Hicks was an intimidating presence even when he wasn't trying. When he heard this news, his frustration threatened to boil over. He moved in close on the nervous sergeant and looked him squarely in the eyes. "He *what*?"

"Disappeared, sir." O'Neal stood there as though the world were about to cave in on his head. And it probably would have if another soldier hadn't stepped in at that very moment and told Hicks that he had a telephone call from the secretary of defense. After a lingering, deadly stare, Hicks turned away to take the call.

I stepped up to O'Neal and asked for clarification. "How in the world can something that large just disappear?"

"We're not sure," he told me. "We're scanning the area now. Believe me, we'll find him."

It didn't take long for Elsie to notice that Sergeant O'Neal had the body of a GI Joe and a movie star's good looks. She slunk in close and looked up into his eyes. "Don't worry, gorgeous, it probably returned to the river."

I shook my head. "I don't think so," I said. From where we were standing, we had an unobstructed view of Manhattan through one of the tent's doorways. It was only a feeling, a hunch, but somehow I was sure that after chasing this gargantuan mutant halfway across the planet, our travels were over. "I mean, look at it," I said, pointing across the river to the dense cluster of skyscrapers under the dark gray sky. "It's perfect. It's an island like the one he comes from, but it's not like any other island in the world. This is a place where he can easily hide. He's there, all right. He's in there somewhere."

Hicks was still speaking on his cellular phone when another soldier ran up to him and gave him some urgent news. The colonel shouted into the phone, "Mr. Secretary, I'll have to call you back." He turned to us. "Channel Twelve caught it on film!"

We rushed into the big tent's main space, the war room, and crowded around a television set. We flipped over to WIDF, Channel 12, just in time to see the spectacular videotape images cameraman Animal Palotti had shot only minutes before. There on that tiny little screen we got our first look at the gigantic reptile. He was only a few inches tall on the television, but our mouths dropped open in amazement when we saw him walking toward us. When the huge foot lifted and then came plummeting down toward the camera, several people gasped and involuntarily backed away.

The screen went black and we were certain the cameraman had been stomped like a ripe grape. But moments later a reporter's smiling face appeared on the screen. It was Charles Caiman. He was out in the rain somewhere, doing a live stand-up report while someone stood behind him holding an umbrella. He seemed positively delighted with the frightening images we'd just seen. "You won't find reporting like that on the other channels!" he chirped. "These images are exclusive to WIDF, shot less than half an hour ago by cameraman Victor Palotti, who, like all of us on the ActionNews team, is willing to risk life and limb to provide you, the viewer, with the kind of footage you've just seen. So stick with us, won't you, as we continue our coverage right after this commercial message."

The noisy WIDF newsroom fell silent as everyone stopped what they were doing and turned to watch the overhead television screens mounted around the room. Spellbound, they watched the huge lizard march directly toward Animal's camera until the giant foot lifted and blotted out the sky. Everyone present held their breath, amazed by what they had seen. But as soon as Caiman finished talking and introduced the station break, the whole room erupted in cheers.

"You the man, Animal!"

"Way to go, Victor!"

Animal had arrived only seconds before the tape went on the air, just in time to see his work on-screen. The staff crowded around him offering him congratulations on a job well done. Animal took a bow.

Audrey and Lucy were nearby, throwing the entire contents of their desks into cardboard boxes, when Animal came over and sat down, grinning like the wild man he was. Audrey was properly impressed.

"Now *that* was great tape. Nice stuff, Animal, but weren't you scared?"

"What are you, kidding me? Of course I was scared. I knew Lucy was gonna kill me."

Lucy picked up the nearest nonlethal weapon she could find, which happened to be a heavy envelope, and used it to whack her daredevil husband across the arm. "You're damn right, you crazy wop. You were only a chihuahua's butt-hair from being squashed by that big ape."

"It's a lizard, Lucy. Not an ape."

"Whatever! From now on, I don't want you going near that thing, you hear me?"

"People! Everyone listen up!" Murray, the balding station manager with the heart of gold, climbed up on a chair to make an announcement. When he had everyone's attention, he updated them. "Everybody should be packed by now. We're going to do the ten o'clock show from the New Jersey station." All the employees groaned. "Which means," he continued, "we have to be completely relocated in two hours. The vans are here, they're parked right out front. Let's start loading up." He hopped down off the chair and told Animal that he was supposed to report to the helipad at the top of the building. He'd be going up in the chopper with Caiman to look for the creature. Lucy got a worried look on her face, but she knew she wouldn't be able to stop him. And being in a helicopter sounded safe enough.

"You guys gonna be all right?" Animal asked, pulling on his leather jacket.

"Yeah, sure. Oh, Vic, Audrey's gonna stay with us tonight. She can't go back to her apartment."

"A threesome? Great."

This time Animal knew what was coming and stepped out of the way before Lucy could whack him with the envelope. They smiled at each other, then moved in close for a kiss good-bye. Lucy whispered, "I'm real proud of you, Victor. I'll see you tonight. And, sweetie?"

"Yeah?"

She whacked him across the arm with the envelope. "Gotcha."

Audrey was staring up at the nearest television monitor. The commercial was over and they were reporting on the army headquarters being set up across the river. For the second time that day she'd noticed her ex-boyfriend, me, walking across a TV screen surrounded by a military escort. And this time I wasn't in far-off Panama. I was right across the Linclon Tunnel in New Jersey. She was watching the film of Elsie, Mendel, and me arriving at the command center.

Although she would later deny it, I believe that this was the moment when her transformation began, the moment when her ambition began to hatch inside the overheated incubator of her brain. The biggest news story to hit New York City in fifty years was unfolding around her, and there was her dear old friend Niko Tatopoulos at the center of the action. She stared at the television, lost in cogitation.

"Hello! Earth to Planet Audrey!" When she snapped out of her trance, Caiman was standing at her desk with an exasperated expression on his face. "My bag, my bag, my bag! How many times do I have to ask?"

"Oh, sorry." She picked up his field case and press ID badge, carrying them for him as he hurried toward the elevators. Her mind was already racing, imagining ways to exploit her connection with someone on the inside of the story. She spoke to her boss in a conspiratorial whisper. "Mr. Caiman, listen, I've got a lead. I know a guy on the inside! One of those experts the army brought in."

"Not now." He wasn't even listening.

Audrey couldn't believe it. She knew someone *on the inside*. For the first time in her career she had a connection, a source, and she was offering this plum to her boss on a silver platter. She shot a look toward Animal, who was marching along with them, but he only shrugged. "Mr. Caiman, I don't think you understand. I'm telling you I *know* one of those scientists the army brought in. At the very least I can get us some great back—"

"Listen, honey," Caiman cut her off, "this is when the big boys go to work, understand?" And with that he stepped into the waiting elevator and flashed the already befuddled Audrey a hand signal she couldn't understand. She stared at him, confused. Then he did it again, yelling, "The bag! Can I please have my bag?"

She gave it to him all right. She flung the carry

case at him hard enough to knock him against the rear wall of the elevator just as the doors started sliding closed. Then she flashed him a hand gesture of her own, one he had no trouble interpreting.

Audrey fumed. She boiled. She stewed. And, after a moment, she looked down and realized she was still holding Caiman's press ID badge—which is when her scheme kicked into high gear.

Only a few minutes later she and Lucy were schlepping their boxes out the front door of the building. They carried them through the rain and loaded them in the waiting vans. One look at the congested street and both women knew those vans weren't going to be in New Jersey for the ten o'clock broadcast. Forty-third Street was jammed solid with traffic from one end to the other.

"Come on, girl, we'll take the subway," Lucy decided.

As they hurried across the street and went down the stairs to the train, Audrey looked up and saw the WIDF news helicopter lifting away from the rooftop helipad.

Inside the chopper, Caiman had already gone live. "Call us courageous or call us foolhardy, but we've decided to take to the skies to keep you, the public, informed during this hour of crisis. We're putting our lives in the hands of Captain Jeremy Myers, WIDF's ActionCopter pilot. And who knows, maybe we'll catch a glimpse of this sizable saurian, this wrecking ball of a reptile, this herpetological horror show that has already caused so much damage to the city of

New York and struck so much fear into the hearts of those who call the place home."

Animal rack-focused past the verbose anchorman to show the mayhem taking place in the streets below. Police and National Guardsmen were out in full force doing everything they could to facilitate the exodus, but it was no use. The entire rain-soaked island was an endless, angry traffic jam.

"City officials," Caiman continued, "are calling this the worst act of destruction ever, much worse than the World Trade Center incident. As you can see, hundreds of thousands of Manhattanites, attempting to comply with the mayor's evacuation order, have taken to the streets, some of them desperately clutching their most treasured possessions in hand. This is the largest emergency evacuation in the long history of New York. And not everyone is happy about it or believes it necessary."

They cut to a man-on-the-street interview. Some middle-aged palooka they'd interviewed outside the office an hour earlier was suddenly showing up in the living rooms of ten million households, offering his uninformed opinion. "What are we running from?" the man asked, disgusted. "Some big lizard? I got cockroaches in my building that could kick the crap out of it."

When Caiman's face popped back on screen— his earphones a tad too roomy for his dwarfish head—he wore the resigned smile of a sympathetic uncle. "If that same gentleman is watching this live broadcast, perhaps the view of this building will change his mind."

Animal swung the camera around to focus on the venerable old concrete-and-glass tower. It was demolished. An enormous hole, roughly twenty stories tall, had been smashed into one side of the structure and through the other side. It was plain to see that the creature had crashed its way through the building. Caiman poked his head into the frame as another helicopter passed by outside.

"I hope your roaches are up to it."

"Look at this mess!" the mayor roared over the noise of the helicopter. "And who do you think they're going to blame? The same one they always blame—*me!*" The view out the passenger compartment's windows was not a pretty sight. The center of Manhattan was already emptying out, but its shores were teeming with huddled masses yearning to get to Jersey and Queens. The commissioner of human resources had called a minute earlier on his car phone to report that looters were working their way down Lexington Avenue. As they flew over the West Side Highway and out across the Hudson, Ebert could see the lines of snarled traffic for several miles. "If this evacuation turns out to be unnecessary, Gene, they're going to roast me alive. They'll string me up from the Statue of Liberty's torch." It was all too horrible to contemplate. The mayor consoled himself by tearing back the wrapping on a candy bar and eating most of it in three furious bites.

Disappointed, his chief aide leaned forward and reminded the corpulent candidate, "Didn't we agree that we weren't going to eat any more sweets until *after* the election?" He reached out to take the candy bar, but Ebert reacted with the fury of a rhino protecting its young. After a brief tussle, he wrested the chocolatey treat away and hissed over his shoulder, "Back off, Gene!"

Mayor Ebert was on his way to the army's command center, having invited himself. When his helicopter landed a few minutes later on a New Jersey helipad, there was a crowd of people waiting for him on the roof under a canopy of umbrellas.

"What's this? Who are these people, Gene? I don't have *time* for this!"

As they stood in the doorway waiting for the stairs to be lowered, Gene leaned in close and explained that they were businesspeople, major stakeholders, merchants and property owners who stood to lose several fortunes if the situation couldn't be resolved quickly.

"Who the hell are these clowns? I don't have time for this nonsense. Screw 'em."

"They're campaign contributors, sir."

Campaign contributors? Well, that was a different story. Candidate Ebert's hectic schedule relented. He ducked under the whirring blades, beaming his sunniest smile, and waded into the crowd for a quick meet-and-greet. After all, these people were his constituents and they were legitimately concerned about the welfare of the city.

"I share your concerns," he shouted to them after he'd shaken most of the hands. "You have my personal assurance that I'm going to be looking out for your interests. We're going to do everything humanly possible to protect your investments and get the city back in business just as soon as possible." With that, he threw his stubby fists in the air and offered the crowd a double thumbs-up.

He was shouldering his way past them toward the elevator, shaking hands without breaking stride, when he ran into a human roadblock. A tall man with a salt-and-pepper grizzle of beard stood directly in the mayor's path. He held a large black umbrella over a long black trench coat, and he moved in on the mayor like a falcon on a field mouse. Reaching into his breast pocket, he produced a business card, twirling it expertly between his fingers as he handed it over.

"La Rochelle Insurance," he said warmly and with a thick French accent. "We represent nearly thirteen percent of the buildings in your city."

The mayor looked up uneasily. He was in a hurry, and something about this hovering Frenchman made him nervous. He chirped an encouraging word before lowering his head and attempting to bull his way past. But the Frenchman cut him off at the pass, sliding deftly into his path once more, this time reaching out to pat the mayor on the back.

"I just wanted to tell you how relieved we are that you are in control of the situation." He patted Ebert on the back of the neck, something the mayor found odd. *Probably just one of those weird French things,* he told himself. "You can count on La Rochelle for support."

"Oh, right, well, thank you. Thanks very much. What was your name?"

The Frenchman only smiled and stepped aside. "Have a nice day."

Mayor Ebert, spotting his opening, plunged forward and continued on his way, completely unaware that he'd just been bugged. Protruding from the collar of his shirt was a pin-sized object that hadn't been there when he stepped off the helicopter.

THREE

A udrey scanned the faces of the people on the subway, wondering if they knew. Wondering if they could tell just by looking at her that, less than thirty minutes before, she had committed the first crime of her entire life—the theft of Caiman's press ID. And could they see that she was on the verge of committing yet another misdeed, a forgery? Each time someone in the crowded train glanced in her direction, she felt an impulse to confess everything. Was this only the beginning? Was she edging out onto the slippery slope of criminality? Would she, in time, become addicted to the reckless thrills of the outlaw lifestyle and end up robbing banks? Where would it all end?

She and Lucy were riding the PATH train toward New Jersey and WIDF's temporary production facilities, which consisted of Big Ed sitting behind the mixing board in the truck while the rest of the staff stood outside with umbrellas. Like most of the news outfits in New York, WIDF had set up shop as close to the command center as they could. Luckily, Animal and Lucy's apartment was only about a mile away.

Lucy examined Caiman's press ID before digging through her purse in which she carried, seemingly, everything. She found a strip of photo-booth pictures that she and Audrey had taken some weeks before, then pulled out a pair of nail scissors. She cut out an almost-square picture of Audrey acting almost serious and found that it fit almost perfectly over the picture of Caiman.

"Well, that'll have to do. It's the only picture of you I've got where you're not acting like a mental patient."

"I'm not sure this is such a good idea," Audrey fretted. "I mean, what if Caiman finds out I took it?"

Lucy stared at her with an angry, don't-even-think-of-going-there facial expression. "Come on! You're finally starting to show a little chutzpah. Don't wimp out on me now. Caiman doesn't even need this pass. Everybody in town knows his face. He won't have problems getting in anywhere."

"Yeah, I suppose." Audrey bit her lip, still doubtful. "But what do you think he'd do if he found out?"

"*Who cares?*" Lucy exploded. All the other passengers looked at them, but Lucy couldn't have cared less. "Look, you gotta ask yourself the following question: How often are you gonna have an ex-boyfriend on the inside of an international story? This is a once-in-a-lifetime opportunity, girlfriend. Now, you gonna do this or not?"

Audrey thought of her three years of slave labor under Caiman's harsh yoke and of how he'd repaid her with an invitation to "dinner." She had tried her best to play by the rules, but now she realized it hadn't gotten her anywhere. Lucy was right, she acknowledged; it was time to take matters into her own hands if she ever expected to make a career for herself as a reporter in this tough-as-nails town. Right then and there she made up her mind. (And take it from someone who knows: Once Audrey makes up her mind about something, she can be a real mule.) She curled her lip back, imitating Edward G. Robinson in an old gangster flick, and laid her cards on the table.

"Yeah, I'm in."

"Good. We need some glue or something to stick your picture on this badge." Lucy had everything else in that purse of hers, but she didn't have glue.

"Foolish me! I left my forgery kit at the office again."

"Hardy-har." Luckily, there was a group of schoolkids a few seats away, and they were carrying backpacks. In her sweet-as-horseradish way, Lucy spoke to one of the boys. "Hey, kid, you got any glue?"

"Maybe," the pudgy thirteen-year-old sniffed. "And what do I get out of it?"

"Will ya get a load of the cheek on this youngster?" she snorted. "How about that warm, fuzzy feeling of knowing you helped out your fellow man?"

"Blow me," the kid shot back.

That cracked up everybody who had followed the exchange, including Audrey. But a minute later, after Lucy had walked over and held a brief but pointed conference with the young scholar, she came back holding not one but *two* containers of glue, one stick and the other liquid. He had offered to throw in his stapler, but Lucy said that wouldn't be necessary.

"My friend Joshua told me that I may keep these," she said politely.

A nondescript man in nondescript clothing came walking through the rain carrying a bag of Yum Yum doughnuts and a large to-go cup of coffee. There was nothing memorable about him. If anyone had happened to stop and ask him for the time, they wouldn't have been able to describe him five minutes later. If anyone happened to ask what he did for a living, he was prepared to explain that he worked for an international insurance agency. Let us call this man Jean-Luc.

A thick ceiling of storm clouds blocked the late afternoon sun, bringing an early twilight to the city. A light but steady rain was falling as Jean-Luc paused on the curb near an ordinary-looking van and pretended to sip the coffee. After a surreptitious glance up and down the block, he knocked the secret knock on the vehicle's rear door. It clicked open, and a second later he evaporated completely from the street.

"*Merci beaucoup,*" said Phillipe Roache as he pulled off his headphones and took possession of the junk food. He had only just arrived himself, still in the suit and tie he'd worn to see the mayor. Now, if what he told me much later is to be trusted, he was seated at the controls of a floor-to-ceiling portable eavesdropping console. Pretty fancy equipment for an insurance agent. He hungrily opened the bag and lifted out a doughnut. Obviously, it wasn't what he'd been expecting. The sight of the powdered-sugar snack seemed to confuse and wound him slightly. He looked up at Jean-Luc. "No croissants?"

"*Il n'y en a pas*—there aren't any."

Warily Roache tore off a sweet, greasy mouthful and grimaced at the taste. To wash it away, he quickly drank from his coffee. But that was even worse than the doughnut. After he succeeded in forcing the bilge down his throat, he complained to Jean-Luc, "You call this coffee?"

"I call this America. *Il n'y a pas de café ici!*" he declared.

The two other men in the van wholeheartedly agreed that there was neither edible food nor potable drink in *les États-Unis*. They haughtily declared that the best reason for a Frenchman to visit the States was so he wouldn't be tempted to go off his diet.

Still regarding the coffee as if it had betrayed

him bitterly, Roache put the headphones back on and listened. He quickly turned up the volume when he heard the mayor storm into the command center screaming, "Tell me this is all a cruel joke!"

Elsie, Mendel, and I were hanging around the edges of our tent headquarters on the banks of the Hudson, waiting to see what would happen next. The top brass from each branch of the military were converging on the site, and the mood of tension in the air seemed to escalate with the arrival of each new officer. They all seemed angry with Hicks for having failed to intercept the creature before it reached American waters and stomped through the front door of the most populous city in the nation. At the same time, none of them wanted to strap himself into the hot seat. So, while Hicks was allowed to continue leading the hunt, his superiors let it be known that they had him on a very short leash. In addition to deploying arms and munitions in the city and monitoring reports from his search teams, Hicks was busy answering the generals' questions.

"What are you calling this thing?" was a question he was asked more than once.

"Dr. Chapman, have you people come up with a name for this thing yet?"

"I hadn't really thought about it," she said, "but since Dr. Tatopoulos was the one who first realized this thing is a distinct species, he should be the one to name it."

I was taken aback, both by Elsie's generosity of spirit and by the fact that everyone in the tent was suddenly looking at me. "I'll have to give it some thought," I said.

"I've got a suggestion," Hicks's immediate supervisor, General Anderson, announced. "Let's call it 'the target.'"

It was loud under the command center's tent. Phones were ringing, printers were spitting out status reports, technicians were speaking into radios, and a hundred people were coming in and out. But the noise level tripled with the arrival of the right honorable mayor of New York City.

"Tell me this is all a cruel joke. Tell me this isn't really happening," Ebert bellowed. He walked to the center of the room and stood surrounded by high-ranking military personnel and government officials, not to mention we three scientists. Other men might have been intimidated into a show of good manners, but Mayor Ebert was indignant. He'd recently learned that the army had no idea where "it" was. "You're telling me that in an election month, I've ordered the evacuation of the entire city, and ten minutes later this thing disappears? My own mother, ladies and gentlemen, is on a train for Pittsburgh. When she finds out this was a false alarm, even *she* won't vote for me!"

Admiral Phelps had a deep, baritone voice. In contrast to the mayor's arm-flapping histrionics, he remained cooler than a cucumber. "We've been monitoring the waters on all sides of the island. As far as we can tell, it hasn't left the area."

"Yes, but what I'm hearing"—Ebert gestured toward his own ears—"is that you don't know for sure. This lizard or whatever could have been long gone by the time you started watching for it! Nobody has even seen it for hours. This evacuation is no longer necessary. Let's call it off."

Colonel Hicks shook his head and explained why that wouldn't be possible. "There's still a very good chance it's in the city. We have reason to believe it may be hiding inside one of the buildings within the sequestered area."

"But you don't know for sure! Do you have any idea what this is costing the city every hour in lost revenues? Do you know how many Upper East Siders are going to spend the night out in the rain?"

Sergeant O'Neal rushed into the tent, stopped a few feet from Hicks, and stood frozen in a rigid salute. I think Colonel Hicks noticed him right away but decided to ignore the interruption. He didn't need any more bad news, especially not in front of all those cranky generals. And especially not midway through Ebert's tirade.

"Mr. Mayor," Hicks growled nicely, "I sympathize with your position. Believe me, I do. But I cannot and will not give the all-clear until we've inspected each and every building inside our perimeter. For the safety of your city's people, I'm sure you'll agree that—"

Whatever Sergeant O'Neal had to report couldn't wait another second. He stepped right into the middle of the heated Hicks-Ebert discussion and resaluted.

"What now?" asked the colonel, popping an antacid tablet into his mouth.

"Excuse me, sir, but inspecting the buildings inside the perimeter might not be enough." O'Neal, an edgy soldier who desperately wanted everything to run smoothly and by the book, stared straight ahead, ramrod erect.

"What is it now?" Hicks asked, although by then we had a fair idea of what the answer was going to be.

"Sir, we've run into a problem, sir."

The question raised by the visiting generals about what the creature should be called makes this an opportune moment to discuss the problem of naming. Up to this point, I have referred to the story's central character as "the creature," "the beast," "the monster," or "the really big lizard." Also, after finding evidence of femoral glands, I knew the animal was a male, so I sometimes called him "him." Confusing? *Why,* the reader might well ask, *don't you simply go ahead and call him Godzilla—after all, that is the name on the cover of the book.*

There are two reasons. First of all, we still hadn't settled on a name among ourselves. We were

using terms like "it" and "the thing" and "the creature." Although we had seen the videotape with the
old Japanese cook repeating the word *gojira,* we
still didn't know what that meant. Secondly, the
name Godzilla is nothing but a butchered mispro-
nunciation of the creature's true historical name. As
we will see, it was the result of one unscrupulous
reporter's misreading, a man who was small in both
spirit and stature. The name Godzilla appears on the
cover of this book against my wishes, and only
because it is the term that has come into common
usage. As someone who constantly has to correct
the way people pronounce my last name, I am perhaps overly sensitive to this issue. I urge all my
readers not to call this animal Godzilla. That's not
his name. No more than my name is Tadapoleus,
Topapodalus, Dopatodolus, or any of the other
things I've been called.

To quote Audrey: "It's Gojira, you moron!"

As soon as O'Neal told us about the problem he'd
discovered, we piled into a set of armored personnel
carriers and tore off toward the city.

Twenty minutes later we were cruising the rain-
streaked streets of Chelsea at better than sixty miles
per hour. On a normal night, Eighth Avenue would
be crowded with pedestrians and taxicabs. But at
eight-fifteen that evening, all the shops were shut
down and the lights turned out. The only people we

saw were the soldiers directing traffic. They stood in dreary pools of light under the street lamps, wearing black rain slickers, and saluted as we whizzed past. The deserted city looked like one large Edward Hopper painting. Up ahead, we could see the lead vehicles in our convoy turning west on Twenty-third Street.

"Um, driver," Elsie ventured, leaned forward, "are you familiar with the term *hydroplaning*?"

"Yes, ma'am."

"Well, I'm young and beautiful and have everything to live for. I don't want to crash and burn."

The guy glanced over his shoulder, gave her a long, curling, easy smile, and promised to "take the corners nice and slow."

We lurched to a stop in Madison Square, where Twenty-third Street and Fifth Avenue meet Broadway (which runs on a diagonal). The Flatiron District takes its name from the Flatiron Building, the famous wedge-shaped landmark on the square that points uptown like the prow of a twenty-one-story-tall ocean liner. The ornate structure was the world's tallest building when it was completed in 1902, ushering in the beginning of New York's skyscraper era. In the early 1900s, according to local legend, strong downdrafts from the building lifted young ladies' long skirts, exposing their ankles and sometimes more. The crowds of young men who gathered in the area to catch glimpses of this forbidden flesh were cleared away with shouts of "Twenty-three skidoo" from the policemen directing traffic. The square is really nothing more than a giant intersection several blocks long. Off to one side is a little patch of trees and benches known as Madison Square Park.

We climbed out of the personnel carriers and found ourselves at the mouth of a subway entrance. Sergeant O'Neal quickly lead the group down the stairs and into the sprawling Twenty-third Street station.

Mendel sneezed. "Subways make me claustrophobic," he told me as we marched down the stairs. "This cannot be good for my allergies."

We hopped over the turnstiles and marched through the underground corridors of the station, listening to our footsteps echo off the walls. I'd been scared in New York's subway system before, but it had always been a fear of other people. Now that we were the only ones down there, the place seemed spookier than ever.

We followed O'Neal down another flight of stairs to one of the northbound platforms. "Lieutenant Plyler and his men were searching the station late this afternoon," he explained, "when they found this."

"Oh, my lord!" exclaimed one of the generals.

"Damn it!" fumed Hicks.

"Uh-oh," worried Dr. Chapman.

"Ah-choo!" sneezed Dr. Craven.

Through the murky fluorescent lighting, we could see that where there had been four parallel train lines moving through four separate tunnels, there was now only a single, very large passageway. Something with enormous power had pushed its way through, carving out a much-enlarged opening. There were claw marks scratched deep into the concrete. Shattered bricks and twisted steel rails were everywhere.

"Dr. Patapopolis, Dr. Craven," Hicks said, staring with displeasure at the wreckage, "you should have told me lizards can dig."

"They pretty much invented the process, sir. About sixty million years ago." I didn't correct his pronunciation.

O'Neal spoke up again, fleshing out his report. "When we learned he could burrow his way through the tunnels, we realized he could have escaped the quarantine zone."

"Christ!" Hicks kicked an aluminum can halfway down the platform. "How many tunnels lead off this island, Sergeant?"

"Sixteen. Only sixteen, sir. We've checked them all. He hasn't used any of them," O'Neal said proudly, glad to have positive news for a change. But Hicks wasn't satisfied.

"Seal them off. Seal every last one of them off."

"And how do you propose we do that, sir?"

"How the hell should I know?" he exploded. "Fill them with cement, brick them up, put land mines in them, bombs, I don't know. But you'd better make sure that goddamned lizard doesn't leave this island! Do I make myself clear?"

"Sir, yes, sir." At that moment O'Neal probably

would have preferred to be facing the enormous lizard instead of his irate commanding officer. Cringing and saluting, he nodded rapidly. The colonel had made himself perfectly clear.

"You know," I said about five minutes later, when Hicks's blood pressure had returned to almost normal, "this creature, he's not an enemy who's come here to attack us. And right now he's probably not even trying to evade us. He's just an animal. Doing, you know, his animal thing."

We were at the edge of the platform closest to the mouth of the newly enlarged tunnel. The colonel had sent a small group of soldiers into the opening and was monitoring their progress when I joined him. The men were forced to proceed slowly, because not only was the ground underfoot churned up, but the destroyed walls were full of jagged fragments poking into their path. Sparking electrical wires hung like deadly snakes from the ceiling. Hicks turned and glanced at me as though I wasn't making much sense. "What exactly are you suggesting?"

"When I need to catch earthworms," I explained, "the best way isn't to chase after them. Instead of digging them out, I make them come to me. I *draw* them to the surface."

The colonel grunted as if that was an interesting idea. "And how do you propose to *draw* this particular critter to the surface?"

That was a good question—one I couldn't answer at the moment. "All we need to do is figure out what it needs and he'll come to us. The problem is, we still don't know what he's looking for." Just then one of the men returned from exploring the first hundred yards of the tunnel.

"What'd you find, soldier?"

"Fish, sir. A couple of hundred of them."

This news puzzled the colonel. "Fish?"

"Yes, sir."

Hicks turned to me, trying to understand. "Let me see if I've got this straight. A two-hundred-foot-tall radioactive mutant lizard swims halfway around the globe and comes to Manhattan because it wants—fish?" He was right. It didn't add up. I was pretty certain the creature we were chasing had other reasons for making the trip, but we didn't have enough information at the time.

"Colonel, I don't understand it, either, but this is our chance to lure him out in the open. If it's fish he wants, let's give him fish."

I could tell he wasn't crazy about the idea. He stood there staring at me for a minute trying to decide if I knew what I was talking about. Either he came to the conclusion that I did or else he simply couldn't think of anything better to do. Five minutes later we were upstairs again, standing in drizzling rain. Hicks used a mobile telephone to order the bait.

Within minutes the square began to buzz with activity. Dozens of army trucks rolled in and dropped off reinforcements. Too many of them, I thought at the time, probably five times the number of soldiers the situation seemed to call for. Rifle crews took positions on several of the surrounding rooftops. Heavy artillery units arrived and positioned themselves strategically about the square. You would have thought a war was about to break out.

In addition to the military, there were scads of firefighters, paramedics, and teams of construction workers sent out to do emergency repairs. A handful of reporters were on hand to cover the situation, but there were only about twenty of them and they were kept tightly corralled inside a small area a block and a half from our position. All together, there must have been two thousand people working to prepare the trap. The noise level was kept to a minimum, however, as everyone concentrated on completing their tasks.

When the groundwork had been laid, Hicks announced that he was headed back to the command center. He would command the operation from there, and invited Elsie, Mendel, and me to come along. "It's not going to be pretty," he told us. "We've got a lot of firepower out here, and the moment the lizard shows itself, we're going to chop him up pretty bad. You'll be able to see everything just as well via the remote monitors."

All three of us quickly refused his invitation. We were curious to see the creature with our own eyes. You don't get very far in the world of professional science unless curiosity rules your life. And after chasing him nonstop for the previous three days, we were determined to observe him—even if just for a moment or two. Hicks could see that we weren't going to budge. "All right, you can stay here and observe so long as you stay out of the way." Soon after that he climbed into a helicopter and lifted away, leaving Sergeant O'Neal in charge of the site.

Then we waited for the fish to arrive.

The amount of fish the colonel had ordered involved more than a trip to the supermarket. It required seizing the entire contents of three local canneries, then arranging the men and machines to transport it all. Given the size of the task and lateness of the hour—it was after ten o'clock at night when Hicks flew away—it's amazing how quickly everything happened. But sitting out there in the rain waiting for something to happen made it feel like an eternity.

We three scientists were essentially superfluous to the proceedings. But that didn't keep us from grabbing the best seats in the house. At the end of the square opposite the Flatiron Building there is another roughly triangular building. On the sidewalk at the base of this structure, a field communications post had been established behind a wall of sandbags. It was filled with electronic equipment and about twenty soldiers to operate all of it. To protect it from the rain, a waterproof tarp had been pitched, supported by metal poles. There were folding chairs, video monitors, radar equipment, and radios—it was definitely where we wanted to watch from. As we sat there waiting for the bait to be brought in, the mood under the tent was a mixture of tension and boredom.

No one was more tense than Mendel, and no one was more bored than Elsie. He was driving her up the walls with his continuous verbal hand wringing.

"Ironic, don't you think? I've written all these books about deadly viruses, lethal solar flares, and pernicious proteins introduced by extraterrestrial species. I've imagined a hundred ways the world could end. I just never thought it would be at the hands of an overgrown iguana." He had armed himself with a pen and yellow notepad but was too jittery to write.

"If you're so scared, why don't you head back to the command center?" she asked. "There's still plenty of time."

"What? And miss this?" He looked at her as though she'd flipped her lid. "Do you know what kind of a book I'll be able to write when this is all over?"

"Well, I think the whole situation is surreal," Dr. Chapman declared, making meaningful eye contact with a boyish-looking technician who was manning the sonar detection scanner. "It's like being invited to a dinner party hosted by Salvador Dali." She reviewed the action up to that point. "A man in a uniform picks up a telephone and tells the person on the other end of the line that he wants a quantity of fish delivered immediately to a public place. He says he will need several tons of fresh raw fish. The person on the phone agrees, as if this request is the type of thing he handles every day. They say good-bye and hang up. Then the table must be set, so all vehicles and personnel are cleared from the center of the square. The dinner guests—that's us—take their seats behind sandbag barricades and wait patiently for the meal to be delivered, a meal none of us intends to eat."

"I don't get it," said the soldier.

"I could learn to live with that," she told him.

The chilly rain showed no signs of letting up, but I wanted to get out from under the low tarp of the communications post and stretch my legs. I strolled over to a bank of sidewalk vending machines and bought myself a refreshing Mountain Dew. As I sipped I pondered. And soon I found myself wandering absentmindedly down an empty side street.

Something continued to bother me. *Why,* I asked myself over and over, *did the creature come here?* Not to Manhattan necessarily—that part was easy. The skyscrapers were taller than any forest, and there was an extensive system of tunnels below the ground for him to dig through. He could have searched the world over and been hard pressed to find a better place to hide himself. But that answer wasn't enough.

If he was hungry for fish, why would he have left the South Pacific for the cooler waters of the

North Atlantic? Was he looking for something more than a hiding place? What instinct had induced this sudden migration? I reminded myself that lizards are not particularly intelligent animals. Although I'm not a herpetologist, I've read enough about them to know they carry many diseases, become docile in captivity, and seem incapable of higher mental functions—rational thought, planning, and emotion. I needed, therefore, to find an extremely simple explanation. The farther I meandered away from the square, the clearer my thinking became. Eventually I hit upon a theory: The reptile had outgrown his natural habitat. His own sheer magnitude had flushed him out into the open. He was a pretty large lizard, and humans must have begun to stumble across him in his island home (and I wonder what happened to them). It had become obvious—even to an animal with a prehistoric IQ—that he needed a better place to hide, somewhere he could keep out of sight while remaining close to his source of food, the sea.

Given the information available to me at the time, it seemed like a plausible theory: His instinct for survival told him he'd outgrown all the hiding places on his island and needed a new home. I still believe that's partially true. Size does matter, as they say. But, as I was soon to discover, there was more motivating this remarkable saurian than size alone.

When I made my way back to the command tent at about eleven-thirty that night, things were start-

ing to happen. We got word that the delivery vehicles were approaching. The sound of distant helicopters echoed through the canyons of skyscrapers.
Hicks's voice came over the radios, demanding constant updates from the harried communications
experts.

"Where are they now?"

"Delta Niner, this is Flatiron," the soldier murmured into his headset microphone. "What is convoy position at present?"

"Sit tight, Flatiron, they're just entering the city.
You're looking at an ETA of approximately ten minutes."

Just about then, on a rooftop in New Jersey, a nondescript man in blue overalls was finishing a
"repair" to a satellite dish. He was on the roof of a
seedy hotel that overlooked the army's command
center. The "repair" he made involved attaching a
boxlike device to the side of the satellite dish. The
box was connected to a cable that disappeared over
the retaining wall, ran down the outside of the hotel,
split off into one of the rooms, and continued down
to street level. From there, the cable ran across the
busy roadway, under a chain-link fence, and directly
into the command center itself, where it became
invisible among the thousands of similar cables.
This man on the roof repacked his tools and, before
standing up to leave, tapped at his earpiece and

spoke into his own lapel. Let us call him Jean-Claude.

"*C'est bon, n'est-ce pas?*" he asked, reaching out and flipping a switch on the device.

"*C'est bon,*" a voice answered. "*C'est okay, très bon.*"

The voice belonged to Phillipe Roache, who was two stories below, sitting inside one of the hotel's dingy rooms. As soon as the device was activated, he could hear and see everything Hicks saw and heard. The crafty team of "insurance agents" had turned the hotel room into a mini command center of their own. Roache sat at the foot of the lumpy bed watching live aerial pictures of Madison Square. The static disrupting the broadcast was the result of the hotel's TV being so old and decrepit. The whole beige room was ratty, faded, and dismal in every way but one—it came with a Mr. Coffee machine. Jean-Luc, who must have been special agent in charge of refreshments, poured some of the fresh brew into a flimsy plastic cup and handed it to his boss. This time Roache had a trick up his sleeve. Out of nowhere, he produced a handful of sugar packets and poured the contents of several into the cup before he dared bring the suspicious liquid to his lips. He stirred the scalding coffee with his bare pinkie and looked up at the television. Quite pleased with the sight of the stolen video feed, he sipped. The taste of the coffee peeled his lips back as though it were paint remover.

"You said this was French roast!" he complained loudly.

Jean-Luc, defeated, held up a bag labeled French roast. *"Plus de crème"* was the only thing he could suggest.

Every muscle of every person in Madison Square tensed the moment we heard the sound of the approaching dump trucks rumbling through the abandoned streets of the city. I was under the tarp roof of the communications post, watching the technicians run through their systems check. O'Neal stood in the rain atop the sandbag barricade in front of the post, directing the last-minute preparations. The only job Elsie, Mendel, and I had been given was to stay out of the way, which was a little frustrating. There we were, a trio of scientists on the verge of witnessing one of the most spectacular events in the entire history of the biological sciences, and we had nothing at all to do. Although there were video cameras positioned around the square to record the scene, I decided to prepare myself in whatever small way I could. I walked back to the vending machines where I'd bought the soda awhile earlier and spent a few bucks on a Kodak Fun Saver, one of those disposable cameras, before jogging back to our outpost.

Hicks was definitely running the show. Although he had returned to the command center, he kept an eye on the preparations via a closed-circuit video feed and had the ability to override all radio frequencies. Whenever he did this, his commands were picked up on all the hundreds of radios and walkie-talkies scattered around the square, and his voice seemed to come from everywhere and nowhere at once, like the invisible ringmaster of a strange circus.

At last the sixteen dump trucks came thundering around the corner, each one filled to the brim with two tons of fish. The soldiers led the vehicles through a complicated automotive ballet until they were arranged in a circle, their tailgates facing the center. The pungent odor of fish was so thick in the air that our eyes began watering. Mendel was probably the only person who welcomed the overpowering aroma. He reported that it was helping to clear his sinus passages.

O'Neal turned around and looked right at me. "I sure hope this plan of yours works."

"I'm kind of hoping the same thing," I told him.

Elsie, a hard-core smart aleck, couldn't resist toying with him. "Sergeant, are you questioning the fact that this lizard is ichthyophagous?"

O'Neal stared at her blankly. "Uh, no. No, I guess I'm not," he said before turning back to the action in the square. I don't think he knew that ichthyophagous means "eating or subsisting on fish."

When everything was ready, O'Neal waved his arm—the signal that the fish dumping should begin. All sixteen tailgates were thrown open simultaneously, and copious amounts of fish began to spill onto the street. Ton after slippery ton of fish—cod, shad, mackerel, salmon, red snapper, fish of every size and shape—poured from the trucks. As the pile spread out sideways, hundreds of soldiers rushed forward and tossed the escapees back onto the center of the pile. Right below the nose of the Flatiron Building, they built an enormous pyramid of sea creatures, twelve feet tall at its peak. It was an amazing, surreal sight. Some onlookers shook their heads in disbelief, and others laughed nervously. I held my nose. If you hadn't known we were trying to lure a two-hundred-foot-tall ichthyophagous lizard into the intersection, you would have thought we were crazy.

The moment the last fish skittered onto the pavement, the trucks were ordered to evacuate the area—an order the drivers were only too happy to obey. As the sound of their motors disappeared down the skyscraper canyons of midtown, the square fell quiet once again. Thousands of soldiers hunkered down behind their barricades and trained their weapons on the enormous stinking pile, which was illuminated by intensely bright spotlights. O'Neal reminded us to stay out of the way before he stepped into the building behind us. He was going to observe the killing from its rooftop.

Except for the constant patter of the rain on the tarp of the communications post, all was silent as we waited for the dragon's arrival. The technicians under the tent sat at their instrument consoles, whispering to their counterparts back at the New Jersey command center. I moved forward to the sandbag barricade and peered out into the square. Almost immediately I noticed a problem. Steam was escaping from the air vents and manhole covers. It wisped a couple of feet into the air before breaking apart in the rain. I asked one of the soldiers next to me if I could borrow his radio.

"Come in, Sergeant O'Neal. This is Nick Tatopoulos. Do you read me? Over."

"What?" he asked, exasperated.

"Sergeant, if you look down, you'll notice steam coming out of the air shafts. The subway's ventilation system must still be operating, and if the air is being forced upward, he'll never be able to smell the bait. Over."

"Damn it, I knew we'd forget something." Then the radio went dead as he switched to another frequency and ordered a squad of his soldiers down into the Twenty-third Street station. As they ran down into the subway, I hoped I was right about the smell not being able to waft down. If I was wrong, they might meet an unexpected visitor below-ground. A couple of minutes after they disappeared, we heard the sound of the big air turbines shutting down.

I figured we had a few minutes before the odor of the fish could penetrate the underground maze of passageways, so I called out to the soldiers around me. "We've got to remove the manhole covers so the scent can waft down!" Before anyone could raise an objection, I ran out into the square.

Opening the vents was a good idea. I only wish I'd thought of it *before* there were thirty-two tons of fish lying in the street. Accompanied by a handful of soldiers in full combat gear, I raced from cover to cover, pausing long enough for the heavy disks to be pried loose and rolled aside. The whole process was taking too long, and as I waited impatiently for one of the lids to be removed, I looked down a side street and noticed it was chock full of manhole covers. "Give me a hook," I demanded. Once I had it, I ran past the edge of the army's defensive perimeter and into one of the dimly lit, unguarded streets. I was fairly certain there was a subway tunnel running directly underfoot, so removing a few of the covers would greatly improve our waft factor.

The cast-iron disks were heavy, but I was pumped with adrenaline and was able to remove them rather easily. I quickly got the hang of it and hurried down the street prying up one after another. I was three quarters of the way to the next cross street and had just unsealed another manhole when I heard something go *thump*. I stood very still, afraid to move, and glanced around.

Half a block ahead of me I saw a pair of parked cars hop into the air like a couple of overweight bull-frogs. Then a delivery van, thirty feet closer, bounced upward for no apparent reason. Something was moving below the surface of the street, something huge, and it was coming toward me. As I watched this curious phenomenon the entire street in front of me began to swell and bulge. The center lifted until it was several feet higher than the sidewalks. A foot-wide crack shot down the street, traveled right between my feet, and continued on toward the square. The bulge in the asphalt moved toward me like a slow wave traveling across the surface of the sea. I knew the beast had caught the scent of the bait and was stealthily forcing its way closer through a too-narrow passageway. I thought of running, but the bulky shape under the ground was still half a block from where I was standing. As I stood over the man-hole I'd opened, I heard something move beneath me. I looked down into the pitch darkness of the hole. I couldn't see anything but heard the sound of breath-ing. It took me a moment to realize what was hap-pening. It was the animal's belly and haunches that were breaking the street apart. Its head and neck were already below me. Just then the creature breathed out through its nose, expelling the dirt and debris that had accumulated in its nostrils. A warm gust of air blew upward out of the hole, bringing with it great scoops of dirty mucus that covered the front of my jacket as though I'd been hit by a cream pie.

It was time to run.

I backpedaled, then turned and raced down the darkened street as fast as my legs would carry me. Up ahead I could see the bright lights of the square and a group of soldiers who still had no idea how close the danger had come. Then the entire street behind me erupted from below. In an explosion of dirt, pipes, and pavement, the creature broke through to street level. Chunks of roadway started hitting me in the back and flying past me. I increased my speed and was nearly back to the well-lit square when my path was suddenly blocked by a huge piece of falling asphalt. A fifteen-foot-tall boulder of debris smashed down out of the air right in front of me. If I'd been a faster runner, it would have crushed me to death. It landed with a heavy thud just outside the square. I was about to swerve around it and keep running when I heard a blood-chilling primordial howl rip through the rainy night. The creature's scream had a raw, ragged, throaty quality that spoke to me in a way no one had been spoken to for the past sixty-five million years. I dashed behind the boulder to hide.

When I peered around the corner, I got my first good look at the creature. My knees went weak and threatened to buckle completely when I saw how staggeringly large it was. Its dark outline towered over me. It was only half a block away, a seemingly endless mass of writhing reptilian flesh. Some of the street lamps were still working, but they only reached as high as the lizard's ankles. It climbed up to street level and stood hunched over in a menacing, prowling posture as the huge feet came plodding softly down the street in my direction. High above, in the murky light that cut through the rainstorm, I could see the head swinging back and forth near the tops of the buildings. Tall armored plates ran down the creature's back, similar to the protective spikes on the back of an ancient stegosaurus, only larger, much larger.

Of course I was terrified. But I was sure this fabulous creature was only moments away from being sliced up beyond recognition by the army's weapons, so I did my best to clear my head and tried to make some useful observations, something I could share with other scientists. I estimated the creature to be ninety feet wide at the haunches and just over a hundred and eighty feet tall—even in his forward-crouching posture. Stretched head to tail, it would have been longer than a football field! Among land animals, it appeared most closely related to a crocodile: It had an elongated, thickly muscled neck that led to a rather flat skull with an extremely powerful jaw. Its rounded shoulders and long arms were abnormally well developed compared to other living reptile species—indeed, for any species that walks upright. He kept these arms folded, tucked tight against his chest, allowing his long clawed fingers, which never stopped moving, to dangle in front of him. Their constant twitching movements gave him a grasping, greedy appearance and generally contributed to his overall frightfulness. Perhaps the most surprising thing I noted was his physical grace. When I'd watched Animal's videotape earlier that afternoon, there had been a lumbering indecisiveness about him. This may have been due to the fact that he'd been surrounded by a great deal of noise and movement. Now, instead of stomping down the street, he came stealing up closer to the square with silent, graceful steps. The ground was not shaking this time, but his tremendous weight compacted the asphalt and left a visible trail behind him. I don't want to anthropomorphize, but I believe he sensed that there is no such thing as a free lunch and that the unexpected cache of fish lying just around the corner was a trap. He crept up to the end of the block and peered carefully into the square. He was almost directly above me now, his great meaty belly sixty feet off the ground and blotting out the sky. One of his clawed, birdlike feet was settled about twenty yards—less than a single one of his strides—from where I was hiding. If he was startled or decided to turn around and retreat, I was in danger of being stepped on. He paused at the threshold of the square, hesitant, evaluating the danger.

My mind was racing with questions about this strangely deformed and mutated creature, which I felt must have been the result of exposure to gene-warpingly high levels of atomic fallout. Its body seemed to be a hodgepodge of parts from other animals: the head and neck of a crocodile, the brawny rear limbs of a Komodo dragon, the dorsal armor and spindly fingers of an iguana. He also had certain avian or birdlike characteristics. The three-toed feet resembled the heavy, slashing claws of an ostrich; also, the armored plates extending from the shoulder blades looked like a stunted set of wings, which, after failing to grow, had turned to bony stumps. He had muscular control over the two main armored plates but most of the time let them flop loosely back and forth as he walked. His arms were held close to his chest, like a boxers.

Overall, it was as if some intelligent force had selected all the most frightening adaptations from the reptile world and blended them seamlessly together to create this towering, dread-inspiring leviathan. I desperately wanted more opportunity to study it before it was killed. But as it sniffed loudly at the bait I realized my time was short. This awesome new species was about to be blown away into extinction. In my frustration I reached into my pocket and pulled out my Fun Saver, determined to record the moment in some small way. I pointed and clicked. To my surprise, the camera's built-in flash lit up the entire block and immediately attracted the creature's attention. Like an enormous whip, the broad neck rolled down to street level, carrying the flattened, horn-scaled head with it. The creature had a pronounced, almost noble chin, which swept by just over my head like a floating semitrailer until it spotted me.

I found myself being scrutinized by a three-foot-tall sparkling eyeball the color of liquid honey. It stared down at me, only a few feet above, and blinked in two directions at once. In addition to the main eyelid's thick sheet of rough flesh, there was a gristly white nictitating membrane, which closed from the sides. The loose, spiky skin on the underside of the throat scraped against the ground, and a soft guttural purring came from deep within the throat. In order to sniff me, the animal repositioned its head and turned one of its slitlike nostrils toward me. The glistening nostril was approximately four feet across and lined by pillows of callused flesh. The warm air pouring out of his lungs swept across my face. I almost lost my self-control when I saw the mouth begin to open. Lizards, I knew, use their tongues to help them smell, but I was afraid a long forked tongue was about to shoot out and wrap me up as a before-dinner snack. He was close enough that I could have reached out and stroked the leathery brown flesh of his snout—something I had no intention of doing. I was careful to keep as much of the asphalt boulder as possible between me and the jagged yellow teeth poking out from the enormous reptilian mouth. As we stood there, it occurred to me that this was the reversal of an age-old scenario: A man notices a lizard and bends down for a closer look, whereupon the lizard darts for shelter under the nearest rock. Only now the lizard was inspecting the man.

I glanced behind me, thinking—foolishly—that I might try to make a run for it (at that point I didn't realize how fast he could move), and saw a handful of soldiers pointing bazookas in my direction. If they fired at the creature, I was going to be caught in the middle. For some reason this idea scared me more that the prospect of being devoured by the megalithic lizard looming over my shoulder. Gently, very gently, I raised my hands and signaled to the men to hold their fire, that everything was fine, nothing to be alarmed about. I eased away from the safety of my boulder and moved closer to the giant snout. My head was only a few inches from one of his teeth, some of which were the size of a rhino's horn.

"Good boy, that's a good lizard," I said. "Now go eat the fish."

I don't know who thought I was crazier, the soldiers or the lizard. In a soothing voice I tried to communicate the idea that I wasn't a threat. And it worked. With a slight grunting noise, the head lifted away toward the building tops and one of his feet sailed almost directly over me. Still moving carefully, he stepped into the open square and began making his way toward the brightly illuminated pile of fish.

I ran as fast as I could back to the communications post, jumped over the barricade of sandbags, and collapsed breathlessly into a chair. "Oh, my God, did you see that?" I asked.

Elsie nodded casually. She'd seen the whole thing but was much more interested in watching the beast prowl up the intersection. Shaking her head in disbelief, she said, "Tell me this creature isn't related to Theropoda." she said. I looked around for Mendel and spotted him huddled at the rear of the tent, dumbstruck by the sight of an animal many times larger than a *Tyrannosaurus rex.* He had a legal pad and a pen in his hands, ready to take notes, but all he could do was stare.

It was out in the open now, its underside brushing the treetops of Madison Square Park and moving away from us toward the Flatiron Building. He kept his hind end high off the ground, tail held straight back for balance, and took small, deliberate steps. Over the radio I heard Sergeant O'Neal muttering something like, "I think we're going to need bigger guns."

Just before it reached the food, the animal stopped one final time to make an inspection of the area. Its broad neck was just flexible enough to allow for a 360-degree scan of the surrounding buildings. There is no doubt that it recognized our presence in the square and the potential threat we represented. But the smell of the fish proved too tempting, and with a last sudden step the beast stabbed his mouth forward and began to dig in. The enormous jaws unhinged and plunged into the pyramid of fish like a steam shovel, scooping up thousands of them in a single bite.

Colonel Hicks, following the action on his video display across the river, immediately sounded the order. His voice boomed over all the hundreds of radios at once: "Fire at will!"

"Fire at will," O'Neal repeated. And a split second later Madison Square erupted like a powder keg. From every angle machine guns and rocket launchers roared. Rapid bursts of flame spit from a thousand gun muzzles, lighting up the sky, and the quiet of the deserted city was ripped apart by the staccato hailstorm of projectiles, all flashing through the air toward the colossal reptilian body in the center. Hundreds of thousands of rounds were fired in the space of a few seconds, and presumably all of them found their target.

Welling up out of the roar of gunfire came an even louder noise, a thunderous, earsplitting animal wail. It sounded like the war cry of some incredibly large, prehistoric bird. At first I thought it must be the animal's shriek of pain, a reaction to its multitudinous wounds. But as the gunfire continued we realized that it was only a screech of annoyance. The long tail and forearms began to flash through the air, swatting at the flying ammunition as if it were a bothersome swarm of mosquitoes. Then this amazing creature did yet another amazing thing: It turned away from the barrage, bent down, and quickly scooped up another huge mouthful of fish!

"Fire the Sidewinders!" Hicks ordered.

"Fire the Sidewinders!" O'Neal said, relaying the orders.

A large truck hidden among the trees of the park raised its multicannon firing mechanism and sent a trio of missiles screaming toward the creature. They whipped across the night sky, leaving a brilliant trail of spark and smoke in their wake. They were headed straight for the creature's chest. He ducked out of their path with a lightning-fast reflex action and they sailed past him, smashing into the venerable old Flatiron Building and demolishing it instantly. The structure blew apart and collapsed in a triangular, fiery mass. Over the radio we could hear Colonel Hicks screaming for more firepower and, behind him, Mayor Ebert roaring in pain over the loss of the historic building.

The lizard was highly agitated now, and its tail

began to thrash ever more violently from side to side. First it flew through the park, snapping trees off at the midpoint of their trunks, then swung the other way and ripped apart the facades of the buildings facing the square. It whizzed back and forth like an armor-plated wrecking ball. After another deafening roar the creature spun around and began to walk straight toward us. The great head lowered until it was just above street level and turned to one side so it could stare at us with one of those enormous honey-colored eyes. There was no doubt he was coming toward the communications post, and he was angry.

"Okay, this is very bad news," Elsie said, backing away from the barricade.

"Let's get out of here!" Mendel yelled. Tossing pen and paper over his shoulder, he broke into a dead run down the sidewalk, heading for the nearest corner. After a split second of indecision, we all decided he had the right idea and took off in several directions at once. I bolted out into the open, planning on cutting across the nearest corner of the park to a set of buildings. Only then did I realize something important about the geography of Madison Square—there is absolutely no place to hide. And the titanic lizard coming up behind me was moving much faster than I had anticipated. Once again I found myself in the wrong place at the wrong time. Luckily, there was a life-size bronze statue of one of America's founding fathers—the great James Madison. I ducked behind the tall cube of granite on which President Madison stood and hoped the monster wouldn't step on me.

As we had feared, he moved directly to the communications post, probably attracted by the lights on the instrument panels and the squawking of the radios. He swiped at it with one of his muscular forepaws, sending everything—crates, computer equipment, and sandbag barricade—flying through the air with such force that the whole mess smashed into the third story of a building half a block away. Explosive shells continued to zip through the air despite the fact that there were now humans in the crossfire. Another Sidewinder missile came sizzling through the air and struck the creature in the back, exploding against his thick armor without causing any visible damage.

As I cowered at the base of the statue, a division of tanks rolled up and swung their turrets around, training them on the enraged beast. Realizing I was directly in the line of fire, I scampered around to the far side of the statue. But this put me in plain sight of the lizard, who charged in my direction. In a blind panic I looked around for an escape route, but it was too late. With astonishing speed, the huge body rushed past me on a collision course with the tanks. As they fired, the monster leaped into the air and jumped directly over them. At the same time, the tip of his tail spanked the statue of President Madison hard across the backside. The mortar shells shot past me overhead and plowed into the front of a building. As I followed their trajectory across the sky, I noticed the heavy statue above me teetering off its base, about to fall on me. I tried to run, but my feet slipped out from under me on the rain-slick pavement and I belly flopped to the ground. A second later—*boom*—the statue crashed to the ground, President Madison's head resting on my chest! His outstretched arms had punctured the asphalt on either side of me. I was pinned to the ground but lucky to be alive.

Craning my neck to the side, I caught a glimpse of the powerful beast galloping away. He headed up Sixth Avenue on all fours, moving with the grace of an overweight gazelle. Within seconds, military vehicles were racing after him in hot pursuit. I tried to get their attention, but they sped away uptown. Realizing I would have to wait for someone to find me, I lay back and let myself get soaked by the rain. During the melee, someone had dropped a walkie-talkie on the ground not far from me. It was resting face up in a puddle of rainwater only a few feet away, just beyond my reach. I could hear Hicks shouting through the static.

"Will somebody tell me what the hell is going on over there?"

For the next several minutes I listened to the walkie-talkie, following the drama that was unfolding a few blocks uptown. I suppose I could have attracted the attention of some of the soldiers in the square, but as

I lay there listening to the pursuit unfold over the radio, I forgot my own predicament. I wish I could have watched the chase with my own eyes.

The pursuit vehicles raced in a tight pack up Sixth Avenue at about a hundred miles per hour. At that speed, they were approximately three times slower than their prey. (After analyzing all the relevant evidence, Dr. Chapman puts the creature's top speed at between three and five hundred miles per hour!) They would have had absolutely no chance of catching up to the rapid reptile except for the fact that it seemed indecisive at certain points. It slowed down and stopped a few times, looking around for the best escape route. Or was it taking time to study its new surroundings? In any case, the pursuit vehicles announced over the radio that the creature had veered off to the west. With shouts of "Faster, faster," they watched the enormous brown tail disappearing around a corner several blocks ahead.

"It's turning left around . . . maybe Thirty-fourth Street," a soldier in the lead vehicle reported. "We need backup!" The drivers accelerated, weaving back and forth across the boulevard to avoid the giant potholes the lizard had torn into the street. When they came to Thirty-fourth and began turning left, they found a nasty little surprise waiting for them.

The lizard was crouched down lying in wait. Its fleshy snout was resting on the ground a few yards behind the crosswalk, like a battleship stopped at a traffic light. It was too late for the Jeeps to do anything but skid out of control toward the beast's great maw. A sudden sideways flick of his head allowed him to point one of his steely eyes down at them. The radio filled with inarticulate shouting as the vehicles fishtailed and crashed into one another. "Back up! Back the hell up!" the commanding officer yelled at his men. Gunfire erupted. But before the drivers could shift into reverse and get out of the intersection, the beast did it for them.

According to the survivors, the animal did something unprecedented in the annals of saurian behavior. He inhaled deeply, causing a dramatic expansion of his own rib cage. Then he forced the air out of his mighty lungs, generating a gale-force wind. This phenomenon, which I would later be unlucky enough to observe firsthand, has come to be called "the power breath." And, however shocking this behavior might be to herpetologists, it should be noted that there arc very good anatomical reasons for its being possible. Aquatic reptiles, as is well known, have extremely well-developed lungs and are capable of spending long periods of time submerged in water. Owners of iguanas and various "dragon"-like reptiles report their pets sometimes heave great hissing sighs, but never had they seen this great breathing ability used as a defensive mechanism.

The power breath was strong enough to blow everything—and everyone—clean out of the intersection. The foul-smelling wind picked up the Jeeps and the soldiers and sent them all tumbling far down the next block like so many children's toys caught up in a sudden tornado. All radio transmission ceased for several seconds, and the creature was able to escape to another part of the city without being directly observed.

It took a couple of minutes until he was spotted again. A second convoy of Jeeps found him standing at the mother of all intersections, the so-called crossroads of the world: Broadway and Forty-second Street, Times Square. Even with the city deserted, the lights of the intersection were bright enough to illuminate the two-hundred-foot-tall brute as though he were starring in a Broadway show. Standing out in the open, he seemed to be confused by the bright lights. His head whipped this way and that, seemingly in search of an escape route or a place to hide from his bite-sized tormentors. Before he could decide, his dilemma got a whole lot worse. A group of Apache helicopters lifted over the rooftops of some nearby buildings. These lethal flying machines swooped down on him like a pack of ancient pterodactyls. But they packed considerably more of a punch.

"We've got a good look at him now," one of the pilots said calmly into his microphone. "He's out in the open and we are locked on."

Hicks shouted furiously, "Then *fire,* damn it. Take him down!" He waited through five seconds of silence before demanding an update. "Is it dead yet?"

"He's making a run for it," the lead pilot reported, "heading east. We are in pursuit . . . maintaining visual. Okay, now he's turning onto . . . I think it's Lexington. Got him in our sights."

"Lock him in and fire!" Hicks repeated.

The Apaches let loose a barrage of guided, heat-seeking missiles—at least a dozen of them, which screamed down at their moving target. With a quick glance over his shoulder, the creature saw what was coming. Lightning fast, he darted into another street before the projectiles could reach him. Instead of following him around the corner, as they should have done, the bombs continued in a straight line and smashed into the Chrysler Building. The ensuing explosion ripped into the world-famous landmark, effectively chopping off the top ten stories. A moment later, as the command center watched via live video feed, the gleaming art deco spire went plummeting to the ground, where it crashed and splintered into ten billion pieces.

"I thought you were locked on," Hicks said to the pilot. "What happened?"

"I don't know, sir. The heat-seekers aren't functioning properly.They won't lock on. And the target isn't showing up on thermoscan."

Duh! If I hadn't been locked in an embrace with one of our founding fathers, I would have grabbed the walkie-talkie and reminded them of the obvious fact that lizards, no matter how large, are cold-blooded animals. He wouldn't be any warmer than the exterior surfaces of the buildings he was moving past. In fact, given the heating systems and incidental energy consumption inside the structures, they must have been slightly warmer than his leathery skin.

Again the helicopters lost visual contact and searched the area for several minutes before finding a likely hiding place—a hollowed-out skyscraper. As the lead pilot described it, the structure looked as if the creature had crashed through one wall of the building and was cowering behind the drapery of collapsed walls and twisted iron bars. The dark, heavily armed birds dropped straight down and hovered in front of the building, which had been gutted up to the fifteenth floor. Then they pumped it full of explosive shells, approximately sixty missiles in four seconds. The forty-story building was quickly torn to shreds and collapsed into a smoking pile of rubble. Their goal accomplished, the gunners ceased fire and waited for the dust to clear so they could inspect the demolished building for signs of the dead animal.

"Okay, it looks good," came the report. "It looks good from this angle. Appears to be a kill."

Think again. There was another forty-plus-story building standing right behind them, just across the street. Without any advance warning, the beast suddenly erupted from within. Exploding out through the chaos of flying glass and broken marble, the screeching leviathan appeared once more. It pounced at the hovering helicopters, lifting its jaws skyward and snapping up two of the huge flying machines in one powerful bite!

Before the two remaining copters had time to pull up, one of the reptile's enormous fore claws slashed through the night and batted one of them out of the air. It burst into flame even before it shattered like a glass egg on the ground.

That left one pilot still hovering within the beast's striking range. Most people would have turned tail and gotten the hell out of there. But this guy had ice water in his veins. His voice remained calm as he explained what had happened, then reported that he was circling around to make another attack on the animal.

By the time he looped once around and swooped in for the kill, the beast had disappeared again. The pilot dipped down into the canyon formed by the walls of the midtown skyscrapers and patrolled for the animal. As the chopper hunted, Hicks was yelling at the pilot not to let the creature escape. "Echo Four, don't lose that lizard. Where the hell is he?"

"I don't know, Colonel. He was right here a second ago, but now he's gone."

"How is that possible?"

"I don't know, sir, but he's vanished."

That was almost correct. *Masked* would have been closer to the truth. As the helicopter cruised between the tall buildings, the pilot reported seeing something, an indistinct shape of some sort, ahead of him. The creature hadn't vanished, but he had become nearly invisible. Taking advantage of his gray-brown skin tone, he had pressed himself against the side of a stone-gray building. Keeping perfectly still, he was able to hide himself—even though he was out in the open.

"Oh, Jesus!" the pilot yelled when he realized what the strange shape was. He was skimming through the air even with the tenth story of the buildings around him when he recognized the indistinct shape for what it was. He lowered the nose of the Apache and gunned the engine, shooting forward at top speed (almost two hundred miles per hour). Suddenly the hunter had become the hunted.

The helicopter was too low in the canyon to climb, which would have slowed his forward momentum. Instead, he raced into the first intersection at breakneck speed and banked wildly to the left. The twenty-story-tall lizard was right behind him, like a Doberman chasing a dragonfly. Jaws snapping at the tail of his prey, the creature charged furiously through the streets, keeping pace. At the next intersection the pilot banked right, almost clipping his rotor blades on the corner building. Buildings behind him exploded as the lizard plowed through them. The helicopter swerved wildly through the obstacle course of the city, staying a heartbeat ahead of extinction.

After two hard turns without catching sight of the creature behind him, the pilot allowed himself to take a breath and began climbing toward the rooftops. With audible relief in his voice, he said, "Wow! That boy is quick!" The sky ahead of him suddenly turned bright pink. "He's real quick, but I think I outra—"

Too late, the pilot understood that the pink color of the sky was the wide-open mouth of the lizard. He had outguessed the pilot and was waiting for him around that last corner, his great jaws unhinged. He simply waited for the Apache to fly into his mouth before snapping down and crushing it utterly. Witnesses on the ground say the animal chewed the big machine once or twice before spitting it out and moving on.

"Dr. Nick, are you all right?"

"Yeah, I'm fine," I said, "but I'm stuck."

Sergeant O'Neal and a few of his men hoisted the statue up high enough off the ground for me to shimmy my way out to freedom. All of us were pretty stunned by what had happened. For a minute we stood around surveying the scene. It was a mess. The street was torn up, and half of the buildings in the square were either decimated or badly damaged. The historic Flatiron Building was a total loss. And there was still a huge amount of fish lying in the street.

O'Neal stood there muttering and shaking his head. I don't blame him for not wanting to face Hicks after the Flatiron fiasco. Even though we had no way of anticipating how impossibly fast and powerful the animal was, or how well his thick scales would protect him from the weapons, somebody was going to get an earful. Somebody—we all knew it was going to be O'Neal—was going to get blamed and bawled out for things having gone so horribly wrong.

I noticed something on the ground. It was a puddle but didn't look like rainwater. I knelt down and dipped my fingers into it. To my surprise, it had the metallic smell and taste of blood. From my vantage point, I didn't think the army had put a scratch on the reptilian mutant, but there it was—blood on the street. Fumbling through the pockets of my coat, I found a glass sample tube and scooped up some of the viscous, red-brown liquid.

"Damn!" O'Neal kicked a stray fish toward a squashed truck. "I can't believe it! He did all this damage and we did *nothing* to him."

"That's not true," I observed, looking up as I put the blood sample in my pocket. "We fed him."

The trip from New Jersey to the Flatiron Building had taken less than fifteen minutes. The journey back took an hour and a half. While O'Neal's troops combed the square for evidence and salvaged pieces of equipment, I climbed into one of the personnel carriers and fell asleep.

When I woke up, we were back in New Jersey near the front gates of the command center. It must have been two-thirty in the morning, but the place was swarming with people. There were scores of reporters, dozens of nervous city officials, and hundreds of evacuated Manhattanites gathered around the perimeter of the brightly lit military compound, all of them waiting for news. It was a real circus.

Our convoy slowed to about one mile per hour as the crowd reluctantly parted to let us pass. Television camera crews, taking advantage of our presence, started filming immediately, broadcasting live and using our return as a background for their stand-up reports. I rolled down my window and listened, catching snatches of what the reporters were saying as we rolled past.

One said, ". . . but at this point that is only a rumor. It may be some time before we can confirm that this havoc-wreaking animal is indeed a lost dinosaur. . . ."

Another said, "The president today declared a state of emergency and has issued disaster relief funds to New York City. Mayor Ebert claimed it was his get-tough policy with . . ."

A third, rather puny reporter in his fifties stepped onto a stack of phone books before he spoke into the camera with avuncular concern. His face looked familiar to me, but at the time I didn't recognize him as Charles "Let's Have Dinner" Caiman. "Maintaining a total media blackout, officials here remain silent this evening about their progress—or lack of it—in bringing this blood-thirsty monster under control. As you can see in this live shot, reporters from around the globe have descended on . . ."

As we inched past him, a blinking red light on a

nearby building caught my eye: R$_X$ NEVER CLOSES. R$_X$ NEVER CLOSES.

It was a twenty-four-hour pharmacy, one of those oft-overlooked miracles of convenience. It reminded me that, less than a week earlier, I'd been in the Ukraine, where such things simply do not exist. For some unconscious reason, I reached into my pocket and began twirling the beaker of blood I'd collected between my fingers. Then I got an idea. It started out small, nothing more than a personal joke, really, but it quickly blossomed into a full-blown theory. I had to get out of the truck. I leaned forward and spoke to the soldier behind the wheel as if he were a cabbie.

"It's okay, driver, I'll get out here."

He told me I couldn't do that, that I had to wait until we were inside the compound, and that I would have to get it approved by the colonel. But I was on a mission and there wasn't much he could do to stop me without abandoning his vehicle. I hopped out and quickly sliced my way between the news crews toward the blinking red sign. When I reached the sidewalk, I noticed a street vendor who had set up shop under a doorway. He had a display table full of trinkets: dinosaur toys, key rings, coffee mugs, and of course T-shirts. One of them was actually very cool. It featured a freeze-frame image taken from Animal Palotti's daring footage of the creature, the shot where the huge gray paw was coming down on top of the camera. I thought about buying one but figured I'd better see how much my trip to the pharmacy was going to cost first.

I complimented the nondescript salesman. "It's amazing how fast you got these T-shirts made up."

"It is our job," he replied. I think he had a French accent.

A bell over the door tinkled as I stepped into the pharmacy. The place seemed deserted. "Hello?" I rang the bell on the counter a couple of times before a woman in a wrinkled smock shuffled out from the back room.

"Can I help you?"

"Yes. I need a home pregnancy test. I'm looking for one that tests for gonadotropic hormones, but if you don't have any, one of the clomiphene citrate kits will do the trick."

She laid one package after another on the counter. She carried six different over-the-counter brands. "This is all we got," she informed me. I heard the bell tinkle on the door as another customer entered the shop.

Without reading the labels, I reached for my wallet. "I'll take them all. One of each." I wasn't going to be able to afford the T-shirt. As the pharmacist was accepting my money, I heard a woman's voice come over my shoulder.

"You must have quite a harem."

I recognized the voice and froze stiff for a moment before turning around to see who it was. She wore a long raincoat over a red dress and a dark beret over blond ringlet curls. She was dripping wet and even more darling than I remembered. The sight of her sent a quick, arrow-sharp pain shooting through my chest.

"Audrey? Is that you? Wow. Hi. Hello. You look . . ." I almost said *incredibly beautiful*, but caught myself in time. "You look . . . wow, how've you been?"

"Good to see you, Nick."

"Here's your change." The pharmacist poured a few coins into my palm and handed me my bag full of test kits. Something was different about Audrey. She seemed more determined, more direct than I remembered her. I assumed it was the result of her success in her new career. She had an official press badge and everything.

"So you made it."

"What?" She looked confused, so I pointed to the photo ID she was wearing on her trench coat.

"You're a reporter. That's what you always wanted to be, right? I'm happy for you. Really, I am."

"Yeah, well . . ." She didn't seem quite convinced, but at the time I thought she was just being modest. We stepped outside and stood under the overhang of the drugstore's doorway, keeping out of the rain. "And you? Are you still picking apart cockroaches?"

That was a hell of a way to say hello after eight years. I felt condescended to. "I'm into earthworms now," I answered testily, "but I don't want to *bore* you with my work. I know invertebrate biology isn't exactly your bag." My tone of voice must have betrayed some of my bitterness.

"You're still mad at me."

"Ha!" I scoffed. "Mad? I'm not mad. Why would I be mad? You think I'm still mad?" I tried to make it sound as though it were the most ridiculous idea I'd ever heard and dismissed the whole matter with an imperious wave of the hand.

Then I changed my mind. "Well, yes," I admitted, "you left without so much as a phone call. No letter, no nothing. Maybe it was wrong to ask you what I asked you, but I think you should have . . . you could have at least . . . yeah, I guess I am still a little mad."

"That was eight years ago, Nick." She made it sound like an eternity. "Some people change, you know."

"Most people don't," I said bluntly.

"Well, I'm sorry you feel that way." She turned up her collar and walked out into the rain.

Good riddance, I thought. *I have every right to be angry.* You see, Audrey and I had met when our campus newspaper sent her to cover a protest rally I'd organized. There had been an instant attraction, a chemical bonding. We became inseparable pals, and one thing led to another. We practically lived at each other's apartments. And four years later, on the verge of graduating, we were still going strong. At least I thought so. One morning as we were walking up the hill to class, I told her how much I loved her and how I couldn't imagine my life without her and asked her to be my wife. To show you how out of touch with reality I was, I was expecting her to say, *Yes, of course I'll marry you, Nick darling,* without even blinking. Instead she reacted with shock and told me she'd need some time to think it over. She had to decide whether she wanted to spend the rest of her life with a guy whose idea of a hot Saturday night was renting a National Geographic video about gastropods (it's excellent, by the way). She didn't say how much time she would need to mull the question over. But it was apparently quite a while, because I hadn't seen or spoken to her since that day. Rather than do the right thing and tell me the truth, Audrey skipped town. She even missed the graduation ceremony so she wouldn't have to face me. Who wouldn't be angry?

Although I had every right to be angry, it was painful watching her disappear into the crowd, and I suddenly regretted my haughty attitude. I didn't want it to be another eight years before I saw her again, before I could at least hear why she'd left me in the lurch like that.

"Audrey, wait!" I ran down the sidewalk and caught up to her. "You're right. It's been a long time. Can I offer you a cup of tea or something?"

She hesitated. "Sure. I'd, er, like that." She hesitated again. "One thing, though. Who'd you get pregnant?"

"It's a long story." I smiled and we headed off to search for that cup of tea. Unfortunately, nothing was open. We walked around in the light rain for a

Godzilla's claws tear through the side of
a Japanese fish-processing ship.

Dr. Nick Tatopoulos (Matthew Broderick) is forcibly
recruited for the adventure of his life.

"Here's your sample. Study it."

A dock explodes as Godzilla arrives in New York.

Godzilla's foot smashes down on cars
on a New York City street.

Will Animal survive his close encounter
with Godzilla?

Animal gets the shot (and the scarc) of his life.

Godzilla's movement through the city
leaves destruction everywhere.

Godzilla's appearance sends crowds into a panic.

Nick is frozen in awe at his really close
encounter with Godzilla.

Godzilla's toenails dwarf both people and cars.

The top of the Chrysler Building lies in ruins
following a near-miss aerial strike at Godzilla.

Even massive firepower can't stop Godzilla.

A torpedo explosion in New York Harbor
appears to mark the end of Godzilla.

The startling discovery of Godzilla's nest.

Baby Godzillas are always hungry—after all,
they've got some serious growing to do!

while, chatting, catching up. She was asking all the questions, and I did most of the talking. I told her who I was working for and described a few of my earthworm-related misadventures in the good old Ukraine. She seemed genuinely curious about what I'd been up to, and it felt so good to talk to her that I'm afraid I rambled on and on without asking her any questions about what *she'd* been doing all that time. Or was that her plan?

Still, I hadn't forgotten why I'd gone into the drugstore in the first place. Eventually I steered us back to the command center and told the guards at the entrance gate that she was with me on official business. We headed for my tent. The army had set up individual tents for Mendel, Elsie, and me, each of them stocked with all sorts of advanced scientific equipment. We continued to chat while I prepped the blood sample for testing. It was a little tricky because all the kits I'd purchased were designed for testing urine, but I knew how to get around that.

"I still can't believe it," she said, pouring some coffee from one of the lab beakers. "Remember that time we chained ourselves to those railroad tracks? I was terrified of being arrested, but you—you were such a militant. You practically ran the whole nuclear freeze movement in the state of Ohio, and now look at you. You cut your hair, shaved your beard, and now you look so . . . I don't know . . . *establishment.* It's kind of ironic, if you don't mind my saying so. How does a guy go from being an antinuke activist to working for the Nuclear Regulatory Commission?"

"When you and I used to attend rallies in college," I explained, mixing fluids, "we helped to create awareness and mobilize public opinion. But now that I'm on the inside, I can actually affect policy. Real change." I looked up from my work and said pointedly, "I may have put down my picket sign and cut my hair, but I never lost my idealism." I needed some tweezers and popped open my tool kit. I'd forgotten about the photos of Audrey taped to the inside of the box. I snatched the tweezers up and slammed the lid closed before she saw them. Although I was trying to focus on my work, talking to her was stirring up a lot of murky emotions that had settled to the bottom of my heart long ago. I didn't know whether to be more hurt by the suggestion that I had somehow sold out or the hint in her voice that she thought I looked better with the beard.

"And exactly what changes are you trying to effect?"

"Well, I've been doing some rather groundbreaking work, actually. I'm tracking mutations in earthworm morphology caused by nuclear contamination in and around the Chernobyl power station. They're getting bigger all the time. And, at the same time, I'm preparing a census for the government, cataloging new species that have been created as a result of man-made changes to the environment."

"Human-made, you mean?"

"Right, sorry. Human-made changes to the

environment—in particular, changes brought on by an increase in the levels of radiological contamination."

She sipped her coffee, feigning innocence, while I continued working. "Is that what you think created this lizard? Nuclear contamination?"

It didn't occur to me that I ought to be careful about what I told her. When we were in college I used to tell her everything, and I guess I fell back into that old habit. Although she was now a member of the press, I was relating to her like, well, like Audrey, my old and trusted friend. "Yes, contamination, definitely. Specifically, the fallout from French tests in the South Pacific. I found this blood sample earlier this evening after it—"

"Blood sample? My God, Nick, how close did you get to that thing?"

I took my eye away from the microscope lens and thought for a moment. "I got . . . pretty close." The slide I was examining looked good. I poked an eyedropper into the blood sample and suctioned up a few cc's of the serum, which by that point was a milky yellow color.

"What else did you find out?"

Distracted by my work, I told her more than I should have. "Well, we know he eats tons of fish. He's a member of the reptile class, obviously. He displays physiological traits associated with Theropoda, a suborder of prehistoric dinosaur. But he seems to be a hybrid of some sort. Not only is he a genetic combination of at least three different species, but his DNA has obviously been exposed to high levels of radiation. The gene mutation is pretty darn spectacular. In fact, he's probably the first example of an entirely new species. He's a burrower, he's amphibious, he's relatively young, and . . ." I squeezed a drop of the yellow, hormone-rich fluid onto the white litmus paper of the test kit. The paper turned dark red at once. I felt a rush of goose bumps erupt on the back of my neck as I announced, "And he's *pregnant*."

"*He* is pregnant?" Audrey asked, understandably confused.

Immediately I began preparations for a more rigorous test to confirm the results of my experiment. "Obviously, these tests weren't designed to be given to giant lizards, but fundamentally they look for the same hormonal patterns that would indicate pregnancy in a human female. And according to this test, our friend is very, very pregnant."

"I don't get it," she said suspiciously. "You just said it's the first of its kind. If that's true, how can it have babies? Doesn't it need, like, a mate?"

I started thinking out loud. "Not necessarily. Keep in mind that this creature is an aberration, a mutant. We don't know how it reproduces. Some species are actually born pregnant. Or it might be a hermaphrodite. Or, more likely, it might reproduce asexually."

"Where's the fun in that?" she asked.

I decided to ignore that question and continued thinking out loud. "I've been asking myself why—

why would he travel all this way, almost exactly halfway around the world? But now it makes perfect sense. Think of all the different species that migrate great distances in order to bear their young. That's why he came to New York—he's nesting!"

"Nesting?" The idea made her uneasy.

"Yes! And Audrey, do you realize that most species of lizards lay up to a dozen eggs at a time?"

"No, I didn't realize that."

"Think about it: a *dozen* eggs. It means our problems might be only beginning." I grabbed my sample materials and marched out into the rain. Of course, I needed to verify these astonishing findings before presenting them to Colonel Hicks and the others. I hurried toward the army's mobile laboratory, an ambulance-sized truck that was parked close by. They had a very sophisticated chemistry lab inside staffed by an expert crew. I was halfway there before it dawned on me that I'd abandoned Audrey without a word. Then the most curious thing happened. I experienced a vague sense of déjà vu. I felt guilty about having become so excited about my work that I'd failed to even ask her to wait for me, and this triggered a memory. I recalled that in the weeks before I'd asked her to marry me, I'd been immersed in a series of experiments on the digestive system of *Reticulitermes flavipes,* a type of leech. The work had been so exhilarating that I could scarcely talk or think of anything that spring but leeches. In fact, I believe I started talking about it right after she told me she'd need time to consider my proposal. I wondered if that had anything to do with her sudden disappearance. And there I was, eight years later, doing the exact same thing all over again. I dashed back to the tent and explained.

"Forgive me, but I've got to run these things over to the lab in order to confirm all of this. Be right back." And once again I disappeared into the downpour.

So there she was. Audrey Timmonds, the fledgling reporter who only hours before had been told she didn't have what it takes to be a professional reporter in a survival-of-the-fittest town like New York, was alone in a tent full of information pertaining to the biggest news story of the year, the decade, maybe the century. She must have felt like the kid in the proverbial candy store, surrounded on all sides by temptation. She began to poke around, examining some of the materials I'd left scattered on the desktop. One item in particular caught her attention, a videotape labeled FIRST SIGHTING. After a look over her shoulder, she inserted the tape into the machine and pushed play. It contained most of the information we'd gathered up to that point on the origins and movement of the creature: the old cook in the hospital bed screaming "*Gojira, Gojira*"; the decimated village in Panama; the ruined ship on the beach in Jamaica. It was all information that Colonel Hicks had warned me not to discuss with anyone.

After she'd fast-forwarded through the video, Audrey ejected the tape and did the right thing. She

put it back in its case and put the case back where
she'd found it. A reporter like Caiman wouldn't
have thought twice about putting the tape under his
jacket and rushing back to the studio with it. But
Audrey wasn't the kind of person who would stab
an old friend in the back just to get a story. She sat
down and sipped her coffee, waiting for me to
return.

As she sat there she must have remembered
how Animal and Lucy had laughed at her in the
diner, telling her she wasn't tough enough for the
journalism jungle. Something happened to dear,
sweet, innocent Audrey Timmonds while she
waited for me to return. A change came over her, a
mutation that had nothing to do with nuclear contamination. Metaphorical fangs grew beneath her
lips; her fingernails morphed into dagger-sharp
claws. She set down her coffee cup and glanced outside to make sure no one was looking, then committed her third—and most serious—crime of the day.
She grabbed the videotape, buried it in the folds of
her trench coat, and fled into the rain.

Very soon thereafter I came back and found her
missing. In her haste, she hadn't even taken her
bright red umbrella. I looked around the tent, then
went to the door and shouted her name into the
downpour. She was nowhere to be found. Once
again she'd suddenly disappeared from my life
without explanation, without even leaving a note.
And this time, I thought to myself, she was probably
gone forever. *Some people change,* she'd said. But

after all those years, one thing had apparently remained the same: Audrey Timmonds wasn't interested in spending her time with a boring worm guy.

Ed, the tech wizard who ran WIDF's mixing board, was sitting at the controls of the station's studio-on-wheels. Audrey was hanging over his shoulder, scrunched into the narrow aisle behind him. Their eyes were on one of the monitors where a recently shot videotaped image of Audrey was doing a stand-up report. Animal Palotti hovered nearby, helping himself to Ed's cache of junk food, watching the tape he'd shot for his blond friend only moments before. He did not seem entirely pleased with the situation.

Audrey in the truck silently mouthed the words Audrey on the screen was saying as the report drew to a close: ". . . the disturbing prospect of Gojira giving birth to a dozen offspring. Which is why, in this case, all the king's horses and all the king's men may not be able to put the Big Apple together again. Audrey Timmonds, WIDF, New York."

"Bee-yoo-tee-ful," Big Ed declared as soon as the tape was over. "Good report! By the way, you owe me breakfast for mixing it."

"I should have pulled my hair back," Audrey worried. "Victor, what do you think? Was it okay?"

"Real good, a real good piece," Animal said between mouthfuls of a muffin, "but I'm curious. How did you get hold of this footage? And how'd you learn so much stuff about the lizard?" The way he asked the question let Audrey know he suspected the truth.

"Like you said, good guys finish last—first law of the jungle." With that she slid her clawed hands through the sleeves of her coat and headed outside. It was coming down cats and dogs, which wouldn't have bothered the old Audrey. But the new one quickly decided she wasn't going to look like a drenched rat the next time she stood before the cameras. As she headed down the stairs of the mobile studio, she reached out and snagged the umbrella away from a woman who was heading inside— "Hey, thanks so much!"—and got away before the lady could do anything about it. She ran out into the rain and quickly spotted her station manager.

"Murray! Come here for a minute."

He was stooped over under a large umbrella that was being held by a much shorter man, Charles Caiman. Both of them looked annoyed by the interruption. Murray waved Audrey over to join them, but she stood her ground. She didn't want to be anywhere close to the slimy, repellent Caiman—especially since she was wearing his doctored press ID pinned to the lapel of her coat.

"Murray!"

"Not now, Audrey!"

"Yes, Murray, right now." The power in her voice surprised both men. Reluctantly he asked Caiman to wait for a second while he dealt with the situation.

"What? What do you want?" he asked, joining her under her freshly purloined umbrella.

Audrey smiled her most wicked smile. "I've got exclusive footage of other places this thing has attacked, and oodles"—that didn't sound tough enough—"um, I mean a *shitload* of background information."

Suddenly Murray was very interested. "You do? Whose story is this?"

"Mine!" she told him proudly. "All mine!" In addition to her ill-gotten video and the information she'd learned from me, Audrey had gone onto the Internet to see what other stray facts she could find to beef up her already meaty story. The most important discovery she'd made concerned the strange word the *Kobayashi Maru*'s cook had uttered time and again: *Gojira*.

She had surfed her way to some obscure corner of the World Wide Web and found an on-line encyclopedia of Oriental mythology. She scanned through page after page until she happened across a brief description of an ancient Japanese sea monster, one that supposedly attacked ships that ventured too far out to sea. This legendary chimera was known by the name of Gojira.

> Massively you dwell, O Dragon of the
>   Triple World,
> In the great iron cage of the sea,
> [But] When the dead mists of the half-
>   eaten moon stir the waters

[and] Open your cage, you rise in
    effulgent glory,
A great flash of livingness, eye and
    wind, tongue [and] water,
To swallow the wayward sailor's floating
    world.
Spare our ship, O dragon, [remain]
    embedded in stone,
Humbly [we] speak [your] name, Gojira.

—Sixteenth-century
Japanese sailor's prayer

"All right, then," Murray said, "let's not stand here putzing around. Let's go have a look at this report." And the two of them hurried away, leaving Caiman standing there by himself wondering what was going on.

FOUR

Dawn broke reluctantly over New Jersey. The disheartened sun was barely able to force its way through the gunmetal gray rain clouds, which continued to hang like a cast-iron skillet over the entire eastern seaboard. Someone in a seedy hotel room pulled aside a beige curtain just far enough to spy down on the army's military headquarters.

"Taisez-vous," said Jean-Claude. He stepped away from the window of their fleabag hotel room, which overlooked the tents of the command center. The team of so-called insurance agents was eating a breakfast of toast and *café américain.* They must have been in a collectively foul mood after sleeping for only two hours on the lumpy mattress and stained carpet.

"Even the butter is horrible here!" complained one of the Jeans, a paper napkin tucked nerdily into his collar to protect his shirt. The other men grumbled sleepily, agreeing that it tasted funny.

Roache examined one of the foil-wrapped pats and announced to everyone's surprise that the butter had been imported from, of all places, France. After that the men ate in silence. In time Roache shuffled over to the main surveillance console and switched it on to see if the new day had begun inside the command center's war room. It had.

A major strategy session was just getting under way. It was 7:03 A.M. I remember, because I was late. I'd stopped by the mobile lab to pick up the printed results of the chemical analysis they'd done on the blood sample I'd given them. The report confirmed my suspicions of the night before.

Colonel Hicks was standing at the head of a large square table, explaining, with as much confidence as he could muster, his Plan C. Seated around the table staring back at him skeptically were high-ranking representatives from the nation's armed services—including General Anderson, who had read him the riot act only moments before the meeting began. He was furious that Hicks had let the situation get so far out of control.

Also present at the meeting were several political figures, most notably Mayor Ebert (who hadn't slept a wink) and the governor of New York. Elsie and Mendel sat near the head of the table, to Hicks's immediate left.

When I slipped quietly into the tent, the colonel was standing at a large map of the area explaining to his audience the previous night's wild chase through Manhattan. Black X's on the map showed the positions of severely damaged buildings. There were at least forty of these *X*'s clogging the midtown area. Things weren't going very well for Hicks. When I entered, he seemed both relieved that I'd made it and angry that I wasn't on time. I think he was counting on me to help him assure the military brass that everything humanly possible was being done. A Marine Corps general interrupted the presentation as I closed up my bright red umbrella.

"Colonel Hicks, what makes you think another attempt to gun this lizard down is going to be any more successful than the last one? You've already done a hell of a lot of damage to the city."

"Naturally, we want to do as little physical damage to the city as we can." Hicks went back to his map and pointed to a large green section. "What we'd like to do is lure him out into a more open area, such as this section of Central Park, where we'll be able to get a clear shot at him and bring him down without damaging any more structures."

Mayor Ebert grumbled, "Last time you destroyed several historical landmarks and you didn't even scratch him!"

"That's not entirely true. Our worm guy— excuse me, I mean Dr. Tatopoulos here—found blood. Isn't that right, Doctor?"

Every eye in the room turned to me. I could tell Hicks was hoping I'd help get him off the hook. I tried to break the bad news slowly. "Well, yes. Yes, I did find blood." It just wasn't the kind of blood they thought.

"So you see," the colonel interrupted me, "we did more than scratch him. And now that we understand what we're up against, all we have to do is lure him into open terrain and use weapons that don't rely on heat-seeking technology. I spoke to Fort Bragg this morning and they're sending up—"

"Um, excuse me, sir," I interrupted his interruption, "but despite the very fine job the army did last night, the situation has gotten to be a wee bit more complicated. You see, the blood I recovered after the creature left the square reveals that it is either about to lay eggs or already has."

The governor of the great state of New York arched an eyebrow. "Are you trying to tell us there's *another* one of these things out there? Or maybe a whole population of them? And if so, where are they all hiding?"

"No, sir. I don't think that's the case. I think he's the only one."

"Then how the hell can it be pregnant?" Mayor Ebert demanded loudly. His aide, Gene, quickly whispered something in his ear. "Right. What is this thing, the virgin lizard?"

His remark caused a smattering of laughter from the military bigwigs. And Mendel found it pretty entertaining as well. He tried to share a laugh with Elsie, but she looked away from him, disgusted. I hadn't had a chance to share my findings with them before the meeting. I knew that no one at the conference table would be laughing once they understood the full implications of my discovery. If

I was right, we were staring down the barrel of a worldwide catastrophe much worse than the human race had ever faced before. The writing on the wall seemed to spell out our own annihilation as the dominant species on earth. I explained.

"Actually, Mr. Mayor, there's some truth to your joke. I believe this *is* a virgin lizard, which makes the situation a whole lot more dangerous. From what I can gather, the creature, like some amphibians, reproduces asexually. That's why it is absolutely imperative that we find the nest as quickly as possible. If we don't get there in time, as many as ten to twelve more of these creatures could be born. And each of them will, in turn, be capable of laying ten to twelve of its own eggs." At the time I thought these numbers were slightly inflated because they didn't take into account the large number of losses reptile broods typically experience, but since I needed to convince the generals that this was no laughing matter, I let the exaggeration stand. "Because the creature has no natural enemies except us, its population could increase at a geometric rate. In a matter of only a few years, we could find ourselves facing an enormous number of these animals."

This news hit Hicks like a punch in the gut. He let out a long sigh, then reached up and rubbed the dark circles under his eyes. It was clear he hadn't slept the night before, and he was looking the worse for wear. After a moment of contemplation he announced a slight modification to his Plan C. "We go after the creature. We kill it. Then we begin hunting for the nest."

I shook my head. "By then it may be too late. These eggs are going to hatch very quickly."

"How could you possibly know that?" Mendel asked, ready to debunk my theory.

"I was going to ask that same question," said General Anderson, highly dubious.

The answer was simple. "The fish. The fish we found down in the subway. He's not gathering all that food just for himself. He's stockpiling it, preparing to feed his young."

There was a long pause around the conference table while the idea sank in. We were having a devil of a time dealing with just one of these reptiles. What were we going to do with ten or twelve of them?

Of course, none of us sitting under the green tarpaulin roof of the command center had the slightest suspicion that the place was bugged or that the whole conversation was being monitored by a group of nondescript foreign men who claimed to be insurance adjusters. As we sat there discussing these highly classified subjects, a man in a nearby seedy hotel room was handing another man a dossier. The documents and photographs inside this folder concerned a certain American biologist whose name he couldn't quite pronounce. "Tatata . . . Topopup . . . *Je ne sais quoi*!"

The man with the salt-and-pepper beard, who accepted the dossier, studied the name carefully before examining the file. "Tatopoulos."

Inside, there were photographs of me along with a complete record of my employment history. They even had my college transcripts!

The conference inside the command center broke down into several private discussions. Half the people in the room seemed not to believe what I was telling them. In the middle of the confusion, one of the governor's aides entered the tent and whispered something into his boss's ear. The governor listened and nodded.

Hicks stood at the head of the table and called for everyone's attention. As soon as he had it, he began explaining Plan D. "If Dr. Tatopoulos is right, we must act quickly before this situation escalates beyond our control. We can send Divisions A, C, and F"—he indicated their current positions on the map—"down into the subways to begin a thorough sweep. Meanwhile—"

General Anderson, who had been scowling in disbelief the whole time, leaned across the table and cut the colonel off with a venomous hiss. "Correct me if I'm wrong, Colonel Hicks, but you seem to be suggesting we divide our efforts and open up a whole new front based solely on some wild theory."

"Nick has come through for us before," Hicks

replied. "I have every confidence in him, and if he feels strongly—"

Anderson interrupted again, this time venting all his pent-up frustration. "Come through for you? Colonel, maybe you need another cup of coffee. Your whole campaign has been one disaster after another. You weren't even able to prevent this thing from coming to Manhattan!"

"Excuse me, gentlemen," the governor interjected diplomatically.

"Ahem," Elsie coughed.

"Gentlemen *and* Dr. Chapman, my assistant has just informed me there's a news report I think we should see."

A soldier turned on the television set, and we saw the WIDF ActionNews logo appear on the screen. It was replaced a moment later by the image of an elderly Japanese man in a hospital bed screaming, "Gojira! Gojira!" The image froze, allowing us to study the terror that filled the old man's eyes.

Right away I knew something was horribly wrong.

A moment later anchorman Charles Caiman's surgically enhanced face replaced the sailor's. "From an old Japanese sailor's song called 'Godzilla'"—I have no idea how he mangled the pronunciation so badly—"a mythological sea dragon who attacked ancient sailors, to our own modern day terror. Who is this Godzilla? Where did he come from? And why has he come here? Find out in my special report."

(As I would learn much later, Audrey and Animal were at that very moment watching the same televised report in a crowded bar less than a mile from the command center. When she realized what was happening, that Caiman had stolen her story, Audrey began cursing him wildly and throwing handfuls of pretzels at the television screen. As an embarrassed Animal dragged her kicking and screaming out of the bar, she yelled at the smugly grinning image of Caiman, "And it's *Gojira*, you moron!")

In the command center, all attention was on the television screen and WIDF's report. A series of computerized maps popped up, giving the story a visual component. "A direct path can be traced backward from Manhattan to Jamaica to Panama and eventually all the way back to French Polynesia, where the French government has been conducting nuclear tests for many years."

It quickly became clear that someone close to the military effort, someone on the inside, had leaked this information to the press. I heard a pencil snap in two and glanced over at Hicks, who was bright red, burning with anger and embarrassment.

"A member of the expert scientific team the army has assembled to deal with this unprecedented situation, Dr. Nick Padapadamus, believes the creature is nesting, using Manhattan's towering skyscrapers and deep subway tunnels as ground zero for the cultivation of an entirely new species."

The moment he heard my name, General

Anderson swiveled around in his chair and exploded. *"You went to the press with this?"*

I was stunned. "No, no, I didn't . . . I-I didn't talk to anyone."

"They mentioned you by name!"

"Yes, yes, they did. But no, no, I didn't . . . I didn't go to them."

Calmly, far too calmly, Hicks asked me whether I'd given my copy of the videotape to anyone.

"No, no," I assured him, "it's still in my tent." I knew exactly where I'd left it, right on top of the . . . and then it dawned on me what must have happened. "Oh, God, she took it."

Everyone around the table stared at me in disbelief, thinking I had betrayed them. I knew it wasn't going to do any good trying to defend myself, so I didn't even try to explain the whole thing about running into Audrey and how I hadn't seen her for so many years and why I'd invited her past the military cordon. So I just stared straight ahead and waited for what I knew was coming next.

"Pack up your stuff, Doctor," General Anderson growled as he glowered at me, "and get the hell out. You are officially off this project as of *now!*"

It was the worst hour of my life. I was humiliated, deeply embarrassed, angry with myself that I'd let everyone down, worried about what this might mean for my future, and deeply wounded by Audrey. I didn't understand how she could do such a thing—it felt as though she'd swooped down out of the blue just long enough to rip my heart out. General Anderson had given me half an hour to pack all my equipment and personal effects. I didn't want to find out what would happen if I ran over the deadline, so after hastily packing up my scientific instruments, I literally threw my other possessions into my duffle bag just as two soldiers arrived to escort me off the grounds.

Elsie came into the tent as I was preparing to leave. "I'm sorry about all this."

"I really didn't give that tape to anyone."

"I believe you," she said. I think she meant it.

"Look, Elsie, make sure Hicks finds that nest before it's too late."

"I'll try," she said, extending a hand. "Bye, worm guy."

It was still raining as if it would never end when I walked outside. About five minutes earlier I'd realized the army wasn't going to provide any transportation. They were going to toss me and my bags out the front gate. After that I'd be on my own. I called a cab company, but the dispatcher told me I might have to wait for quite a while, even after I explained that it was an emergency. So I was surprised and relieved to see a yellow taxicab parked right outside my tent.

"You got here awfully fast," I said.

The driver rolled down his window a quarter of an inch. "Where to?" he asked in a nondescript foreign accent.

"Newark Airport. I've got a lot of luggage back here." I was hinting that he might want to come around back and give me a hand. Instead, the trunk popped open automatically and the driver rolled up his window. *I hate this town,* I thought.

And as I was loading my rain-soaked possessions into the trunk, who should come jogging up to me but Ms. Audrey Timmonds, reporter at large.

"You're leaving? Why?" She seemed so authentically surprised that it was almost possible to believe her innocent-little-Audrey act. But I ignored her and kept packing. I was convinced she was no longer the wide-eyed apple-pie girl next door she once had been. Now it was only a sham, a way to sink her claws deeper into a story. "Is this because of me? Because of the story?"

"Well, what did you *think* was going to happen?" I snarled.

She looked at the ground. "You never said it was off the record."

What nerve! I came very close to losing my temper. "I shouldn't have to, Miss Big Shot Reporter. You were supposed to be my friend. I trusted you."

"Oh, Nick, I'm so sorry. I'm really, really, really, really, really sorry. I didn't mean for it to turn out like this." She seemed to be sincere, and I had trouble staying quite as mad, especially after she confessed the truth to me. "Look, I lied to you. I'm not really a reporter. I'm just an assistant to a reporter. When we broke up and I came to New

York, I was so sure I was going to make it. But it's eight years later and I'm still at the bottom of the ladder. That's why I needed this story so bad. I wanted to tell you the truth, but you're so successful—you have this glamorous, exciting life—and I . . . I just didn't want you to know I was such a failure."

I could see that she was ashamed of what she had done. Teardrops merged with raindrops and dripped down her cheeks. But no amount of crying was going to erase the fact that she'd betrayed me in cold blood. "So you thought that made it okay to steal my videotape? And use all the things I said to you?"

"No! That was a terrible thing to do. I never should have done it, and I'm sorry."

I threw my last bag into the trunk and yanked open the cab's back door. I got in and turned to her for one last word. "Well, good luck in your new career. I think you really have what it takes." I slammed the door closed in her face for dramatic effect and was pleased when the driver peeled away the moment I was inside. She'd remember *that*, I congratulated myself.

But within seconds I'd turned around in my seat and was looking through the rear window. Audrey didn't move, just stood there in the pouring rain watching the cab drive away. I knew that this time it was probably final—the last time I would ever see her.

Once we were on the road, I sank back in the

seat and contemplated the horrible turn my life had taken. Not only was I humiliated, angry, and wet, but I was certain this episode was going to permanently damage my reputation. My research grants were in danger. I found myself longing to return to Chernobyl and my trustworthy worms. Then another nasty possibility loomed on the horizon: Maybe by the time I returned to Ukraine, the NRC would pull the plug on my unfinished work there. I didn't know General Anderson well, but he didn't seem like the type of man who would be satisfied with banishing me from the command center. I imagined him getting on the phone with the commissioner and demanding that my contract be rescinded. I felt as though I were trapped in a nightmare, watching my entire life go up in flames. With such pleasant thoughts drifting through my mind, I'm surprised I noticed that my driver missed the turn for the airport. Despite the huge sign pointing to the left, he veered right. I leaned forward and saw we were heading into a rundown district of warehouses and factories. I knocked on the partition glass.

"Excuse me, I don't think this is the way to the airport."

He ignored me and continued to drive.

"Hey, buddy, where do you think you're going? Do you speak English?"

Again I knocked on the glass barrier and again he ignored me. Another conspiracy theory began to bloom in my head: The reason you never hear of anyone ratting out the U.S. Army is because they deal with breaches of security swiftly and severely. The reason the cab had arrived so quickly wasn't because some dispatcher took pity on me, but because General Anderson had told someone to *take care of me!*

I reached for the door handle. I was prepared to jump out of the moving car and make a run for it. But they'd thought of everything: both doors were locked from the outside.

"All right, that's it. Stop this car *right now!*" To my surprise, the driver obliged. He stepped on the brake and the cab skidded to a stop. "Let me out of here," I demanded. "Unlock these doors."

The cabbie turned around to face me. He had heavy-lidded eyes and a salt-and-pepper beard. In a French accent he said, "I'm afraid I cannot do what you ask."

I gasped. He was the same guy we'd run into on the beach in Jamaica, the one who smoked in hospital rooms. "Hey, I know you. You're that guy, the insurance salesman."

He reached into his breast pocket and pulled out a laminated identification card. He twirled it between his fingers briefly before laying it over the back of the seat for me to inspect. It looked official, but it was completely in French. He introduced himself under his true identity. "Agent Phillipe Roache, DGSE."

"Never heard of it."

"The French Secret Service."

"Oh."

"I thought you might want to know that your friends in the American military have decided *not* to look for the nest. They're going to waste too much time trying to kill the creature first."

The way he said this made me believe him at once. But the circumstances were so fishy, I felt the need to be skeptical. "What? Are you sure? How could you possibly know that?"

"We know. Trust me."

"Trust you? You lock me in the back of a cab, hijack me out to an abandoned warehouse district, then you have the gall to ask me to trust you?"

"Yes."

"And why in the world would I trust you?"

"Because you're the only one who wants to find the nest as much as I do."

The man had a point. If the army wasn't going to go after the nest, someone had to do it. I thought about the possibility of the enormous reptile rearing ten little ones just like him—or perhaps they'd be even larger—and I made a decision that although Roache wasn't the type of man anyone could trust completely, I would at least listen to what he had to say. I sat back in the seat and he drove deeper into the rows of unused warehouses.

Over the next eighteen hours I was going to learn many things about this French secret agent. But I already sensed how intelligent, perceptive, and highly skilled he was. I am certain that under less stressful circumstances, he would have noticed the news van that had been following us ever since we left the command center.

A large door rolled open and we drove into a warehouse. The door rolled closed behind us, pushed by a couple of men dressed in U.S. Army combat fatigues. Stepping out of the cab, I took a look around the warehouse and saw that these fellows meant business. Although there couldn't have been more than fifteen of them, they had stockpiled an arsenal that was, in its own way, every bit as impressive as the one the U.S. Army had brought to town. In addition to lots of high-tech communications and tracking equipment, there were crates full of rifles, rockets, bazookas, and grenades, and a fleet of assorted vehicles—a couple of jeeps, an army limousine identical to the ones I'd seen screeching into and out of the command center, and even a tank! I hoped they weren't planning on using the tank. The men moved about the room busily engaged in all sorts of tasks.

I was impressed. "How did you get all of this stuff into the country?" I asked, assuming they'd used some sort of diplomatic immunity to smuggle the goods past customs.

"This is America." Roache shrugged. "There is nothing you cannot buy."

Along one wall there were several racks of military uniforms—enough of them to dress every man in the room as a lieutenant colonel or a GI, depending on what the situation called for. As with the weapons and the vehicles, they'd tried to find at least one of everything, allowing them to improvise their way through a wide variety of scenarios. I wondered if all of this was really necessary. "Why all the secrecy?" I asked Roache. "Why aren't you guys working *with* the American government?"

He lit a cigarette and gave me a Mona Lisa smirk. "Sorry, *mon ami,* but I am not permitted to speak of such things."

"Hey, wait a minute," I complained, feeling we were getting off on the wrong foot. "You said you wanted my trust. Then I need yours."

Roache paused to consider this for a moment. He knew I had a point. And I knew he needed my help. "Nick, I am a patriot. I love my country. Can you understand that?"

"Sure," I said.

"It is my job and my duty to protect my country. Sometimes I must even protect her from herself, from the mistakes she has made. Mistakes we don't want the world to know about."

"You're talking about the tests in the Pacific?"

"*Oui.* As you may know, this testing done by my country has left a horrible mess. We are here to help clean it up the best we can."

He led me quickly past the indoor parking lot of military vehicles. Despite the wide selection, the one they seemed to be preparing for their assault on the nest was a white Humvee. A discussion was under way, all in fast-moving French, about how to make the vehicle look more realistic. One of the men brought over photos of a similar Humvee parked outside the command center and called his comrades' attention to various details, including the serial numbers and a couple of small dents. Striving for authenticity, one man went to get the paint and stencils, while the others carefully kicked dents into the fenders.

Roache led me back to the center of the room and introduced me to a man who was eavesdropping on the command center through a set of headphones. His name was Jean-Louis. Or Jean-Marc, or something like that. It seemed like all of the men were named Jean-something, and I couldn't keep them all straight. He scribbled something down on a notepad, then spoke to Roache mostly in English.

"They are planning to set the trap *ce soir* at eight-thirty."

"Where?"

"*Dans le* northern sector *du* Central Park."

Upon hearing this news, Roache took me to a large map of the city thumbtacked to the side of a huge wooden crate. He scratched his beard, contemplating the army's strategy, before turning to me. "If Godzilla accepts the fish again, it will give us some time to find the nest undefended. We know how to get into the city. We just do not know where to start looking for the nest."

I told him the creature's name was Gojira, but I don't think he cared one way or the other. As we were studying the map, a cracking sound diverted everyone's attention to a set of open windows above. Everyone stopped. We waited in silence, wondering if someone could be up there spying on us. But there were no more noises, so we returned to our discussion.

"Here." I plunked my finger down on the map. "The Twenty-third Street subway station."

"*Pourquoi?*"

"Well, this is where we first found the fish and discovered he was burrowing through the subway tunnels. With a little luck, we'll be able to follow his trail directly from there to the nest."

"So you're in?"

In? I scanned the faces of the other men in the room, then looked over at the ample stockpile of firearms. I wasn't quite sure what he meant by *in,* but I knew that whatever it meant, I was going to say yes. If there was a nest, it had to be destroyed as quickly as possible. "Are you kidding? I always wanted to join the French Foreign Legion. I'm in. Definitely in."

Roache and the assorted Jeans got a chuckle out of my enlistment speech, but everyone stopped laughing when we heard the noise on the roof again. This time a search party was immediately sent outside for a look around. When they returned without having found anything unusual, we decided it must have been the building settling or some birds keeping themselves out of the rain.

● ● ●

Victor Palotti parked his van illegally in a neighbor's driveway and jogged up the block toward his brownstone apartment. It was raining hard. As he came up the steps he couldn't help noticing the fifteen strangers milling around on his front porch, chatting and drinking coffee.

"How ya doin'?" whispered a bearded man holding a sleeping child in his arms.

"Hello." A Korean lady he'd never seen before raised her coffee cup toward him in greeting. Who were these people, and why did they look so at home in his home? He smiled halfheartedly and moved past them into his apartment.

It was even more crowded inside. People he didn't recognize were crowded onto his sofa watching his television set. Others where playing a game of Scrabble at his kitchen table. This made Animal uncomfortable. It wasn't so much that he wanted them all to get out; he just wanted to know what the heck was going on. And he knew how to find out.

"Lucy!"

A second later his wife, her maternal instinct running in high gear, stepped out of the kitchen wearing an apron and holding a pot of decaf in one hand and a pot of regular in the other. "Hi, hon." She pecked Animal on the lips before turning away to offer a refill to some guy in a business suit who was talking on a mobile phone.

"Who are these people?"

"What? I couldn't just let them sleep on the street. They're people who live in Manhattan. All the hotels are full from here to Pennsylvania. Ma'am, would you like more coffee?"

"You're nuts, you know that?"

"Ain't that why you married me?" She smiled.

Animal shook his head and couldn't help but smile back. It took him a minute to remember why he'd driven through the rain like a madman all the way from Newark. "Where's Audrey?"

"In the bedroom. Crying her eyes out because of you."

"Because of me? What did I do now?"

"All that you-gotta-be-vicious-to-get-ahead stuff you filled her head with."

"You were the one—"

"Whatever. Go in there and talk to her. She's all broken up."

As Lucy waded deeper into the crowd, offering refills, Animal pushed his way toward the back of the apartment and opened the door to the Jungle. The Jungle was the couple's bedroom. It got its name as a result of Lucy's choice of wallpaper: lush pink and red flowers dripping over a dark green background.

Audrey sat in the bed, awash in discarded tissues, her red eyes focused on the television. She was watching a news broadcast and weeping. As WIDF returned from a commercial for an exciting new toilet bowl cleaning product, the screen filled with the words THEY CALL HIM GODZILLA!

"It's Gojira, you morons!" she sniffled. Not only had Caiman stolen her report right out from under her, but he also had the whole country mispronouncing the creature's name.

General Anderson was holding a live news conference. "Contrary to what you may have heard, we have no reliable information that leads us to believe there are any eggs. These reports were the result of some very irresponsible reporting. In fact, they came from a woman who was only posing as a reporter but had no valid credentials. At the present time, we . . ."

"Waaaaaaah!" Audrey broke into a fresh set of tears and punched a nearby pillow. "It's all my fault. What have I done, Animal? What have I become? I just wanted to be tough, but look at me. This isn't me. I don't do things like this."

Animal came over and sat on the edge of the bed, not knowing exactly what to say. "Yeah, well, you know. We all make mistakes, Aud." He was trying to comfort her, but obviously that wasn't what she needed to hear. As soon as she heard the word *mistake* she let out a loud moan and covered her head with a pillow. Just then a stranger walked out of the Jungle's bathroom, a long-haired biker dude in reflective sunglasses who trucked out to the living room.

"Yo," the guy said on his way out.

"Yo," replied Animal.

"Yeah, we all make mistakes," Audrey was saying, "but I just screwed up royally with the only man who ever really cared about me."

"Maybe not."

Audrey blew her nose and tossed another tissue on the bed. "What do you mean?"

"If you could make it all up to him, would you?"

"Of course I would. Why? What are you talking about?"

"Good. Listen up. I saw the two of you talking today when that cab came to pick him up. Then I followed him. I was going to, I don't know, try and talk some sense into him—tell him what a big mistake he was making by not giving you another chance."

"You did? That's so nice."

"Yeah, whatever. But then the cab suddenly pulls into this warehouse area, right?"

"Yeah?"

"Yeah. So I climbed up on the roof and looked inside. And get this. The warehouse is packed with guns and trucks and a bunch of French wackos who want to try to sneak into the city tonight."

Audrey gasped. "Is he crazy?"

"You tell me."

Audrey chewed on her lower lip, concentrating, trying to make sense of this news. In a flash she realized what must be happening. "They're going after the nest!"

"Exactamundo. And it occurred to me that if he finds it, you should be the one to show the world that he was right all along, that the army should have listened to him in the first place."

"Wait a sec. You want *me* to follow him and a bunch of French wackos into the city?"

Animal was already digging through the closet, retrieving extra videocassettes and spare battery packs and throwing them into a backpack. "We both will. I'll go with you. C'mon, it'll be fun!"

"Fun?" she asked, evidently doubting it. "I don't know about this. I've already made such a mess of things. And the authorities have the whole island blocked off. I saw a story where some kids were trying to sneak in and—"

Animal lifted the window and interrupted her. "Look, Audrey. I'm going after them. You can come with me or not." Audrey sat in bed wrestling with her demons as Animal lifted his bag of gear out onto the fire escape. When she asked him what he was doing, he looked embarrassed. "I think it would be safer if I didn't go through the front. If Lucy finds out, she'll hurt me."

When I stepped out of the rest room, I was dressed in full combat uniform: camouflage fatigues, helmet, boots, the whole works. But no gun. They told me I would look more authentic if I carried a rifle, but I didn't want one.

Roache had five of his men lined up and standing at attention. He walked down the line like a drill sergeant, scrutinizing each one of them. He adjusted the tilt of a helmet here, loosened a collar there. He thought one of the men looked too clean, so he took the man's jacket and rubbed it on the ground before giving it back to him. When at last he seemed satisfied with the team's appearance, he handed each man a stick of gum and sent him to the Humvee. Then agent Roache turned his sights on me. Apparently I already had the look he was searching for. "*Pas mal,*" he said. We were ready to rock and roll.

I was riding shotgun and he was driving. The five "soldiers" fit very comfortably into the back of the roomy vehicle, all of them masticating with gusto. I had to ask. "What's with the chewing gum?"

"It makes us look more American."

I turned and studied the squad of faux American GIs. They were really pounding the Wrigley's, as the expression goes. To my mind, they all looked a few years too old and a few pounds too thin to pass for U.S. soldiers. It was going to be a tough sell, I decided, gum or not.

I said to Roache, "You'd better let me do all the talking."

He shrugged and we sped out of the warehouse.

Every entrance to the city had been sealed off tight. The army had established fortified checkpoints at all the bridges and tunnels. Police barricades held back the crowds of irritated Manhattanites who were waiting to go home. An armada of Coast Guard ships made sure no one tried to float, row, or swim to the city. National Guardsmen patrolled the shores of the island and the shores opposite. There was absolutely no way to get in.

Unless you were Animal. He drove to Lucy's

brother's house and, after ten minutes of furious shouting, came outside grinning like a lunatic. "Everything's under control," he announced. "We're in."

A few minutes later he and Audrey were rolling
through a run-down section of Hoboken. The view
of Manhattan was obscured by the continuous rain
and the grimy industrial buildings. About two hundred yards before they encountered one of the
army's ubiquitous shoreline checkpoints, Animal
killed the headlights and pulled the van onto an
embankment.

"This is it."

Audrey, realizing she was in the middle of
nowhere, asked Animal how *this* could be *it*. But he
was already at the back doors. He grabbed his gear
bag and took off at a jog along a broken-down
chain-link fence. He wasn't going to wait. Audrey
sucked in a deep breath and straightened her beret in
the mirror. "Time for the big boys to go to work."
Then she jumped out into the elements and took off
in pursuit of her cameraman.

They slipped through a tear in the fence and
hurried across a muddy field littered with weeds and
discarded steel track. In the middle of the lot was a
tall concrete building in the shape of a cube. A sign
on the door gave the address as EXIT 2677 and the
property owner as the PORT AUTHORITY. Animal dug
a key out of his pocket and inserted it into the rusty
door lock.

"What is this place?"

"It's a way down to the tracks. A service

entrance. Lucy's brother works for the Port Authority."

"Animal! The army shut down all the train stations. They're guarding the entrances."

"Exactly," he grunted, having a little trouble with the key. "The entrance is way over there. They won't be guarding the platforms." After some coaxing, the key turned and clicked. They stepped inside and let the heavy door slam behind them.

"You have got to be kidding me," Audrey said in the pitch-black.

Animal switched on his flashlight, handed her one of her own, then started down a steep flight of narrow stairs that took them deep, deep underground. At the bottom of the stairs they found a rusty metal door. They pushed it open and found themselves in an equipment room. Another door at the far side of the room led them out onto the boarding platform.

"See? I told you there wouldn't be nobody down here," Animal said, as if he'd been sure of it all along. He hopped down onto the tracks and took a long look into the mouth of the tunnel that would lead them below the Hudson River. "Looks good. We can follow this tunnel to the Twenty-third Street station."

"I thought you said this was going to be fun," Audrey reminded him, lowering herself off the platform. "Aren't there rats and things down here?"

"At the moment I'm a little more worried about lizards. Big, ugly, nasty, large lizards."

• • •

There was a long line of military traffic waiting to pass through the checkpoint at the Lincoln Tunnel. Instead of waving army personnel through, the guards were stopping every vehicle and talking to the drivers. It would have been a long wait if Roache hadn't pulled into the lanes of oncoming traffic and raced to the front of the line. He snaked expertly back into line only a few car lengths from the checkpoint. We pulled in behind a dump truck filled with fish, bait for the second trap. Several of the drivers waiting in the line honked their horns at us angrily.

"I thought the plan was to blend in," I reminded him, "not call any attention to ourselves."

"Americans hate to wait in line," he told me. "I'm driving like an American."

When we pulled even with the barricade, a meaty midwestern MP with a clipboard leaned in the driver's-side window and glanced around at the gum-chewing infantrymen. "Who you boys with?" he asked our driver.

"Uh, we're with the Three-two," I piped up.

"I didn't ask you, soldier," he snapped, scanning his clipboard.

I had no idea whether there was any such thing as the Three-two. It was just the first thing that came to mind. I knew I'd better distract him from the list on his clipboard before he realized our unit didn't exist. "Sergeant O'Neal just called down for us to join them, sir." As soon as I mentioned O'Neal's name, the MP's ears perked up and he stared straight at me. I was sure I'd said something wrong. He looked at the gray in Roache's beard, sizing him up carefully before asking, "You got a problem talkin'?"

I was certain that once Roache spoke, the MP would hear his French accent and our cover would be blown. If Roache was nervous, he didn't show it. He gave the soldier a lazy, sideways glance and answered the question in a dead-on Southern drawl. "Why, no, sir, I'm just fine."

The beefy soldier was still skeptical, but there were a couple hundred vehicles stacked up behind us. He stepped back and waved us through. "All right, keep it moving."

"Thank you, thank you very much," Roache said, hamming it up.

As soon as we pulled away, the grin I'd been suppressing broke through. Talk about staying cool under pressure! "Hey, that wasn't too bad," I told him. "Where'd you learn to talk like that?"

"Elvis Presley movies," he informed me. "He was the King!"

After a very long walk, Animal found something on the ground that told him they had reached Manhattan. At a gore point, where the tracks split off in two directions, half a dozen lemon yellow disks lay scattered on the tracks, each one about ten inches tall. They looked like high-tech plastic mushrooms sprouting in the darkness of the dank passageway. "Aud, watch your step around here." He used his flashlight to show her where the danger was.

"What are those?"

"Those would have to be land mines," surmised Animal, who had never actually seen one before. "They must've booby-trapped it so our friend can't use the tunnels. Don't worry, they only bite if you step on them." He hopped over the mines and pressed on. Audrey approached the explosive devices with all the confidence of a first-time tightrope walker. She gulped hard, stepped mincingly between the disks, then ran to catch up with Animal.

As the Frenchmen and I drove through the eerie, ghost-town-like streets of Manhattan, we listened in on one of the army's protected radio frequencies. O'Neal was supervising a second delivery of fish, this one even more massive than the first. A large meadow at the northern end of Central Park, between the reservoir and the Lasker Rink, was being flooded with spotlights and seafood. One of the interesting things we overheard was an angry exchange between the leaders of two heavy artillery units. They both wanted a place on the front line, the perimeter of the park. But the army had brought in so many troops—from as far away as the Carolinas—that there wasn't room for all of them. Colonel Hicks had pulled out all the stops, determined not to suffer another humiliating embarrassment at the hands of a lizard. But we weren't heading to the park.

We turned south and headed downtown. It was dusk, the hour when the gray, rain-streaked day was fading to black, rain-soaked night. As we passed block after block of empty shops and apartment buildings, I thought I could see candles flickering behind the curtains in some of the windows. Every now and again a vaguely human shape darted across the street far ahead of our headlights or disappeared into a darkened doorway as we approached. As we drove along we realized that a handful of people continued to elude the evacuation's dragnet.

When we rolled into Madison Square, we were surprised to find a large contingent of soldiers still guarding the rubble-strewn intersection. They had all the entrances to the Twenty-third Street station guarded. Obviously, we couldn't risk a face-to-face encounter with them, so Roache sped right past them, circling back only after we were well out of their sight. We would have to find another way down into the subway system.

Within minutes we had slipped underground and were traveling through an undamaged tunnel, which was pitch-black except for our flashlights. The Frenchmen kept the pace somewhere between a fast march and a slow jog. Before long we came into the Twenty-third Street station—or what was left of it. At first I didn't even recognize it because the place had been utterly torn apart and destroyed. We were standing at the bottom of a hundred-foot-deep pit of mangled concrete. The platform where I'd stood with Hicks and O'Neal the day before was gone. Evidently, Gojira had been back.

Our flashlights revealed that the station was much deeper and complex than I'd thought. Train tunnels moved off in different directions at different distances below the ground. It reminded me that Manhattan not only reaches to impossible heights with its skyscrapers, but also goes down to surprising depths with its network of tunnels. After some scouting around, I came across a pile of fish. I recognized it as the same pile O'Neal's soldiers had found the day before. Judging from the odors permeating the passageway, the finny carcasses weren't getting any fresher. I discussed this discovery with Roache and we decided to begin our search for the nest with this tunnel. We set out through the lizard-enlarged train tube, moving more slowly now because our path was littered with a thousand dangers: boulder-sized clods of earth, pools of sewer water, bent train rails, and live electrical wires.

Suddenly all the air pressure in the tunnel changed, and a background noise, a humming sound that had been vibrating the walls, cut off. It left us with the feeling of being marooned in a vacuum of silence.

"They've switched off the ventilation system," I whispered. "They're calling him to dinner."

Roache looked at me with those world-weary eyes and cracked a bad joke. "Let's hope we are not the hors d'oeuvres."

The seven of us pushed nervously onward, keeping to the center of the tunnel for the most part, pausing occasionally to decide the best way around a barrier of debris. Then we heard a noise that froze us in place. It was a muffled screeching sound that came out of the darkness and vibrated the walls around us. It seemed to come out of the earth itself. We realized it must be Gojira's voice in an adjoining tunnel. Before we could discuss our next move, the ground began to tremble. The shaking quickly intensified, and years of accumulated dust spilled onto us from the pipes and beams above. Sections of the walls buckled and began to collapse. The overhead pipes clanked against one another, and the animal's roaring got louder.

Suddenly something was in the tunnel with us. We trained our flashlights on the source of the sound and saw Gojira's giant claws breaking out a new entrance. In an energetic fury the six-foot-long talons scraped away earth, concrete, and steel. After only a few seconds the opening was large enough for him to squeeze into the tunnel. He did, and came barreling toward us like a runaway subway train.

A large drainage pipe intersected the subway tunnel near our position. It was tall enough to accommodate a man standing upright. We hurried over to the mouth of it, but I lingered in the tunnel, mesmerized by the giant lizard's agility. I felt a hand grab me by the collar and yank me out of harm's way. One of the Frenchmen pulled me into the pipe a moment before the animal blasted past us, the sides of his body scraping hard against the tunnel walls.

Audrey and Animal were only a hundred yards away. They'd watched us from above as we entered the Twenty-third Street station, ducking out of the way when our flashlights moved close. After we moved off down the tunnel, they decided to climb down to our level and follow us. The way down was through a subway car that had been parked at the top level. Now it was dangling over the side, a natural bridge to the bottom of the hollowed-out station. No sooner had they made the nerve-wracking trip to the bottom and stepped out of the car than they found five hundred tons of lizard rushing toward them.

"Animal, let's get out of here!" Audrey screamed. But the fearless newsman ignored the advancing earthquake and stood in the middle of the tracks, camera rolling. Finally Audrey began pulling him out of the path of danger.

"All right, all right already!" He lowered the camera from his eye just as the creature became visible in the distance, filling the tunnel like a flash flood of flesh and teeth. At the last possible moment they jumped back into a broken-down subway car. With a metal-shredding jolt, Gojira grazed the car as he hurtled past them. Through the rattling, broken windows, they got the same close-up view of the lizard's brawny, scale-covered flanks I'd seen only a moment before.

"Shoot! Shoot it!" Audrey yelled. Animal, whose jaw had fallen wide open, recovered in time to capture some close-up images of the hind legs and tail moving by. Once the creature moved away down the tunnel, the two of them broke into sighs of relief and nervous laughter, tickled that they were still alive.

"I guess we go this way," I said, pulling my T-shirt up to cover my nose and mouth against the thick fog of dust hanging in the air. The creature was already long gone, probably drawn northward by the scent of the fish in Central Park. I don't know why, but I had a hunch we should follow him. One of the men suggested we head in the opposite direction, reasoning that the beast might have come from the nest after smelling the food.

Roache turned to me. "What do you think?"

"This tunnel is the first place we found any evidence of him. I think this is where we should begin our search."

That was good enough for him. He pointed north, and that's the way we went. In a minute or two we were back in the Twenty-third Street station, marching past the subway car dangling from one of the upper levels. We hurried along, unaware that we had company.

We wandered through various damaged tunnels, keeping alert for signs of a nest. Moving in a generally northward direction, we passed several ruined subway stations. Eventually, we came into another ruined station. Like the last one, it was several stories deep and looked as though it had been intentionally hollowed out. All the layers of steel and concrete had been smashed down into a carpet of powdery rubble. The destruction was so complete, we all knew the creature had spend a good deal of time in this place.

Jean-Marc spotted something high on the wall. We all pointed our flashlights up to a damaged mosaic and saw that the blue and yellow tiles spelled out ENN STATI.

"This is Penn Station," I said, "or at least it was." It had been one of the largest and busiest train depots in the entire world, but now it was a huge hole in the ground, clawed and stomped to oblivion. High above, at street level, an immense black hole had been torn in the ceiling. There was just enough light coming through the hole to reveal that there was a huge, cavernous space above us. We thought we were looking up into some sort of cave. Sparking electrical wires provided tantalizing glimpses of an enormous blocky shape resting inside the cavern.

"What is up there?" Roache asked.

We pointed our flashlights up at the blocky shape, illuminating a sign that read MADISON SQUARE GARDEN. Then I realized that we were looking at the Jumbotron scoreboard that once hung at the center of the building. It had torn loose from its suspension cables and crashed to the floor of the arena near the immense hole. I asked myself: *If the scoreboard couldn't break through the floor, what did?* As we peered into Madison Square Garden from below, I knew there was a good chance we had discovered the nest. I gulped and turned to the other men. "I guess we should go up there and have a look."

Roache had already started climbing.

FIVE

Meanwhile, in Central Park, the U.S. military was preparing for a showdown of epic proportions with New York City's latest and least desirable immigrant. A new and larger pyramid of fish had been stacked in a soggy meadow near the Lasker Rink, far from the nearest building. It sat out in the open, sparkling brightly under the intense glare of a dozen searchlights, and seemed to be unguarded. It would be a powerful temptation to an ichthyophagous lizard with a family to feed.

But hidden among the trees lining the edges of the park and lurking in the shadows of the nearest buildings were twenty thousand heavily armed soldiers. All nonessential lights had been doused so as not to distract the lizard from the small mountain of fish. With ears and eyes peeled, the army waited anxiously for the confrontation to begin.

High atop a skyscraper, at the south end of the park, one of the perimeter lookouts heard a suspicious rustling noise. He splashed through the rain over to the retaining wall and leaned over it to take a look down Seventh Avenue. A giant, shadowy figure was creeping toward him, advancing one building at a time.

As the soldier peered down, he saw the hunched-forward brute, as heavy as a freight train, stealing cat-quietly up the street. The rustling noise he heard was the reptile's winglike armored plates grazing against the twentieth story of the buildings it passed. He dug for the radio under his rain poncho and reported the sighting.

"Command center, we have visual on the target. He's headed north toward sector five."

Surrounded by phones, video monitors, and assistants, Colonel Hicks stood at the situation table in the command center, watching a computerized schematic of Manhattan. As Gojira approached the edge of Central Park he was picked up by the tracking devices and came to life on Hicks's computer screen as a blinking red light. "Affirmative," Hicks replied to the lookout. "I have him on radar now, heading into sector five. Stand ready, O'Neal."

The twenty-story-high lizard was reluctant to leave the protection of the midtown skyscrapers. He hesitated in the shadows, his wide feet rooted to the ground, his only movement the slow flapping of his bony dorsal fins. After the unexpected trouble his last free meal had cost him, he was being more cautious this second time around. Suddenly, with that astonishing quickness of his, he bolted out into the open. He scampered two blocks closer to the trap, then quickly ducked into a new hiding place, crouching alongside the imposing Dakota apartments.

"Hold your fire," O'Neal's voice said steadily. "We don't shoot until he's clear of the buildings and into the park."

With a series of lightning-fast moves, Gojira wended his way through the maze of streets on the Upper West Side, appearing and disappearing several times as his sense of danger wrestled with his desire to plunge headlong toward the all-you-can-eat smorgasbord the army was tempting him with. Frustrated by his own indecision, he threw his head back and rent the night sky with a high-pitched, screeching howl.

"Come on, you scaly bastard," O'Neal muttered absently, unaware he was still broadcasting. "Get out here where we can see you."

At last the crafty, mutated saurian stepped into the open and tiptoed—as best a five-hundred-ton lizard can tiptoe—slowly toward the food. When he came within a few body lengths of ground zero, O'Neal whispered into his radio, "Prepare to fire." The sound of thousands of guns cocking simultaneously gave the beast a sudden case of cold feet. Hunching low to the ground, he began to slowly back away, turning as he went. He took a few halting steps, still unsure of himself, retreating along the path he'd come in on.

Hicks, miles away but monitoring this U-turn on his computer screen, didn't understand what the hell O'Neal was waiting for. Even though he was only looking at a blinking light moving across his situation board, he understood the creature was about to bolt out of sector five and return to its hiding place. He screamed into the handset of his radio, "Damn it, O'Neal, *fire!* Shoot it down before it gets away again. *Fire!*"

A heartbeat later O'Neal gave the signal. "Fire at will! Fire at will!"

The quiet evening shattered like a fireworks factory, erupting into a pandemonium of gun bursts and rocket fire. From all directions at once, a staccato blaze of muzzle blasts lit up the sky. The deafening racket of grenade launchers and small rockets filled the air. Overwhelming this great din, Gojira screeched once more. This time his tormentors offered more injury than insult. Powerful explosive shells tore deep into the leather of his scale-plated flesh, buffeting the animal's body first one way, then another. In the blink of an eye the hunted animal turned and charged out of the park. He headed south for a mile or so before making a sudden turn onto West Fifty-seventh Street.

A thwacking roar filled the sky as a fresh squadron of Apache helicopters lifted away from their hiding places and over the nearby rooftops. Fearlessly they bore down on the fleeing reptile. According to the rules of engagement, the choppers were to pick their shots carefully. Stray shells had already done more severe damage to the city than Gojira ever would. The Apaches ignored these rules entirely. They'd learned the hard way what could happen to pilots who got too close and used too few rounds of ammunition. The helicopters threw open their gun ports, blasting away with everything they had. Their combined firepower ripped into the creature's flesh and the surrounding buildings with equal savagery. Fountains of blood sprayed from Gojira's wounds.

A contingent of mobile rocket launchers skidded to a halt at the intersection of Fifty-seventh Street and Eighth Avenue, cutting off another potential escape route. Before the vehicles' tires had stopped rolling, the gunnery crews fired, sending a phalanx of missiles streaking through the night just above the pavement. Gojira reacted by deftly throwing himself against the side of a building. He took one of the shells in the back, but the others slipped by him and plowed through the front windows of Manhattan's Planet Hollywood franchise, vaporizing it. Before a second round of rockets could be fired, the enraged beast charged the rocket launchers, trampling and smashing them as he sprinted past. He continued to race westward along Fifty-seventh, crushing parked cars and swiping the buildings with his tail. The Apaches screamed in from above, riddling his back with shells.

"We'll have him pinned down when he gets to the highway," one of the chopper pilots said. But as the animal approached the sheer concrete barricade of the West Side Highway, he increased his speed and sprang high—impossibly high—into the air, hurling himself over the roadway. The pilots remarked that as he soared through the sky, the keeled plates on his shoulder blades flapped like wings. These bony fins were, of course, far too small to affect the heavy creature's aerodynamics, but this attempt to fly was an intriguing clue about his mysterious ancestry. The same genetic memory that makes a flightless barnyard chicken flap its wings when in danger must have been at work in the brain of this overlarge reptile. With a tremendous splash he broke the surface of the Hudson River and plunged into its murky depths.

"Lost him again," reported one of the helicopter pilots.

Hicks threw his head back and pierced the night with a high, screeching howl of his own. "Nooooooooo!" He slammed his fist down, jarring the computerized table before him. "It's just a goddamned lizard! Why can't we kill it?"

Admiral Phelps, a calm, thoughtful man who had largely held his tongue until that moment, flashed Hicks a supremely confident smile. "Not to worry, Colonel. The navy has a little something waiting for him down there."

The navy's "little something" was a trio of nuclear-powered submarines, the *Utah,* the *Indiana,* and the *Anchorage.* All three were poised for battle, certain they could handle whatever an unarmed, semi-intelligent amphibious lizard could throw at them.

With klaxons blaring through the bridge, the captain of the *Utah* studied the massive blip moving across his tracking screen. "This is the *Utah*," he murmured into his microphone. "We have our target on sonar and are proceeding to close in." The captains of the other two subs reported that they were doing the same, following a previously choreographed battle plan.

"This shouldn't take long," one of them said.

"Oh, great. Now what?" Audrey asked.

"I guess we follow them." Animal shrugged. The two of them were standing in the ruined subterranean cathedral that had once been Penn Station. High above, they could see me and my European secret-agent friends walking up a broken escalator and then disappearing into the dark recesses of Madison Square Garden.

The gaping hole in the ceiling was finally within our reach. The Frenchmen and I stacked trash bins and large chunks of debris into a pile, then climbed up and lifted ourselves through the opening. When we were assembled on the floor above, we found ourselves in a foyer of some kind. Although it was pitch dark, our noses told us we were surrounded by fish. Only when we tried to move did we realize the slippery, ripening carcasses were everywhere underfoot.

Roache led the way across the foyer and poked

his flashlight into what looked like a demolished conference room. One of the walls had been ripped out, probably as a result of Gojira's tail swiping at it from the outside. Overturned furniture and construction debris were strewn everywhere. The hole in the wall led to a much larger space beyond. Pointing our flashlights through the hole, we saw a confused clumping of rounded objects. I walked past Roache to investigate and confirmed that we had discovered the nest.

Three enormous eggs, between eight and nine feet tall, were resting peacefully on a bed of broken concrete. Despite their frightening size, I remember feeling a false wave of relief. *Only three of them,* I told myself, thinking that I'd overestimated Gojira's laying power. We moved closer and let our flashlights dance nervously up and down the textured, sticky brown surfaces. The shell exteriors were atypical. Rather than the smooth, spotted appearance of most reptile eggs, these were uniform in color—a rich brown highlighted by many streaks of ivory—and had rough surfaces. I moved closer to investigate and learned that the texturing on the shells was the result of thousands of miniature, overlapping curlicue designs. These raised swirls were largely transparent and exhibited a dull sheen. They appeared to be solid, but when I dragged my finger across the surface, they broke apart like delicate, waterlogged spaghetti. Holding my flashlight close to my moist fingertips, I saw that the curlicues were moving—they were some sort of parasitic, sluglike worms that had infected Gojira's reproductive system. I made sure to wipe my hand clean, since lizards are known to carry many diseases.

Glistening sheets of membrane clung to the shells, connecting them to the floor and each other. Like the eggshells, these draping membranes were a rich shade of brown, but they showed no signs of parasitic life. Lost in my fascination, I circled around one of these nine-foot structures until I was on the far side of it. It was easily wide enough for me to hide behind. I estimated the circumference was fourteen feet. Once I was on the far side of the egg, the flashlights held by the rest of the crew penetrated the partially translucent shell walls, illuminating the bulky embryo within. It was moving.

"Um, Phillipe," I said, gulping, "maybe you should look at this."

Roache followed a path through the rubble until he was standing at my side. I called his attention to the silhouette of a man-sized fetus twitching and wriggling behind the brittle egg wall. "*Merde*," he muttered, and grimaced.

"Well, there's good news and bad news," I told him. "The bad news, obviously, is that these eggs are about to hatch. The good news is there are only three of them. Some species of lizards are capable of laying up to a dozen eggs at once. I thought there would be more."

Jean-Luc's voice came from the doorway. "Nick, you were right. There *are* more." Leaving the trio of eggs undisturbed for the moment, we fol-

lowed him through a short hallway to another set of
doors that pushed open to reveal the main arena of
Madison Square Garden.

We could only see a tiny portion of the arena,
but we knew the place was wrecked. Many of the
seats around us had been crushed flat or torn out of
the concrete floor. Overhead, a chunk of the balcony
had broken loose; it dangled above us, suspended by
thin strands of steel bar. In my immediate vicinity
alone, I could see at least two dozen eggs.

"That's impossible," I remember saying.
"That's got to be more than *twenty* eggs. I've never
heard of any lizard that can do that." Then it hit me:
crocodiles! There is a reason these ghoulish ancient
dragons have survived into the modern era long
after all their Cretaceous brethren had slipped into
extinction: They lay hundreds of eggs at a time.
They are the most fertile and reproductively gifted
members of the class Reptilia. I don't know why I
hadn't thought of it sooner, especially since so many
of Gojira's outward mutations showed crocodilian
influences.

A couple of the men found the main light board
and threw a switch. When the arena's work lights
were turned on and illuminated the damaged audito-
rium, we looked out onto a dramatic and stunning
tableau. There were *hundreds* of eggs. They were
everywhere—in the aisles, in the balconies, in the
entrance tunnels—all of them nine feet tall and
slathered with the same ivory-streaked brown
mucous. From the cheapest seat in the nosebleed

sections all the way down to the courtside chairs, the ruined Garden was teeming with eggs. Needless to say, I was astonished.

"Start counting," Roache told me.

"Four hundred meters and closing fast," a technician reported without emotion.

"*Utah,* you are in the path. You are red and free. Fire when ready," Hicks radioed, giving them the go-ahead.

The submarine's sonar showed a cigar-shaped blip moving straight for the center of the screen. The lights in the narrow, equipment-packed room dimmed in preparation for battle.

"Are we locked on?" the captain asked when the swimming object crossed the three-hundred-meter mark.

"Locked on and ready to fire, sir," the ensign reported.

"Then let's put this bad boy to bed. Fire."

"Fire!" yelled the ensign into his headset. "Fire!"

In a furious frothing of river water, a fifteen-foot torpedo erupted out of its firing tube and sliced away toward its target. With an uncanny ability to detect approaching danger, Gojira swerved abruptly out of harm's way. Unlike the airborne projectiles he'd faced moments before, however, the torpedo followed him.

Downward he dived, until his great belly scraped across the thick pillow of pollution coating the bottom of the river, stirring up a black cloud of toxic silt. The torpedo plunged into the darkness after him.

The chief sonar technician aboard the *Anchorage* followed this fast-paced game of cat and mouse with professional calm until it took a dangerous turn. "Uh-oh!" he said when he realized what was happening. "Sir, he's heading straight for us."

The *Anchorage*'s captain looked over the man's shoulder, studying the sonar display until he reached the same conclusion. "Shit! Full astern!" he bellowed. "Full astern!"

But the swimming saurian and the torpedo that was chasing him were zipping along at over three times the *Anchorage*'s top speed. While they were sitting dead in the water, the engines only just beginning their backward thrust, the sub was rammed from below. Crew and equipment slammed against the floor, then ricocheted off the ceiling as the quarter-mile-long vessel lurched in the water. A split second later, the torpedo hit them square amidships. With a single concussive blast the sub was torn in half. The enormous spray of water that erupted from the river could be seen from the command center, not far to the south.

Hicks leaned over the situation table and hung his head between his arms when the radioman reported, "Sir, we've lost the *Anchorage*."

Standing behind him, Admiral Phelps seethed with anger.

On the bridge of the *Utah,* the sub's captain called for a status report. "Which way is he headed?"

"He's shifted course, sir. He's headed back toward Manhattan."

Without hesitation, the captain ordered the engines to maximum. "He's trying to go ashore. Let's get him before he's out of the water. Full ahead. Close in and lock on."

Coming from another angle, the *Indiana* pursued the same tactic. The ships churned the water, pushing toward the shore in a pincer movement.

The very moment his ensign reported the targeting systems were locked on, the captain shouted the order to fire. Almost simultaneously the two submarines fired one torpedo each. The swimming smart bombs closed in on the target, one from either side.

Boxed in by the warships and knowing what awaited him if he climbed back into the city, Gojira reached the underwater shoreline of Manhattan and began furiously burrowing his way into a large drainage pipe. As his gigantic claws slashed deep into the earth, tearing away at the underwater wall, an enormous turbulence of silt and mud spread through the water, cloaking him completely.

On the bridge of the *Utah,* captain and ensign stared down at the sonar screen, watching the cloud of detritus expand outward around their target. Both men shook their heads at the animal's awesome resourcefulness. "Impact in eight seconds . . . seven . . . six . . ."

No one breathed on either sub or in the command center along the river. The torpedoes disappeared into the cloak of silt.

". . . in three . . . two . . . one . . ."

Not far from the docking space of the Intrepid Sea-Air-Space Museum, almost directly across the Hudson from where Hicks and his superiors were orchestrating the attack, two muffled explosions were followed by a tremendous eruption in the surface of the river. The twin blasts blew a column of water a quarter of a mile into the air.

The next seven and a half seconds seemed an eternity. Everyone who was following the chase—whether on land, in the air, or underwater—held their breath and waited for a report from one of the submarines. Finally the radio squawked and a technician's voice, smooth as butter, told them what had happened.

"This is the *Utah*. We have one very large lizard body sinking to the bottom after a direct hit." On the sonar screen, a huge blip drifted lifelessly toward the riverbed like a cement-shoed gangster.

All hell broke loose in the command center. Everyone threw their hands in the air and cheered at the top of their lungs. Hats and fists and reams of paper were tossed toward the ceiling. Elsie, in her enthusiasm, planted a kiss on Mendel's lips. And Colonel Hicks, the most relieved man in America, turned and accepted congratulations from Admiral Phelps.

"We got him!" Phelps shouted over the noise.

"Finally!" Hicks sighed, wiping his brow.

General Anderson marched up through the mayhem, smiling broadly. He pumped the colonel's hand enthusiastically. "Knew you could do it, Hicks. Wonderful job."

As I moved around the eerie, goop-slathered interior of Madison Square Garden, gathering tissue samples and jotting down notes, the French agents were laying out spools of cable and wiring up several pounds of plastic explosive. I still had my Fun Saver camera and snapped off several pictures of the egg-filled arena. A voice came from directly overhead. Jean-Marc leaned over the balcony's railing and called down to Roache, speaking urgently to him in French.

I couldn't understand a word of it, but I could tell by Roache's reaction that something was very wrong. He ran a hand over his beard, nodding and thinking about what the man had said to him.

"What did he say?" I asked.

Roache kicked a fish out of the way on his way over to where I was examining a nine-foot-tall egg. The smile on his face told me he was about to give me some sort of bad news. "Nick, we have a problem. We don't have enough explosives. We need you to—"

Before he could finish his sentence, an odd sound diverted our attention. Our ears perked up and we waited in silence to see if the noise would repeat itself. It did. What we heard was a slow, sickening, heart-stopping crack. The source of this sound was an egg not twenty feet from where we were standing. We watched in horror as a jagged fracture line opened down the belly of the eggshell. Our feet felt nailed to the floor. We stood there limp-limbed and wide-eyed, watching the thing break apart.

As we slowly backed away, the top of the egg shattered and a glistening gray snout pushed into the air and sniffed hungrily at the odor of fish permeating the room. Its thin, leathery mouth pulled back to reveal a set of perfectly formed incisors. Like its parent's, this creature's teeth were raggedly arranged fangs. But since they were still unused, they were razor sharp and bright white. It was an absolutely fascinating moment, and I cursed the fact that we had not brought along a video camera. Roache was trying to get my attention. He whispered that we should leave the area. But I was too engrossed in this strange miracle of biology and didn't hear him.

A moment later the first of Gojira's spawn emerged into the world. The egg was kicked apart from the inside, and a six-foot-tall baby Gojira squinted uncertainly into the lights of the arena. He stood shakily on his hind legs and looked around him. His leathery gray skin was smoother than his father's, but had that same bluish sheen to it. The bony plates protecting his head, back, and tail had yet to grow to their full size, and there was no evidence of the spectacular, stegosauruslike plates growing from the shoulder blades, but in most ways he was an exact replica of his parent—a chip off the old block. He was still wet with yolk fluids and began cleaning himself with his tongue and claws like a kitten. A moment later he took his first wobbly step away from the shell, then lifted his throat to the ceiling and emitted a squeaky, mewling rendition of his father's famous wail.

It was not cute. If this sounds cute, it's only because I have described it badly. The animal was scientifically extraordinary but in no way endearing. I was half expecting, and half hoping, that Phillipe would open up on the newborn with his automatic rifle and kill it on the spot. When it focused its grapefruit-sized amber eyes on us, I heard Phillipe's voice come over my shoulder.

"I think we should leave now."

"Good idea."

We backed away slowly up the stairs, careful to avoid startling the hatchling with any sudden movements. Even though he was a feeble and tiny infant by the standards of his own species, he looked plenty strong enough to tear a man limb from limb. As we slunk away, the dreadful possibility of imprinting crossed my mind. Imprinting is that phenomenon whereby newly born animals, hatchlings in particular, will adopt the first faces they see in the world as parents, no matter what species they may belong to. This is why you sometimes see baby chicks follow dogs, or even cows, around a barn-yard. Queasily I noted that the big scale-covered baby in front of us was batting its eyelids at Phillipe and me.

Instead of imprinting, the animal followed a different instinct. He turned away from us and ripped into one of the fishes lying nearby. *Born hungry,* I said to myself. *Not a good sign.* As he shook the fish violently back and forth in his jaws, my eyes focused on the small, jagged teeth. If, as I suspected, the species followed the crocodilian form of dental growth, these teeth would be hollow. New and larger teeth would be constantly growing beneath the caps of the present set, keeping up with the increase in body size. Crocodiles go through dozens of sets of teeth in a lifetime.

Again it threw back its head and screeched, a bit louder this time, but apparently not loud enough to be heard at the top of the arena, where Jean-Marc and Jean-Pierre were working. The animal's cry acted as a primordial alarm clock for his siblings. All around the section of seats we were in, egg-shells began to gurgle and crack open. Within the space of a few seconds we were surrounded. We continued stumbling backward up the stairs without once taking our eyes off the fiendish newborns around us.

Of course Phillipe and I were scared half out of our wits, and under the circumstances we tried to remain as quiet as possible. I cannot speak for him, but my only thought at that moment was saving myself, getting out of the arena before these hungry lizards mistook us for edible rag dolls. It never occurred to me to shout a warning to the others, and I'm sure if Phillipe had it to do over again, he would have squeezed off a few rounds at that first baby Gojira. Doing so might have accelerated the hatching process and put us in greater danger, but it would have alerted the members of his team working in the upper levels to what was happening below.

"This is fantastic! Gimme one more second," Animal whispered.

He and Audrey had emerged through the hole in the center of the arena's floor just in time to hear the first cry of the first baby Gojira. Animal, obeying a deeply ingrained instinct of his own, hoisted the camera to his shoulder and began filming. The footage he captured is invaluable. He had just enough time to pan once across the ruined forum before the eggs in the foreground began to break open.

Off camera, Audrey's voice was audible. In a nervous, singsong way she said to the photographer, "Okay, that's enough. Eggs hatch, baby dinosaurs come out. We get the idea." She was standing at one of the concrete passageways leading out of the arena and into the floor-level lobby. While Animal kept his face buried behind the viewfinder, she played lookout, making sure none of the sharp-toothed infants came too close. Baby Gojiras were hatching at a rate of a dozen per minute, a spectacular and terrifying sight. Wobbly on their feet for the first few minutes, they rapidly gained skill and confidence. The videotape shows them, within minutes of birth, beginning to search under the arena's seats for fish. The closest ones were still a safe distance away, but Audrey knew that wouldn't last long. She stepped up behind the camera and began tugging on Animal's shoulder. "C'mon, Victor," she said, obviously out of patience. "Don't you think we have enough?"

Still filming, Animal turned and answered her question. "Y-Yes, enough. D-Definitely enough," he stammered, suddenly very anxious. Looking through the lens, he saw (and filmed) what Audrey didn't see: a rough-skinned baby Gojira, as tall as a grown man, stealing up behind her. The reptile had already wandered out into the concourse lobby and was reentering the arena through the doors Audrey had been guarding. It had a big fish clenched between its teeth and seemed to pose no immediate danger. As Animal continued to speak in unintelligible gasps, Audrey stepped closer to the camera, still unaware of the danger lurking behind her.

"You all right? What's the matter?" She cocked her head to one side, trying to understand.

"Behind you."

When Audrey turned around and realized they had company, her reaction was classic. Rather than grab the sides of her head and let loose a bloodcurdling scream, she greeted the predatory lizard pup politely.

"Oh, hello."

The lizard cocked its head to one side, trying to understand. Then it swallowed the fish in one gulp.

"Let's just be calm. Don't do anything to startle them."

"Them?" Audrey asked.

"Yeah, *them*." Animal, afraid to move, used his eyes to point out another baby Gojira, this one sniffing at a nearby cluster of unhatched eggs. Audrey took a quick look around and spotted a potential escape route: the swinging double doors that led to the team locker rooms. But there were two problems. First, the doors were on the far side of the floor, over a hundred feet away. Second, they were blocked by a pair of eggs. But as the curious creatures closed in on them, nostrils sniffing busily, Audrey realized it was their only hope.

She took Animal by the wrist and the two of them began shuffling toward safety, skirting the enormous pit broken through the center of the playing floor. Their strategy, born of mind-numbing fear, was to keep smiling and keep calm. Although both of them had broken out in a cold sweat, they spoke soothingly to the hungry hatchlings, telling them how nice and sweet and pretty they were. It worked. The two baby Gojiras were content to follow along behind them, bending down now and again to scoop up a fish.

That left them with the problem of getting past the huge pair of eggs blocking the locker-room doors. Although there were several hundred eggs in the stadium, Gojira had laid each one with some care (as evidenced by the fact that not a single one of them had rolled away and broken). The two in question were nestled between the retaining walls in front of the doors. In effect, they guarded the exit like a pair of Humpty Dumpty sentinels. There was barely room to squeeze between them. Animal went first. He turned sideways and tried to step over the narrowest part of the gap, but it was higher than he'd anticipated and he found himself dangling in the air, both feet off the ground. This left him in the dangerous and very uncomfortable position of suffering a double Melvin, an eggshell wedgie. As he struggled, both shells partially collapsed. He landed with the seat of his pants protruding into one shell and his crotch poking into the other. As any man in such a situation would have done, he immediately found a way of making himself a few inches taller than he actually was and hopped to the far side of the barrier. Unfortunately, the embryos in both shells stirred angrily to life, woken from their slumber before they were ready.

Then it was Audrey's turn. Like one of those people who walk over a bed of burning embers without flinching, she marched straight toward the narrow gap with her head held high. Both shells were quivering, emitting unpleasant sounds and leaking viscous yellow fluid down their sides, but

Audrey refused to acknowledge the danger. Turning sideways at the last moment, she brusquely forced her way through the gap. But a leathery brown arm reached out and wrapped its pearl-white claws around her calf.

Audrey yelped, half in pain, half in fear, as she tried to pull her leg away. But the unhatched lizard was strong, and it took a series of well-placed kicks to the elbow before it would let loose of Audrey's leg. The moment she was free, they blasted through the doors and escaped into the hallway.

By the time Phillipe and I inched our way backward to the top of the stairs, we found ourselves surrounded by inquisitive reptilian newborns. They moved clumsily at times, stumbling over their own feet or crashing to the floor as they learned to step over the stadium chairs. Although they had us hemmed in, they seemed to be in no particular hurry. For the moment they were more interested in gobbling up the huge supply of fish Gojira had left for them.

As we slipped quietly out into the hallway, one of the little monsters came trotting up the steps to follow us. I slammed the double doors closed and held them as Phillipe whipped off his belt and wrapped it around the handles, effectively locking them shut. As he put the final cinch on the knot, the lizard who had followed us eyeballed the Frenchman's head through the smallish window. It would have made the perfect mouthful. As soon as he was finished, Phillipe reached into his utility belt and took out his radio. He spoke in English. "Everyone outside! Now! Secure the doors. We have to keep them inside."

Like us, Jean-Luc and Jean-Claude were on the middle level of the stadium. They made it outside in seconds flat and began sliding anything they could find into the door pulls to trap the hungry animals inside. We were aware that this was going to be a next-to-impossible task. All told, there must have been two hundred sets of doors. But at the time it seemed to be our best option.

Unfortunately, Jean-Marc remained unaware of the danger until it was too late. According to Jean-Pierre, who spoke to us by radio, he was in the very last row of the twenty-thousand-seat arena, kneeling in a pile of fish behind one of the sound system's giant speakers. He was too busy wiring up the explosives to notice the proliferation of lizard life in the tiers below. There were very few eggs on the balcony, but the few that there were had begun to open. Jean-Pierre spotted him and yelled across the cavernous arena for him to get outside. When Jean-Marc heard the warning, he stood up and wiped the fish oil off his hands and onto his uniform. He had just begun moving toward the exit when he saw one of the six-foot-tall babies coming up behind him. He froze in place as the animal sniffed him up and down. Realizing he smelled of fish, Jean-Marc tore off his shirt and tossed it aside, then made a mad dash up the stairs toward the nearest door. The man was fast, but the lizard was faster. It romped after him as if it were a game. The lizard stumbled once, his claws poorly suited to the slick concrete stairs, but easily caught up. He pounced from ten feet behind, flying in feet first and tackling the man from behind. Holding him pinned to the ground with its long claws, it sniffed him up and down before play-fully snapping his neck.

Jean-Pierre took refuge in one of the doorways and described the horrific details of what he had seen. He was somewhere on the opposite side of the round building. The last thing we heard from him was that the hallway looked clear and that he would work his way back toward our position. But a few seconds later there was a burst of gunfire and a brief scream. We never found his remains.

Audrey and Animal flew down the long hallway toward a set of doors promising salvation. The large sign hanging above indicated a street-level exit. But when Animal lowered his shoulder and smashed against them, he found out the hard way that they were locked. They were the sort of doors you need a special key to open. Precious moments were wasted before the two of them could admit to themselves the ugly truth of the situation: The doors were not going to open. When they turned around, a group of baby Gojiras was coming through the swinging doors open at the far end of the hallway. The two humans were very, very trapped.

Audrey took Animal by the hand and pulled him straight toward the beasts.

"Audrey, shouldn't we be going the other way?"

But there wasn't any other way. Audrey continued walking toward them, telling Animal, "Pretend you're invisible!" The lizards were advancing toward them, their heads low to the ground and ready to tangle, their long claws clickety-clacking on the hard smooth floor.

"No, seriously," Animal said, "where are we going?" They were nearly face-to-face with the creatures.

"Right here," she said suddenly, pulling open the locker room door just wide enough for them to dart inside. She slammed the door closed behind them in time to avoid the snap of an eleven-inch-wide jaw and locked the door. With a huge sigh of relief she turned her back to the door and collapsed against it. Out in the hallway, the reptiles whined. Like youngsters of all species, they were impatient. First they scraped at the door with their snouts, then battered it with the bony plates at the top of their heads. It wasn't going to hold up very long.

"Great. Now what?"

Animal didn't have an answer off the top of his head. He scanned the room for another way out, but there were no windows and only the one door. There was an equipment manager's cage, but it was locked. There were toilet stalls, but the doors were too flimsy. Suddenly an idea dawned on him. "Hey!"

"What is it?" Audrey asked hopefully.

"This is where the Knicks and Rangers get changed before their games."

"And?"

"That's it. Just kinda cool. Ewing, Willis Reed, Jean Ratelle—the first Ranger to score more than one hundred points in a season. This is where they suited up."

"Thrilling," she said sarcastically. If that was going to be Animal's contribution, Audrey thought, she had better think of something on her own. She brushed past him and climbed onto a table. "What about this thing?" She reached up and put her fingers through the mesh grille over the air-conditioning duct, then yanked downward. It pulled free, bringing a shower of dust down on her head. "Think we can fit up there?"

"Only one way to find out."

We sprinted down the foyer to the next set of doors. I let Phillipe lead the way, since he was the trained secret-service agent. Just like they do in the movies, he advanced the last few feet with his back pressed to the wall, then peeked around the corner behind the barrel of his machine gun. He let out a low, pained moan that signaled bad news. I peeked around the corner behind him.

Baby Gojiras were everywhere. Hundreds of them. They had turned Madison Square Garden into a teeming reptilian nursery. Almost as soon as they could walk, they learned to run. And run they did, seemingly for the sheer physical joy of doing so, clocking speeds of (by my rough estimate) forty to fifty miles per hour. I had hoped that as their numbers increased and the supply of fish dwindled, they might begin to turn on one another. After all, most of the larger reptile species are cannibalistic. But quite the opposite process seemed to be under way. They seemed to be forming themselves into packs.

This was strange behavior indeed. All the larger reptiles, such as Komodo dragons and crocodiles, tend to be solitary hunters. But these swift-footed lizards seemed to have inherited an instinct for group cooperation that made them act more like velociraptors, medium-sized dinosaurs. When I saw this, I realized our chances of leaving the building alive were quickly diminishing. "What would Darwin say about this?" I wondered aloud.

Just then a group of five or six of them ran past the doorway. They were jogging around the main concourse, circling the playing area. The last one in the group noticed us and stopped short, only a few paces away. Its long neck twisted in our direction and the slitlike nostrils sniffed at us. Phillipe stepped around the corner and closed the doors just as the animal charged toward us. It slammed into the doors as Phillipe struggled to hold them closed. He grabbed the flashlight out of his utility belt and tried to wedge it between the handles, but it wouldn't fit. Struggling to hold the animal back, Phillipe looked desperately over his shoulder at me. "Give me something!"

"Like what?"

"I don't know! Give me something quickly!"

I checked my pockets and looked around the foyer, but there were no three-foot-long iron bars lying around. The lizard slammed against the doors again and swiped at my accomplice with its fore claws before the doors closed on him again.

Then I noticed something. It was right in front of me, hanging on the wall: a firebox with a thick, carefully folded hose behind a pane of glass. I kicked out the glass and handed the end of the hose to Phillipe. As he began wrapping it around the handles, he reached around and unsnapped his phone holster. In one movement he took the phone out and threw it to me without looking. It flew like a dart and would have hit me smack between the eyes if I hadn't caught it. Where does a guy learn to throw a phone like that? Is it something the DGSE teaches their agents?

Bang. The lizard threw himself against the doors once more. Phillipe held tight against the rope. "Contact the military," he grunted, "and get them to send a bomber to blow up this building before these things escape."

"What? How am I supposed to do that?" I began

to explain that just because I was an American, it didn't mean I could personally call in the U.S. Army. He cut me off.

"Call 555–7600. Tell them it's a Code Dragonfly. That should get you through."

The guy was amazing. Not only had he planted an electronic listening device on the mayor of New York City, tapped into the U.S. Army's communications network, and fast-talked his way past a heavily guarded checkpoint, he also knew the military's top-secret code word—which, I discovered later, is changed every twenty-four hours. For a brief moment all I could do was stare at him in awe.

"What are you waiting for?"

I snapped out of it and manually speed-dialed the number as this Parisian James Bond took off down the curving concourse to seal the next set of doors. My call didn't go through. I redialed but got the same results over and over. *Bee-bah-bue:* "All circuits are currently busy. Please hang up and try your call again."

Praying for a miracle, I allowed myself to imagine that Hicks and the army were sending in the cavalry, that last-minute reinforcements were about to arrive and save the day. But in recent conversations with Elsie Chapman and Mendel Craven, I learned that nothing could have been further from the truth. The military had no idea of the trouble we were in. In fact, Hicks, flush with his victory over Gojira, had temporarily forgotten about the possibility of a nest altogether.

According to my fellow scientists, the command center was beginning to empty out. Admiral Phelps, after holding a press conference, had hopped on a helicopter and headed back to his headquarters. General Anderson was also gone. But Mayor Ebert was still there. After finishing a very loud telephone call to the head of Manhattan's chamber of commerce, he hung up and marched over to Colonel Hicks, determined to bring an end to the evacuation. It didn't matter that the colonel was huddled in a low-key conference with a bunch of high-ranking military officials. Ebert was on a holy crusade, representing the citizens of New York City, whose anger had reached biblical proportions.

"Do you men have any idea what is going on out there?" the mayor boomed. "We have people who don't want to sleep in the rain again, we have traffic jams, we have pissed-off mobs around the bridges and tunnels. My phones are ringing off the hook with people demanding to be allowed back into Manhattan. And I say: Let my people in!"

Hicks glanced at his watch and tried to placate the irate politician. "We're sending divers into the river now to retrieve the body. We'll rescind the evacuation order as soon as we have him. It won't be much longer."

"That thing's dead," Ebert exclaimed. "Kaput!

What the hell is the problem, what are we waiting for?"

Hicks smiled that stonewalling, pleasant-under-pressure smile of his. "We're doing everything we can. If you'll just be patient for a few more minutes . . ."

Elsie and Mendel could see that he was serious. As soon as Gojira was confirmed dead, Hicks was going to let people back into the city. Perhaps the only reason he hadn't done so already was that Mendel had explained to him that aquatic reptiles could hold their breath under water for long periods of time. The bigger the lizard, the longer it could stay submerged. The remote possibility that Gojira was unconscious but still alive was the only thing holding Hicks back from lifting the barricades. As he turned away from the mayor Elsie intervened. She put her arm under the colonel and steered him away.

"Alex, sweetheart, we need to talk." That raised a few military eyebrows. "Before people are allowed back into the city, we've got to look for the nest."

Hicks knew she was right, but he tried to pass the buck. "That's not been approved," he said.

Elsie's disappointment was written all over her face. "What if Nick is right?" she asked. "What if there *are* eggs that are going to hatch soon? This could be our last chance to do something about it."

Hicks hung his head and thought for a moment. Before General Anderson and the other top brass had left, they had agreed the evacuation would be canceled as soon as Gojira was officially pronounced dead. The idea of searching for the nest had been quashed for lack of evidence. But the possibility had continued to haunt the colonel. Luckily, he had come to trust his three scientists—even after one of them had been unceremoniously booted off the project. Very reluctantly he decided the nest was a dangerous possibility.

"Corporal Elms, organize a search party. I want a complete, block-by-block sweep of the entire city and subway system."

When Mayor Ebert heard these words, he went off like a five-dollar firecracker. He squawked so loudly, they could hear him in Weehawken. "You, sir, do not have the authority to do that!" And, technically, he was correct. Hicks *wasn't* authorized to make that decision. But he ended the politician's tirade before it could swing into high gear. According to Elsie, he put his bulldog face inches away from Ebert's and bared his teeth. With an intimidating whisper, he dared the mayor to try to stop him.

The supply of fish inside the Garden was almost gone and the baby Gojiras began to squabble with one another over those that remained. It wouldn't be long before they began venturing outside the nest in search of other food. As the Frenchmen worked frantically to secure the doors, I was still making phone calls. When I couldn't get through on Roache's cellular, I tried my luck at a bank of pay phones but got the same results. *Bee-bah-bue:* "All circuits are currently busy. Please hang up and try your call again."

Phillipe returned from one of the many concession stands with a couple of extension cords and immediately wrapped one of them around the handles of the nearest door. As he ran past me on the way to the next entrance, he called out, "What did they say?"

"I can't get through. The circuits are jammed."

Jean-Claude and Jean-Luc ran up from opposite directions to report that all the doors on the upper level had been barred, in one way or another, from the outside.

"Good work. Tell Jean-Pierre and—" Phillipe began, before quickly remembering the men were gone. He came to where I was standing, took the pay phone receiver away from my ear, and hung it up. "Nick, you have to go to the outside. My men and I will hold them here as long as we can. You must go and get help."

Clearly we needed help. But I didn't think their staying was going to do much good. And I said so. But Roache was already issuing battle orders. Without another word to me, the three of them took off running in different directions. At that point, we were still unaware that the baby Gojiras had begun to escape the arena. I was reluc-

tant to leave the secret-service men, but there was
no time to argue. I pushed through a set of doors
and took a winding staircase down toward street
level. At that point I was less concerned with my
own safety than with that of the brave, doomed,
hopelessly outnumbered Frenchmen I was leaving
behind. I admired them for doing what was necessary. If the baby Gojiras broke free of the building,
there would be a million places for them to hide
while they grew to full size.

Even before I made it to the bottom of the stairs,
Jean-Luc was dead. Phillipe told me later that a few
seconds after they'd split up, he received word that
the animals had freed themselves. Jean-Luc told
him that one of the barred exit doors had been torn
loose at its hinges, and although none of the baby
Gojiras were in sight, he saw pieces of fish in the
hallway. "Wait, I hear them" were the agent's last
words. As Phillipe listened, he heard the menacing
clickety-clack of lizard claws in the background.
Then the radio went dead and he heard the distant
echo of gunfire.

"Jean-Claude, what happened to Jean-Luc? Can
you see him? Jean-Claude? Jean-Claude?" Nothing
more was heard from either man, and I can only
imagine the grisly way they met their end.

I tore down the stairwell and burst through the
door at the bottom. As it swung closed and locked
behind me, I realized I didn't know which way to
go. The curving hallways of the round building
offered no clues. I took a guess and headed left,

keeping my eyes peeled for an exit. Finally I spotted one and increased my speed. If I was lucky, I told myself, there would be soldiers stationed nearby, and they would use their radios to call for backup. But my plan was interrupted by a loud crash ahead. One of the unsecured doors into the stadium blasted open and a dozen scaly, man-eating infants spilled into the hallway, tripping and falling over one another. They sprang up immediately, demonstrating the wicked agility they'd inherited from their father. I slammed on the brakes and slid to a halt, then quietly began backing away. The baby Gojiras watched me curiously but allowed me to escape. Once I had backpedaled around the bend in the room, I turned and broke into a full run. But I didn't get very far. Another pack of them was coming from the other direction, and I found myself surrounded.

I raced over to an elevator and pounded on the call button. The little light popped on, and I heard the gears and pulleys groan sluggishly to life.

"Come on, come on," I begged, pecking mercilessly at the call button. Like a herd of musclebound ostriches, the reptiles came trotting toward me from either direction. "Not good. This is not good." My heart tried to climb out of my throat when they started sniffing at me with those infernally wriggling nostrils. I began to despair of the doors ever opening when, at the last possible moment, came the soothing little *pling* and the doors rolled open. I leaped inside. Frantic to escape,

I held my finger down on the door-close button, which, of course, made absolutely no difference at all. "Why don't these things ever work?" I yelled. The noise excited one of the creatures, and it rushed toward me just as the doors began slowly rolling closed.

He thrust his snout into the elevator and snapped at me. His razor-sharp teeth sheared a button off the front of my uniform. The doors closed and put the bold baby Gojira in a headlock. Panicked, I kicked him several times in the head with my boot and stomped down on his flat, bony forehead. Eventually I succeeded in pushing him away from the elevator and the doors sealed. I took a breath for the first time in thirty seconds as the elevator jerked upward. Only then did I realize that in my frantic attempt to close the doors, I'd punched every single button on the control panel.

The doors opened again at the mezzanine level. Directly in front of me was another group of the agile, hungry lizards. They had ransacked one of the snack bars, and the one closest to the elevator was tearing into a ten-pound plastic bag of popcorn. He seemed as surprised as I was, but not one tenth as scared. He dropped the bag of junk food and wriggled his fleshy nostrils in my direction, sensing a more nutritious meal. Once again I beat a tattoo on the door-close button, smiling idiotically at the creatures.

"Oops," I said, apologizing for the interruption, "wrong floor."

When at last I returned to the midlevel concourse where I'd left my companions, I found something worse than hungry man-sized lizards. There was an automatic rifle pointed at my head and a finger on the trigger.

"Hey, it's only me!" I said. Roache lowered the gun and we both took a deep breath.

"What happened?"

"They're loose," I panted. "I couldn't even get to the lobby. There are too many of them. They're all over the place." As I spoke I flipped open his cellular phone and hit redial. *Bee-bah-bue:* "All circuits are currently busy. Please hang up and try your call again."

We heard another noise. It was directly overhead and seemed to be coming from one of the big ventilation ducts. The barrel of Phillipe's rifle followed his eyes toward the ceiling, and suddenly the entire vent collapsed. Yelling and screaming, two bodies spilled onto the floor. I recognized the one in the beret and, despite the circumstances, felt strangely glad to see her.

In a flash Phillipe had the muzzle of his gun butted against the back of Animal's skull. "Who the hell are you?" he demanded. The cameraman lifted his hands in the air and closed his eyes as tightly as he could.

"It's okay. I know her," I broke in.

The secret-service operative glanced in my direction and seemed impressed. He mistakenly assumed the two of them were somehow working with me. But he didn't extend them a very warm welcome. He took the gun away from Animal's head but quickly stepped over him to where the video camera was lying on the floor and crunched it with his boot. The camera broke into several pieces.

Animal was furious. "Yo, Frenchie, what gives? Why'd you do that?"

Roache looked at him with those heavy-lidded eyes and explained, "No cameras."

"What are you doing here?" I asked Audrey, helping her up.

She didn't seem all that happy to see me. "I thought you said there'd only be ten or twelve eggs." As if it were somehow my fault.

"I was wrong," I admitted.

We heard snouts thumping against a nearby locked door. The lizards, eager to expand their hunting grounds, were reacting with increased frustration to boundaries and obstacles. Almost immediately the thumping intensified. Very soon our quiet hallway would be a saurian stomping ground.

"Do you have a radio?" Phillipe asked. "A walkie-talkie? Anything we can use to contact the outside?" They didn't.

"What about the phones?"

"All the circuits are overloaded."

For a moment we stood there considering our options, listening to the horde on the other side of the doors becoming more and more aggressive.

Suddenly Audrey lit up. "I know! I know a way. I know how you can get a message out of here." She was awfully pleased with herself, but the smile disappeared when the door gave way and the first baby Gojira tumbled headlong into the hallway. Its claws couldn't find much traction on the smooth floor tiles. One by one his nestmates followed him into the corridor.

"This way," Audrey cried as she took off running. We chased after her, and the baby Gojiras chased after us. Their razor claws clicked against the hard floor as they came barreling toward us, filling the hallway with their screeching. Unbelievably, Animal turned back. He couldn't bear to leave the scene without retrieving what he'd come for. He wanted the videotape out of his camera, but by the time he got it, the herd was nearly on top of him. He jammed the tape into the pocket of his jacket, threw a trash can into their path, and broke into a mad sprint. He was truly a maniac.

At the end of the hall Audrey took us through a door that led to a carpeted hallway. As soon as Phillipe made it through, I slammed the door closed, certain Audrey's cameraman friend was lunch meat. Just to make sure, I peered through the small pane of security glass and saw him come tearing around the corner. The lizards, on the verge of pouncing, lost their footing as they made the turn and went crashing into one another. Even after this lucky break, Animal barely made it inside before the animals caught up to him. I deadbolted the door a split second before the leader of the pack tried to bite me through the glass.

We hurried down the carpeted corridor past the luxury boxes that overlooked the arena. They didn't look especially luxurious, just like a bunch of cells with corporate-looking furniture, full bars, and ceiling-mounted television sets. Without looking back, Audrey explained where we were headed.

"Come on, the broadcast booth is right over here."

"How do you know?" I couldn't help asking.

"Our station covers the Ranger games."

We looked back down the hallway. The dead-bolted door was still holding, but we could see it wouldn't keep them back for long. The animals were screeching in frustration on the other side, testing the strength of their new claws by ripping into the metal. Realizing there was not a moment to lose, Audrey tried to pull the door of the broadcast booth open. It was locked.

"Stand aside," Animal warned us. He lowered his shoulder and plowed into the door. It didn't budge an inch, and the cameraman folded over in pain.

Gently and politely Phillipe pushed him aside and used his machine gun to shoot the lock to pieces. He then held the door open and invited us to enter. I felt around on the wall until I found the switch plate and turned on the lights. By the time I turned around and saw that we were in a room crammed full of audio and video equipment, Audrey was already seated at the room's computer terminal, booting up.

"The computer here is on an intranet," she told

us. "It's a direct feed into the WIDF computer system."

I didn't want to rain on her parade, but I'd been on the phone for the last twenty minutes and knew the circuits were flooded. "Your station isn't going to have an easier time contacting the military than I did. They'll just get a busy signal."

I knew I'd stumped her momentarily because she started chewing her lip.

"Hold on a sec," Animal said, a light bulb going on above his head. He looked at me. "You were on the inside. You were working for them. Didn't they monitor the news broadcasts?"

"That's right. They did."

"Then what the hell, we'll go live! We'll broadcast right from here. Hopefully they'll see it." He switched on the room's television set. Charles Caiman's talking head filled the screen. He was out in the rain doing a live stand-up report. From the end of the hallway we heard the screech of metal shredding. Phillipe immediately began pushing furniture and equipment toward the only entrance to the broadcast booth.

SIX

Big Ed dribbled mustard down the front of his brand-new shirt. Mumbling a string of curses, he set aside his sandwich and reached for a paper napkin. After moistening it with a bit of diet soda, he did his best to daub the stain away. He was seated in the same spot he'd been in almost continuously for the past twenty-four hours: a swivel chair parked in front of the mixing board inside WIDF's mobile studio. On the main monitor he could see Charlie Caiman doing a live stand-up.

"So while the immediate danger may be over, the pain continues. It is an anguish that city officials are saying could be with us for weeks, months, or even *years* to come, as the citizens of New York begin to pick up the pieces of their shattered—"

"Yeah, yeah, whatever." Ed turned down the volume. Caiman was hard enough to listen to when he had something to say, but for the last hour he'd been rehashing the same couple of ideas—just filling time until the evacuation order was lifted. When Ed lowered the sound, he realized his computer was beeping at him. He rolled his chair gracefully down the narrow workspace and checked the screen. *New mail: Urgent!*

He double-clicked the icon and read the message that popped up. It said: *Ed, pick up transponder CFX 2 and watch the feed.*

"What?" he grunted in disbelief. "There ain't no Ranger game on tonight." Convinced someone was playing a joke, he adjusted a couple of knobs on the board and plugged in one of the spare monitors. When he saw Audrey Timmonds pacing through the frame, he knew it wasn't a joke. She seemed to be in the middle of a continuous monologue.

". . . which is why, Ed, if you're watching this, you have to put us on live. Please. It's urgent! I know, if you're hearing this, you're probably thinking, *She's crazy,* but I'm not. Just do it, Ed. Break into whatever you've got rolling now." She glanced at the television set. "Come on, Ed. Caiman's just rambling. Please, trust me."

He scoffed at the monitor. "Ain't no way I'm putting you on live, cupcake." Even though he shared Audrey's opinion that Caiman was a despicable slimeball for stealing her sensational story, Ed wasn't going to risk his job just to help her get some sort of twisted revenge, which is what he figured she was up to.

"Eddie, break us in, baby!" Animal's voice filtered through the monitor from somewhere offscreen.

"Screw you, Vic," Ed sang back. He finished wiping the mustard from his shirt, then reached once more for his sandwich and gnawed off a big mouthful. Chewing patiently, he watched to see what Audrey would do next. She kept her eyes on the television set in the broadcast booth, waiting for her image to replace the one of the endlessly yammering Caiman. But it wasn't happening.

She gave up. "He's not going to do it."

"Oh, yes, he will," Animal's voice said.

"Oh, no, I won't," Ed said through his mouthful, as if Animal could hear him.

Animal's face briefly appeared in front of the camera. "Hey, doughnut boy, pay attention here. I got something I want you to see." Animal stepped out of frame, picked up the camera, brought it to the windows overlooking the arena, and tilted it downward.

Cavorting through the aisles of the loge section, a couple hundred baby Gojiras were running around. Some were searching ever more frantically for their next meal; others appeared content to play some prehistoric version of tag. Ed's eyes nearly popped out of his head when he saw Madison Square Garden transformed into a ruined, Cretaceous-era playground. His jaw dropped open at the hinges and his new shirt was ruined forever.

Elsie and Mendel tell me the mood inside the command center was festive. As some of the soldiers began dismantling equipment and preparing it for shipment, others stood around watching the television. O'Neal had returned and had been forgiven by Hicks for any blunders, real or imagined, he might have committed during the wild hunt for Gojira. The two of them were sitting around the main conference table and O'Neal was telling entertaining anecdotes about confronting the battleship-sized saurian invader. The military's sweep through the city was getting under way, and so far no evidence of a nest had been reported. Elsie wandered over to the television set and joined the crowd of enlisted men gathered around it. They cheered loudly when one of the local reporters began talking about the fine job they had done. In fact, they were tuned to WIDF and the reporter on the screen was none other than Charles Caiman. He had been talking for a long, long time, switching subjects freely in a desperate attempt to find something, anything, to talk about. Eventually he turned to the subject of the military and began waxing poetic over the phenomenal job they'd done.

". . . a selfless sort of bravery in the face of danger that is, in this reporter's opinion, something we can all be very proud of indeed. From the lonely foot soldier patrolling the shores of Staten Island to those fearless men on the front lines, some of whom laid down their lives pursuing Godzilla through the streets and tunnels of Manhattan, our boys in uniform have once again proved beyond a shadow of—"

"Are we on? Is this live?" Audrey's image abruptly replaced Caiman's on television screens across the region. The soldiers around the television in the command center let out a collective groan of disappointment with the interruption but continued watching. The blond woman on the screen stood in the darkened room and seemed to be somewhat confused.

"We're really on?"

"Yeah, go!" Animal yelled from offscreen.

Audrey sucked in a quick breath and turned to the camera, a completely different person. It was really quite impressive. In less than a second she transformed herself from a nervous wreck into a carefully composed reporter. "Hello, this Audrey Timmonds with a late-breaking report of the utmost importance. We are coming to you live from the broadcast booth high atop the western sideline of Madison Square Garden with important news concerning the fate of the city. I'm here with one of the world's leading experts on radiation contamination, Dr. Niko Tatopoulos, who has discovered Gojira's lair. Doctor, could you step in here and tell us what you believe is happening?"

Huh? I hadn't thought I would need to say anything, and suddenly I felt very awkward. Audrey and Animal both waved me forward. Reluctantly I stepped toward the camera. Before I got there, Phillipe took me by the arm and whispered to me: "Don't say anything about me or my men. Don't mention that we tried to explode the building ourselves."

I nodded and stepped into frame. Realizing that I was on television made me nervous. I smiled tensely.

Audrey did her best to make me feel at ease and

repeated the question. "Doctor Tatopoulos, can you explain to our audience what is going on here?"

I felt myself start to sweat. I cleared my throat, smiled nervously, then tried to explain. "Well, um, we've located the creature's nest. Um, it's here in Madison Square Garden and it's, um, large. Really large. Larger than we expected. And we've discovered eggs, um, hundreds of very large eggs, which began hatching only moments ago." Just then the door at the end of the hall broke free of its hinges and slammed to the floor like a sonic boom. "In fact," I said, glancing away toward the sound, "I think I hear them coming now."

Elsie and Mendel bolted toward the conference table and interrupted one of O'Neal's stories. They both started talking at once, too flabbergasted by what they'd seen on the television to speak in clear sentences. The sight of all those baby Gojiras had scared Elsie so badly, it took her a long time to notice that Mendel was holding her hand. (According to Mendel, *she* was the one who wouldn't let go of *his* hand.)

"You'll never believe . . . on the news, they're everywhere . . . it's incredible."

"They're trapped, surrounded . . . they're going to kill him . . . we've got to hurry."

"What the hell are you two talking about?" Hicks asked.

Rather than wasting time trying to explain, Elsie

and Mendel each took an arm and hoisted the colonel out of his chair, pulling him across the room. They shoved their way through the crowd of enlisted men watching the broadcast and stood him in front of the television set. When he looked at the screen, he saw me. I was still being interviewed by Audrey.

"So that's why, um, if the military is listening, they should destroy this building, you know, immediately. Before any of these animals escape. In fact, if it's possible, the entire block should probably be destroyed, just to make sure. Because it's bad. The situation, I mean. It's very serious. If only one of these youngsters gets out of—"

"Oh, my God!" Audrey screamed, but quickly regained her composure. "Excuse me, Doctor, but they're coming!" She issued an order to her cameraman: "Shoot it!"

Animal whipped the camera around toward the hallway windows. Agent Roache, I noticed, quickly ducked out of the way, making sure not to be photographed. Through the tinted Plexiglas, dark shapes prowled up to the door of the broadcast booth. A gang of eight or ten baby Gojiras came hunting down the hallway, sniffing us out.

I have to admit, the sight of those little bruisers closing in on us made me very nervous. In fact, I was on the verge of losing my cool completely. Luckily, Audrey sensed this and kept me focused. She pulled me in front of the camera and continued the interview. "Doctor, tell us what will happen if Madison Square Garden *isn't* destroyed."

"It would be catastrophic. No, we have to blow it up. If these creatures are able to escape into the outside world, they'll find places to hide. They'll grow up and, uh, multiply! If that happens, it won't be very long until a whole new species—a very dangerous species—will emerge. One that could replace us as the, you know, the dominant species of this planet."

By the time I finished stammering, Hicks was already on the hotline with the same man he'd spoken to when he needed several tons of fish. "That's right," he yelled into the receiver. "I want those F-18s turned around. And I want them to blow up Madison Square Garden. And no, I am not drunk!"

He slammed down the phone and was drawn back to the television by the hypnotic image of the baby Gojira hunting party and the dramatic pickle my companions and I found ourselves in. Elsie, Mendel, and nearly everyone else under the command center tent watched transfixed as Audrey stepped up to bring her report to a close.

"Regardless of what happens to us, the important thing is that this building is destroyed before these little Gojiras can break out into the city. We'll do everything we can to help contain them in here. You do what you have to do out there. Good luck to all of us. Broadcasting live from Madison Square Garden, this is reporter Audrey Timmonds for WIDF ActionNews."

"And out," Animal said switching off the camera. "Very nice."

For a moment I forgot about the man-eating

lizards and stood there marveling at Audrey. I was impressed by how smoothly and professionally she'd conducted herself under fire. She was a natural in front of the camera, and her report (I would learn later) had left audiences breathless, stunned, and wanting to see more. Her closing statement, asking that the Garden be destroyed, brought tears to the eyes of many viewers. She was finally a legitimate reporter, one of the big boys. I was just sorry her first appearance on television looked like it was going be her last.

But she'd accomplished something far more important than jump-starting her career. Without her quick thinking, we never would have made it to the broadcast booth, and the outside world—the military in particular—wouldn't have learned about the nest until it was too late. It's no exaggeration to say that she helped save the human race.

A few hours before, I'd thought she was a blood-sucking, back-stabbing parasite of a news-hound with no regard for the well-being of others. But she had proved me wrong in spades. She really was that bright-eyed, small-town girl I'd fallen in love with so many years before. And I was proud to be her friend.

With all these thoughts racing through my mind, I searched for the words to explain my feelings. "Audrey, I . . ." But when our eyes met, I realized she already knew what I was going to say. At least I think so. So I summed it all up in a single word: "Thanks."

She smiled, and I sensed that we were on the verge of reconciling eight years of unspoken conflict, that we would finally put all the anger, guilt, and hard feelings behind us. But as the words began to take shape on our quivering lips, the computer bleeped. We turned to see what it was.

Animal was at the terminal, reading the message. "Well, the good news is our friends in the military were watching and they got the message. The bad news is they're going to give us what we asked for." He turned around and flashed a sarcastic smile. "We've got precisely five and a half minutes to get out of the building before . . . kaboom."

Crash! The newborn killers out in the hallway were anxious to join us in the booth. A pair of them were nuzzled against the hallway door, the only way in or out, while the others moved farther down the corridor. The hallway was too narrow for them to get a running start and blow through the glass. But they were clever like their father and found another way to reach us. They invaded the luxury boxes on either side of the broadcast booth and began pushing against the flimsy walls. All that was separating us from these crafty predators were thin sheets of plasterboard and glass.

"Okay, the party's over," Roache announced. "Now it's time to leave."

"Yeah, right!" Animal and Audrey looked at the Frenchman as though he were making a sick joke. I smiled with relief when I saw him tying a spool of coaxial cable to the leg of a heavy steel table. I didn't know what he had in mind, but I already knew him well enough to trust that he had a few tricks left up his sleeve. My smile quickly vanished when he pointed his machine gun at me. I raised my hands as though it were a stick-up.

"Step out of the way, *s'il vous plaît.*"

I obliged, and he sprayed the windows facing the arena with bullets. He used his boot to clear the last jagged pieces away, then tossed the spool of cable out the window.

"Anyone care to join me?" he asked dryly. The lizards, saliva dripping freely from their jagged teeth, pressed their faces against the glass. The walls were beginning to collapse. Given the circumstances, Roache had made us an offer we couldn't refuse. With the skill of an alpine climbing instructor, he rappeled backward out of the window with one hand on the cable and the other firing his semiautomatic at unseen beasts below.

"This guy's good," Audrey observed.

"You have no idea," I told her.

But there wasn't time to stand around applauding the Frenchman's skills. The baby Gojiras were thrashing wildly in the luxury boxes around us. Audrey hopped onto the windowsill, firmly grasped the cable, and took a deep breath, poised at the edge. I waited for her to push off and lower herself over the side, but she hesitated. I assumed she was worried about falling and breaking her neck on the concrete below, but that wasn't the reason she lingered. She reached out and grabbed me by the lapel of my coat, pulling me toward her.

"Just in case I don't get a chance to do this later,"

she said. Then she planted a big wet kiss right on my lips. For a second or two I didn't care that there were flesh-eating, hunger-crazed reptiles closing in on us. I just wanted the kiss to go on.

But that feeling ended when the windows on both sides of us shattered. Scaly gray heads thrust into the booth, screeching and hissing and examining us hungrily with glowing eyes. Audrey yelped once and vanished over the side. The animals flew into a frenzy, throwing themselves against the walls, snapping their jaws closed in anticipation of their first live meal. I took hold of the cable and dumped myself over the side just as one of the creatures was getting up a head of steam, preparing to leap feet first through the broken window. The last thing I saw was that madman of a cameraman, still struggling to dislodge the booth's video camera from its heavy tripod. I think he took his job a little too seriously.

When I was halfway down the eighty-foot drop, the booth above me swelled with a cacophony of screams—both animal and Animal. I thought for sure we'd lost him, but when I looked up I saw Vic Palotti—video camera in hand—doing a swan dive over the windowsill. Somehow he managed to reach back and grab the cable, but only with his free hand and not very tightly. I cringed and shut my eyes as all 180 pounds of him came plummeting down on top of me.

The next thing I knew I was picking myself up off the floor in a great deal of pain.

"Nick, buddy, thanks for breaking my fall."

At that point in our relationship we hadn't even been properly introduced. But I was already getting a sense of how he'd earned his nickname. "Don't mention it," I replied with a grimace, massaging the lump that was sprouting on the top of my head.

We had a whole balcony of stadium seats to ourselves. The nearest pack of baby Gojiras was halfway across the stadium. The burst of gunfire Phillipe had fired on his way down must have startled the creatures and sent them running. Now it was eerily silent. Fish guts and fragmented eggshells were everywhere. Although we couldn't see any of them, we knew the creatures were lurking nearby. Carefully, nervously, we followed Phillipe up the stairs toward the nearest set of doors to the lobby. They had been torn from their hinges and trampled on. Agent Roache reached into his flak jacket and nonchalantly pulled out a second machine gun. Doubly armed, he led the way through the short tunnel and into the lobby.

As we feared, there was a welcoming committee waiting to greet us. Only thirty yards to our left, a pack of baby Gojiras, perhaps a dozen strong, stood there licking their chops. I was surprised to see a couple of them standing on one foot, rather like flamingoes do when they are at rest. As soon as we stepped into the open, twelve sets of nostrils lifted into the air and began wriggling. Drawn by the scent of our flesh, they dipped their long necks close to the ground and began to advance.

"This way," Phillipe shouted, setting off at an easy jog. As we began to run, the lizards' predatory instincts kicked in and they gave chase. The *clickety-clack* noise of their long claws on the floor was unnerving. Without looking back, we could hear them steadily gaining on us, so we increased our speed. In fact, we broke into an all-out sprint. But the powerfully muscled infants were much, much faster than we were. Phillipe, who was leading the way, surveyed the curving foyer and pointed to a set of escalators up ahead. He called over his shoulder for us to hurry.

I was running as fast as I could but lagged behind the others. Now, I've always thought of myself as a decent athlete and fairly fleet of foot. But it was painfully obvious to me that no matter how hard I ran, I simply couldn't keep pace with middle-aged Phillipe, Animal, who was weighed down with a camera, or Audrey, who wasn't even wearing running shoes. But as I fought to stay ahead of the growling animals, there was no room in my brain for embarrassment. A single, screaming idea dominated my thinking: get away. I was running on pure survival instinct. I don't even remember seeing the bank of coin-operated candy dispensers along the wall. I just remember reaching out with both hands and desperately trying to throw some obstacle into their path. When the machines tipped over and hit the floor, all the glass shattered and thousands upon thousands of jawbreakers and gumballs spread out across the hard floor. When the baby Gojiras stepped on them, their feet went out from under them. Their limbs sprawled out in awkward directions and they hit the floor hard.

Watching them try to get up again was like seeing an old Keystone Kops movie.

It bought a little time. And we needed every second, because we knew that somewhere in the sky over Manhattan, jets were approaching. Jets with enough firepower aboard them to vaporize half the city. We didn't want to be inside the building when they arrived.

When they got to the top of the escalator, Phillipe, Audrey, and Animal didn't head down the stairs. They pulled up short and peered over the edge, obviously surprised by something on the floor below. As I caught up with them the Garden's aging but still magnificent main lobby, all chrome and polished marble, opened up around me. It was a beautiful space, with bronze sculptures and colorful murals and three enormous art-deco chandeliers. But the most beautiful sight of all was the set of exit doors at the far end of the lobby.

Of course, it wasn't the beauty of the lobby that caused us to stop running. It was the sheer number of baby Gojiras crowded onto the floor below. There must have been four hundred of them, wall-to-wall lizards. Some of them were tearing into a Taco Bell stand, but most of them were milling around like spectators at some sold-out sporting event. None of them noticed us at first. But they smelled us almost immediately. The ones closest to us twitched their nostrils, then searched with their eyes until they found us. Within two seconds every lizard in the lobby had stopped what it was doing and whipped around to look at us. And everything became deathly quiet. The two species stood and stared at each other. I felt as though I were in a Hitchcock movie right before all hell breaks loose.

"How much time do we have left?" Audrey whispered.

I checked my watch. "Less than thirty seconds." The hunting party was coming up behind us after finally crossing the great gumball barrier. They came marching carefully toward us, afraid we might have other tricks. We all stared across the room at the exit doors. They were so close—only fifty yards from the bottom of the escalator—and yet so very far away. To reach them, we would have to wade into the lake of lizards. It would be like someone with a nosebleed trying to swim past a school of piranha.

"Twenty seconds," I reminded everyone.

Leave it to a Frenchman to feel arrogantly confident in the face of overwhelming odds. Phillipe glanced over his shoulder at us and asked, in that matter-of-fact, secret-service way of his, "Well, what are we waiting for? Let's go!"

He started down the escalator as casually as if he were trotting off to visit the men's room. And because we didn't know what else to do, we followed him. Halfway down the steps he raised both his machine guns and fired a short burst of ammunition toward the ceiling. As you can imagine, he was an expert marksman. The bullets sliced through the cables supporting the closest of the huge chandeliers. In a blur of crystal and iron, the lighting fixture plummeted earthward and shattered on the floor with a violent crash.

Almost as quickly as the shards of glass exploded outward, the startled lizards darted to the sides of the room, giving the chandelier a wide berth. It was all the opening we needed. We raced away from the bottom step and out into the lobby, moving in a line. Somehow I once again ended up at the rear.

The animals quickly recovered from their initial fright, and when they saw us running they instinctively pursued us. They rushed toward us in a ferocious shoulder-to-shoulder wave. The sound of claws was everywhere, and through the seat of my pants I felt their teeth snapping closer and closer.

Phillipe's guns blazed again, and the second chandelier exploded in the center of the floor. Again the animals shied away from the noise and flying debris, but not nearly as far as the first time. I put my head down and ran for everything I was worth. After a third round of gun blasts, the last chandelier crashed not far from the exit doors.

Animal and Audrey reached the doors first and got them to open. When I barreled past Phillipe, he looked like John Wayne defending the sands of Iwo Jima. His feet spread wide, he had a machine gun blazing in each hand. While he held them back, I dashed outside, where it was still raining. When he followed me, we slammed the doors closed.

The doors had large glass panels set into them. Looking through them, we saw a stampede of linebacker-sized saurians heading our way. Their blood lust aroused, they were determined to hunt us down. All four of us wedged our bodies against the doors and somehow managed to withstand their initial shoulder-crunching onslaught. They surged against the doors, pushing with ever greater force. We grunted and shoved and used all our strength to keep the doors closed. My shoulder and face were pressed against the glass. Only millimeters away was the slobbering, frustration-crazed face of a baby Gojira. He tried repeatedly to throw his powerful jaws over my head and bite down, but he only succeeded in leaving deep scratch marks in the glass. I was thinking, *We can do it, we can hold them inside until the bombers get here*.

But, of course, we wanted to eat our cake and have it, too. We wanted to lock them inside *and* get the hell away from the building before it went up in smoke. Phillipe, resourceful to the end, tried to shove one of his guns between the door handles. But it wasn't easy. The lizards began head-butting the inside of the doors, forcing them open a few inches at a time. Then the glass broke and the razor-toothed monster that I had been staring at poked its head outside. The jaws opened over Audrey's head. She ducked at the last minute, just as Phillipe got the gun wedged into the slot. As we backed away, the gun barrel began to bend out of shape. The metal wasn't strong enough to hold the rambunctious youngsters back for long, but we hoped it would be long enough.

We were all drenched in sweat and our legs felt like rubber. We'd used every ounce of our strength to fight our way out of the nest. I was sure I couldn't run another step. I bent over and rested my hands on my knees, trying to catch my breath. The radio on Phillipe's belt began functioning once we were out in the open again. We heard the military pilots speaking back and forth.

"Stallion fifteen, this is Fox six. We are targeted and locked."

"Fire at will."

"Roger that. Missiles are away."

As soon as I heard those words I somehow found an extra reserve of energy I didn't think I had. "Run!" I yelled, and broke into another breathless, all-out sprint. Although I started out in the lead, the others ran past me on both sides. We ran across some sort of patio, down a long flight of rain-slick stairs, past the entrance to Penn Station, and out across another open pavilion. We were almost to the street, a totally deserted stretch of Seventh Avenue, when the missiles flashed past overhead, streaking in the opposite direction. Audrey stumbled, and as I came up from behind I scooped her up. We were running hand in hand when we heard the missiles penetrate the roof of the world's best-known sports arena. We were halfway across the boulevard when the building blew to smithereens behind us. The force of the blast hit us before the sound reached our ears. There was a blinding flare of light, and for a split second I thought, *Hey, I'm finally running really fast*. Then I realized my feet were no longer in contact with the ground. The blast had picked all of us up and was hurling us toward the next sidewalk.

Landing was painful.

Although I didn't get a chance to see the explosion itself, I have since watched it on tape. Most everyone has seen the tape I'm referring to. It's that black-and-white digital video image made by an F-18's automated tracking system, which has been played several hundred times on television. It shows the three Tomahawk missiles entering through the roof of Madison Square Garden with "surgical precision" and the incredibly powerful explosion that ensued. A moment after the roof shattered upward, the walls of the round building blew outward in unison. The sheer power of the explosion made the sturdy old Garden look like nothing more than a wooden barrel filled with gunpowder. In less than two seconds the twelve-story landmark was obliterated, reduced to an open pit of smoldering ashes.

I'd landed on my head. Even before I opened my eyes, I reached up and began examining my scalp ever so tenderly with my fingertips. Now I had a second lump to match the one Animal had given me earlier. It was painful, but I didn't really mind. I was just delighted—and more than a little surprised—simply to be alive. The street around us was in bad shape: All the cars parked on the Garden side of Seventh Avenue were overturned or burning, or both. And the blast had blown out every window for blocks around. We were lying four abreast in the wet street. It was raining pretty hard.

I turned back and looked at the boiling mountain of flame coming from the hole in the ground that had, a moment before, been Gojira's nest. As the remaining chunks of wall crumbled and collapsed, a gruesome noise filled the air—the painful screams of young lizards roasting alive. Their tortured cries echoed through the empty streets like the shrieking of all the souls in hell. Slowly the pitiful sound died away, and soon all was silent except for the crackle of the flames and the pattering of the rain.

I sat up rubbing my head and checked to see if Audrey was hurt. "Are you okay?" I asked her. She said she was fine, a little shaken up, maybe, but not injured. I noticed that she was staring at me with an expression I didn't recognize. "Aud, you look a little funny. Are you sure you're all right?"

"No, I'm fine," she assured me. "It's just that . . . somehow I never imagined your life was this exciting."

"Oh, you'd be surprised," I told her.

Then she took me completely by surprise. "Nick," she said, "I'd like to find out."

I did a quick double take. For a second I thought she might be saying that we should try getting together again. But that would have been too good to be true. Surely she meant something else, something more platonic. Or did she? She leaned in, bringing that angelic face of hers closer and closer to mine. When our eyes met, she was so close, it almost seemed as though we were going to kiss. And then . . . well, I could go on, but I doubt whether anyone is very interested in the love life of some boring worm guy. Let's just say that Audrey and I spent a couple of minutes getting reacquainted.

With a great deal of moaning and groaning, Animal scraped himself off the pavement. Like the rest of us, he had bruises all over after a long tumble across the asphalt. But he forgot his own pain when he saw his video camera lying in the street. Like a mother concerned for her injured baby, he ran over and scooped the machine up in his arms. Part of the plastic housing had broken off, but the camera was still working. Greatly relieved, he turned to check on Phillipe. "Yo, Frenchie, *comment allez-vous* or whatever? You okay?"

"I could use a coffee," he answered groggily. The wily undercover agent forced his battered body into a sitting position. He was several years older than the rest of us and it was beginning to show. A drip of blood rolled down the side of his face from a fresh abrasion above his left eye. "Good French coffee," he specified.

"You got it, my treat," Animal said, helping him to his feet. The radio on Phillipe's belt continued to pick up the army's "secure" communications. As we watched Madison Square Garden burn down to a huge glowing bowl in the earth, we kept one ear tuned to the radio. Amid the flurry of messages, we heard Hicks speaking from the command center to the pilots of the F-18s, congratulating them on the job they'd done. Then we heard O'Neal. He was headed into the city with a convoy of armored vehicles to "search for survivors." It wasn't clear if they meant surviving baby Gojiras or the four of us. In either case, we would soon have a ride back to New Jersey.

Ignoring the rain, I put my arm around Audrey and we walked a little closer to the fire. It resembled nothing so much as the red-orange caldera of an active volcano and was actually quite a beautiful sight. All in all, it was a happy ending. We had succeeded in destroying the nest, Audrey had filed a dynamite news report, Animal had shot several minutes of historic pictures, Phillipe had protected his country's reputation—and best of all, I had my girl back after eight long, lonesome years.

Still, none of us felt like celebrating. The mangled corpses of baby Gojiras lay in the street, strewn around the gigantic fire pit. And Gojira himself was dead. We heard on the radio that they were dredging the river for his body.

My emotions were mixed when I learned that it was all over. On the one hand, I was glad the animals were dead. It meant the millions of people who lived in Manhattan could come home and not worry about being eaten alive (not by reptiles, anyhow). But at the same time I was sorry this new and spectacular species had been sent into extinction only a few days after it was first discovered. If only there had been more time, we might have been able to capture one of the infants alive and raise it in captivity. It's well known that Komodo dragons, fierce predators in the wild, are quite docile in captivity. One of Gojira's children would have made quite an attraction at the Bronx Zoo's petting zoo!

Phillipe came up and asked if he could speak to me in private. As Audrey went to check on Animal, the man with the salt-and-pepper beard scanned the streets in both directions, knowing the U.S. Army was going to arrive any moment. "Nick, I have to go."

It didn't surprise me. Even though he had saved New York City from total destruction, he would be in a world of trouble if anyone found out. He had hidden himself from the camera while we were in the broadcast booth, and there was no other physical evidence linking him to the action. If he slipped away before the army arrived, no one would ever have to know the heroic role he had played. He was, after all, a foreign agent conducting a secret war on U.S. soil—not the kind of thing France would want published in the newspapers. I knew it wouldn't do any good trying to talk him out of it, so I shook his hand and told him to stay in touch.

Then he walked over to have a word with Animal, probably about the videotape in his camera. There were plenty of shots of Phillipe leading the escape from the nest. I knew Animal wasn't going to hand over that tape without an argument, so I watched with interest to see what would happen. But before the subject ever came up, we felt the ground begin to shake.

Then we heard that famous wailing cry, something between a lion's roar and the shriek of a prehistoric eagle. We knew in a heartbeat that Gojira was still alive. But the sound was muffled and seemed to come from far away. It echoed in all directions around the deserted city. Only when the ground began to shake more violently did we realize that he was below us, using the subway system again to move underground.

We turned toward the smoking lava pit that had been Madison Square Garden and saw something begin to stir the pot of glowing embers. Chunks of burning debris were thrown high in the air as a huge shape thrashed around in the crater. Then a huge gray head with piercing amber eyes burst out of the smoldering wreckage.

A moment before, I'd been inwardly mourning his demise. But when I saw him rise through the ashes like a mythological phoenix, I groaned out loud. It had already been a long night, and it looked like it was going to get a lot longer.

In one fluid motion, he climbed up out of Penn Station and into the burning Garden, then lifted his torso and long neck several stories into the air. Great cascades of blood poured down his flanks and dripped into the pavement as he lumbered up onto the street and towered over us. The navy's torpedoes had sheared away large patches of his scaly armor, and he stood above us partially denuded, war-torn. He bent down and nuzzled gently at something on the ground in one place after another, becoming more agitated all the while. We realized what he was doing: inspecting the burned and battered bodies of his children, looking desperately for one of them to show a sign of life. But they were all as dead as could be. When Gojira understood this, he arched his back, threw his neck back, and howled into the sky. This time the scream was different. It sounded like a cry of suffering.

The hair on the back of my neck stood up. He was screaming out in pain over the bodies of his dead children. The sound cut through me like a cold blade and resonated in some primordial part of my nervous system. For the first time I thought I saw an expression cross the huge saurian's face—the nostrils flared, the nictitating membranes closed over the eyes, and the lower jaw quivered. It was impossible not to feel a pang of sympathy for this poor grieving father. And my heart would have gone out to him except for one thing: He was going to kill us.

The titanic lizard wheeled its great head in our direction and glared down at us with those burning honey-colored eyes. All the pain on his face gathered itself into a fireball of hatred. The eyes stretched wide open, the tail began to lash back and forth, and its mouth gaped to reveal the ragged teeth set in his glistening pink gums.

"He looks angry," I hypothesized.

"Thanks, Einstein. Couldn't've figured that out by myself," Animal shot back.

We were in a vulnerable, exposed position facing a wrathful and highly lethal enemy. Naturally, in such a situation, we turned to Phillipe for leadership. "What do we do now?"

The secret agent took quick stock of the situation and dispensed his expert opinion. "Running would be a good idea."

And run we did, scrambling into a nearby alley only a moment before the enraged animal pounced in our direction. His nose smashed against the buildings at the head of the alley as we ran for our lives. On both sides were the service entrances to large office buildings and apartment houses. Before we got very far, Gojira began bulldozing his way toward us, using his brute strength and burrowing skills to rip apart the structures behind us. Even with those huge obstacles in his way, he was gaining on us!

Audrey stumbled on the wet ground and fell. I hydroplaned to a halt, then hurried back to help her. By the time she was on her feet again, we were caught in a shower of flying building materials. I took a brick in the head, adding yet another lump to my growing collection. Leaning on each other, we ran blindly through the downpour. Phillipe called to us over the raging sea noise and waved us into an even narrower space between two adjoining buildings. We made it into this narrow passageway—it wasn't more than six feet wide—only a moment before a huge clawed foot smashed down in the alleyway behind us. I threw a glance over my shoulder and saw that Gojira had gotten himself temporarily stuck, his body far too wide for the narrow alley.

We ran between the buildings until we came out into another street. Desperately I searched everywhere for signs of the military. I wanted to see tanks and rocket launchers converging from every direction. But the street showed no signs of activity.

Phillipe bolted across the street and yanked open the door of an abandoned yellow cab. In a blur of movement he drew a screwdriver from his utility belt, popped the ignition device off the steering column, and hot-wired the car. The whole process couldn't have taken more than fifteen seconds. The guy was amazing.

Even before we realized exactly what he was up to, we followed him across the street and started piling into the cab. We weren't completely inside when the engine turned over and Agent Roache put the pedal to the metal. Animal's feet dragged along on the street as the tires spun and the car fishtailed out into the center of the road.

Fortunately, he was able to pull himself in as we sped away.

Unfortunately, our escape route was blocked by the sudden appearance of a giant three-toed foot that spread across two of the street's four lanes. There was no time to stop or turn around. We were already going too fast. Phillipe tried to swerve around it, but it was too late even for that. The view out the front windshield became one big toenail, and the next thing we knew, we were moving upward. The curved claw formed a ramp that sent us airborne, flying ten feet in the air. The vehicle bottomed out hard when we landed on the other side of the foot.

I don't think Phillipe so much as blinked. He gunned the engine once more and accelerated up the street as the creature roared in frustration. I watched the speedometer needle climb past fifty, then sixty, then seventy, and it occurred to me that a crash at that speed would leave us just as dead as would a stomp from an irate megaton lizard. I buckled my seat belt just before Phillipe hit the brakes and swerved around a corner.

Even though I knew I wouldn't like what I saw, I spun around to look out the back window. At first all I could see of Gojira, fifty yards behind and closing, were his powerful legs. Then the window filled with nostrils and teeth as he snapped at us. One bite would have crushed the cab like an aluminum can.

If Phillipe was fearless, Animal was just plain crazy. As he watched the giant jaws thrashing only a few feet away, he maintained his concentration on another project: He was determined to get the video camera he'd taken from the broadcast booth powered up. When the red light finally blinked on, he hoisted the camera to his shoulder and started filming. "Better step on it, Frenchie, we got company back here!"

"Which way should I go?" the driver demanded, careening into a fresh turn.

"Cut uptown!" Audrey gasped. "Take Fifty-seventh to Eighth."

"Are you nuts?" Animal asked her. "Take the FDR, *mon ami*."

Like a clap of thunder, the jaws snapped closed again, inches from the cab's back end. Phillipe swerved onto a new street.

"The FDR? In the rain? Absolutely not. Phillipe, take the West Side Highway."

"The West Side Highway's under construction," Animal pointed out.

"Yes, I know that, Animal, but there isn't any traffic today, so it won't slow us down."

"*Make up your minds!*" the Frenchman roared.

Audrey and Animal, in unison: "Take Broadway!"

Phillipe immediately swung the taxi into a long skidding turn before blasting off once more in the direction we'd come from. Up ahead we could see the smoking pit of the now defunct Madison Square Garden. We were going around in circles, I realized. It looked as though it would only be a matter of time before Gojira caught us and exacted his revenge.

Finally military backup arrived. A small convoy of Humvees, the vehicles sent out to search for us and bring us back to New Jersey, rolled into the intersection ahead of us. At the time, Phillipe had the cab moving at about ninety miles per hour and was still accelerating. The driver of the lead Humvee slammed on his brakes to avoid plowing into us. The vehicles behind him reacted too late and they piled up like dominoes in a chain-reaction crash. As we rocketed past, a rain-spattered blur of yellow, I caught a glimpse of Sergeant O'Neal sitting inside the lead vehicle. Perhaps it was my imagination, but I thought I saw his lips form the words "What the hell?"

I spun around to look out the rear window. Gojira, still pursuing us, came through the intersection a second after we'd shot past and stepped down on the front bumper of O'Neal's vehicle, flattening it.

It must have been with huge reluctance that the sergeant picked up the radio handset and called in to the command center to tell Colonel Hicks the bad news: "He's back."

Inside the cab, it took a moment for my brain to

register what I'd just seen. I blinked and turned to Phillipe. "That was O'Neal. I know him. Turn back."

He flashed me an incredulous look. "What are you talking about? I can't turn around now."

I reached forward and pulled the cab's license off the dashboard. It was stamped with the vehicle's registration number: MN44. Although Phillipe must have thought I'd lost my marbles, I wasn't going to take no for an answer.

"Do it!" I yelled, "Turn around now!"

There was no time to argue. Perhaps he sensed I knew what I was doing. Perhaps not. In either case, he tapped down on the brake pedal with the precise amount of force necessary to send the cab into a graceful 180-degree slide.

"I hope you know what you're doing," he said without taking his eyes off the two-hundred-foot-tall lizard flailing toward us down the boulevard.

Actually, I knew exactly what I was doing. Every taxicab in New York City has its own radio frequency, all 12,187 of them. Once O'Neal had our cab's call numbers, it would be a simple matter of finding the company's headquarters, breaking in, locating the vehicle roster, adjusting the bandwidth setting on the radio, and speaking into the microphone. So you see, I knew what I was doing. I just had no idea whether there would be time.

Phillipe hit the gas and we shot forward into the mouth of danger. If the beast had simply lain down, our cab would have been flattened under his plated belly like a bloody banana peel. But it was personal now, and he wasn't going to be satisfied with killing us indirectly. Instead, he fumbled for us with his fore claws, intent on picking us up. He might have succeeded if he hadn't been charging forward at full speed. Like a professional stunt driver, Agent Roache swerved his way between the leviathan's grasping fingers, raced past his hind legs, and narrowly avoided a swipe of the tail.

Who could blame poor Sergeant O'Neal for looking nauseated and confused? Not only was there a mysterious taxicab joyriding through the evacuated midtown district, but it had an incredibly large and destructive reptile chasing it—a reptile that had been pronounced dead more than two hours earlier. Before he saw us roaring toward him for the second time, he'd been on the horn to Hicks, explaining the latest change in the situation and asking for the F-18 jet fighters to be sent back to the city.

As we flashed into the intersection and swerved around the squashed nose of his Humvee, O'Neal dropped his radio and ran. He and his men scattered in all directions for cover. I leaned as far out the window as I dared, trying to show them I was me, and tossed the cab's ID plate onto the street. A second later Gojira followed us past the spot, this time stepping on the back half of O'Neal's car.

SEVEN

I t didn't surprise me to learn Phillipe Roache was a phenomenal driver. He hurled the car in one direction after another, zigzagging through the slippery streets without once losing control. He kept the furious creature off balance and half a block behind by turning at nearly every corner, using the street grid to his advantage. By a circuitous route we reached Broadway and headed north up the wide-open roadway.

When we'd driven a couple of miles without catching sight of our nemesis, we slowed down to about seventy miles per hour. Although I'm not superstitious, I cringed and tried not to listen when Animal looked out the back window and announced, "Hey, I think you lost him."

The rest of us moaned, fearing that Animal had just given the beast his cue to come back onstage. And indeed, Gojira stepped out from between a pair of buildings several blocks in front of us. In the backseat, Audrey reached over and swatted Animal on the forehead. "Why'd you have to say that?"

We were hemmed in by skyscrapers on either side. Rather than speeding forward to the next corner, Phillipe brought the cab to a gradual halt. He shifted into reverse but didn't back up just yet. As we idled in the middle of the avenue we looked ahead and saw the lizard lower himself to his forepaws and settle into a crouch. He seemed to be breathing heavily, and for a moment I allowed myself the optimistic delusion that the loss of blood was sapping his energy. Perhaps if we drove around long enough, he would simply collapse.

Too late I realized what he was preparing to do. He sucked in a long drink of oxygen, his flanks ballooning outward, then exhaled. He forced the air out of his lungs with all his strength, sending a tornado-force blast of power breath in our direction. This foul-smelling wind lifted cars into the air, bent street signs back, and shattered all the plate-glass windows. The whole swirling mess blew toward us. A newspaper-vending machine tore free of the sidewalk and smashed down on the hood of the cab. Phillipe gunned the motor and we rocketed backward, avoiding the worst of the airborne debris. Just as I was scraping myself off the dashboard, he slammed on the brakes, and my neck snapped halfway into the backseat. Shifting on the fly, he ground the transmission into drive and squealed into another narrow alleyway.

Our path was cluttered with dumpsters, card-

board boxes, locked chain-link fences, and all manner of large, impassable obstacles. Obviously, we
were trapped. I was already deciding which way to
run when Phillipe stopped the car. But he showed no
signs of pulling over. In fact, he accelerated and
blasted his way through one barrier after another.
By the time we slammed through a locked gate and
bounced into the next street, both fenders were mangled and the bumper, which had nearly come
through the window at us, was lying across the bent
hood, interfering with the windshield wipers.
Phillipe reached out the window and tossed it aside.
Believe it or not, the headlights were still working.

"This time I'm pretty sure we lost him," Animal
chipped in.

"Shut up!" we all screamed at once. Murphy's
Law asserted itself once more and the creature,
walking erect this time, leaped into the intersection
behind us. He sucked another storm into his lungs,
then unleashed it in our direction. This time his
power breath was strong enough to tear big chunks
of asphalt right off the street. We felt the wind lifting the rear of our cab into the air as Phillipe jerked
the steering wheel violently to the right and sent us
sliding around another corner.

The next thing I knew, we were headed up Park
Avenue at 130 miles per hour, which is a pretty good
speed to be going if you're trying to get away from
a man-eating lizard. Unless, of course, the man-
eating lizard is faster, in which case it's a terrible
speed, especially in the rain, because it makes veer-

ing into side streets utterly impossible. I looked behind and saw Gojira was gaining on us.

"Gotta slow down, French Fry, gotta turn again," Animal offered from the backseat. I glanced over at Phillipe, wondering what new surprise he would pull out of his bag of tricks to save us this time. But he had his eyes locked on the rearview mirror, and for the first time I noticed him sweating. It's a bad thing when the secret-service agent you're depending on to save your life begins to perspire. It can only mean you're running low on options. I knew I'd better do something, and do it fast.

"In there!" I yelled. "Go into that tunnel." We were coming up on a construction site of some sort. Behind a herd of sawhorse roadblocks was the entrance to the Park Avenue midtown express tunnel. The work lights outside had been left on, and this drew my attention. Phillipe reacted at once, veering over mounds of loose earth and crashing through barricades. We shot down the entrance ramp and into the tunnel just before a set of six-foot-long claws stabbed through the night and sank into the pavement.

Almost as soon as we were inside, we screeched to a halt. The inside of the tunnel was packed with bulldozers and other equipment. This time there would be no driving right through it. Phillipe deftly flipped the car around in another 180-degree skid.

"Can you teach me to do that?" Animal asked.

The driver grunted noncommittally and looked through the front window down the telescope of the tunnel. Just outside, five hundred tons of enraged lizard was throwing a monumental temper tantrum. He knew he had us trapped. He let loose several of those trumpeting shrieks and dug great heaps of earth away from the entrance with his fore claws. Every few seconds the claws disappeared from our view, only to be replaced a second later by a gigantic eye, burning bright with hate. We were in big trouble.

"Now what do we do, smart guy?"

That was a darn good question. I wasn't quite sure. But, for the moment at least, I seemed to be the person in charge. "Turn out the headlights," I said to Phillipe, thinking out loud.

He did, and we were plunged into a darkness so complete, we could have been parked at the bottom of an inkwell. My companions made a series of moaning noises to express their displeasure with how things were going, but at least for the time being we were safe. Every time Gojira moved away from the mouth of the tunnel, enough light filtered in to allow us to see one another. But I, for one, kept my eyes on him. The work lights outside lit him from below. We sat there for several minutes, mostly in the pitch blackness, as the angry giant stood guard over the only escape route. We were in no particular hurry to go anywhere. Once again all the light was blotted out when Gojira lay down, belly first, sealing off the tunnel. That's when the cab's radio crackled to life.

"Dr. Tatata, Dr. Totato . . . Nick! Nick, can you hear me?"

I groped around the dashboard until I found the radio. "O'Neal, is that you?"

"That was a pretty nice trick with the license. I'm sitting in the office of the cab company right now. Where are you?"

"You've got to help us," I told him. "We're in the, the . . . where are we, Audrey?"

"Park Avenue midtown tunnel."

"We're in the Park Avenue midtown tunnel and he's got us pinned down in here. We're safe as long as he doesn't ou—*oooouuuuwhoooo*!" I screamed. The cab was moving. Gojira had hyperextended one of his long arms and his claws were scraping against the front bumper and hood. Phillipe threw the car into reverse and sent us plowing fifteen feet backward through whatever machinery or equipment lay behind us.

"Nick? . . . Nick, you still there?"

I couldn't speak; none of us could. We sat frozen in the grip of fear, listening to those six-foot fingernails straining to reach the cab. We held our breath until the light at the end of the tunnel appeared once more. The arm pulled away and once again we were inspected by the giant eyeball.

"Nick, can you hear me?" I heard him add to someone with him, "I think we lost them."

"Yes, no, go ahead. We're here."

"Listen, you guys have to lure him out into the open. Somewhere we can get a clear shot at him. Maybe take him into Central Park, or out onto the FDR Drive. Think you can do that?"

"Why the hell not?" Animal said sarcastically. "Do they want us to wash him up while we're at it? Get him to brush his teeth, maybe? Give him a manicure?"

I was a little confused. "Can't you just, you know, blow him up? I mean, he's right outside the entrance. He doesn't look like he's going anywhere."

Phillipe and O'Neal answered my question in stereo. "The F-18s can't get a good look at him unless he's out in plain sight."

So much for my brilliant plan. I thought that once O'Neal had our frequency, he'd be able to rush in with the cavalry and rescue us. Instead he was asking us to bring the beast to the cavalry. Luckily I came up with another idea.

"Where's the nearest suspension bridge?"

"Brooklyn," Audrey said.

I explained what I was thinking to O'Neal and asked him if that would work. He responded that if it worked, my strategy would be "super-duper." He really said that.

"All right," I said, taking a deep breath and staring down the tunnel, "let's go!"

Nothing happened. Finally I heard Phillipe's voice ask, "And how exactly would you like us to do that?" I hadn't exactly *forgotten* that Gojira was blocking our path; I was merely choosing to ignore him temporarily. The big lizard had started digging again, intent on reaching us and making us pay for our crimes. He'd spiked his head into the narrow opening and was burrowing, forcing his way slowly forward. The walls of the tunnel began to give way. The next time he reached for us, there would be nowhere to hide.

"Does this cab have high beams?" I asked.

"No. You gotta be kidding me," groaned a less-than-encouraging voice from the backseat.

But I was quite serious. Without another word, Phillipe adopted my plan and gunned the engine. The cab peeled out and we shot forward through the darkness. Twenty, forty, sixty miles per hour. We were driving blind on a collision course with the creature's head. I don't know how Phillipe avoided smashing into the walls. Maybe that's another thing he learned at the secret agent academy. When he sensed that a head-on collision was imminent, he switched on the brights. I reached over and held down the horn.

Startled by the sudden noise and light, Gojira flinched. He pulled his head away from the tunnel just enough to allow us to blast like a cannonball out of the entrance. We flew, literally, over a ramp and bottomed out again in the dirt of the construction site, skidding sideways. This slowed our forward momentum to a tire-spinning crawl. Gojira spun around and his huge hands began feeling for us on the ground. We were sitting ducks, dead in the water. But the high beams must have blinded him momentarily. Otherwise he would have snatched us up and done whatever he was planning to do. The tires eventually found some traction and we got out onto the pavement once again.

"Which way?" our taxi driver demanded.

Audrey and Animal couldn't agree. They shouted conflicting directions, then they shouted at each other, then again at Phillipe, arguing vehemently over the best way to reach our destination. I think all New Yorkers are like that. It was another testament to Phillipe's skill not only that he was able to steer a course toward the bridge, but that he didn't stop the car and order the two of them to get out. It was about midnight, and the city was so empty and still, it felt like we were racing through a graveyard. We had been moving south with no sign of our pursuer for a couple of minutes when Phillipe caught a glimpse of him.

"We've got company," he announced stonily, eyes on the mirror.

Suddenly the arguing stopped and the cab was dead quiet again except for the whine of the overheated engine. We all whipped around and looked through the back window. Gojira was galloping up behind us, moving like no other animal I'd ever seen. He used his powerful back legs to kick himself forward in great kangaroolike thrusts, a couple of city blocks at a time, and landed on his forepaws, balancing himself in the air long enough for the hind legs to coil again for another leap. He'd given us a head start but was quickly closing the gap.

"Straight ahead, baby," Animal yelled. "Faster."

But Phillipe eased off the gas and turned onto a side street. In an exhibition of superior driving skill, he took us on an evasive, zigzagging route through the East Village, Little Italy, and Chinatown. He cut either right or left at every second intersection, leaving me feeling nauseous and totally turned around. I had no idea where we were when he doused the headlights and rolled up to a deserted intersection.

"City hall," Animal said, leaning over the seat back. "Perfect. I thought you didn't know where you were going."

Phillipe shrugged. "Just lucky."

None of us quite believed that. Then Audrey, after looking out each of the windows, uttered those famous last words: "I think we lost him!" The one surefire way to make Gojira appear out of nowhere was to say those words. We all panicked a little bit when she spoke them. Phillipe slapped himself in the forehead, Animal groaned, and I turned around and said, "Oh, really?"

"Yeah, really," she said, scanning in all directions. "See for yourself."

We looked around and saw that, for the time being, Audrey appeared to be right. He had followed us around that first right-hand turn but hadn't been seen since. The coast looked clear, not a saurian in sight. We rolled down all the windows and listened for the sound of smashing buildings but couldn't hear anything louder than the rain and the hissing of our leaking radiator.

Audrey pointed out a brightly lit road sign with a big arrow looming in the distance. "Brooklyn Bridge, thataway." It was only then that I realized

Phillipe had driven us exactly where we needed to be. The green illuminated sign was set on an elevated roadway, the bridge's long entrance ramp. We edged out into the intersection, close to Pace University, and saw the first of the bridge's twin Gothic towers rising into the sky. One thing was clear: As soon as we got onto the ramp, we'd be out in the open again, completely exposed. Making matters worse, the half-mile path had tall buildings on both sides. Even though they were set back from the road, we knew Gojira could be lurking behind any one of them, waiting to pounce on us when we drove by.

On the other hand, he might *not* be.

"Let's not overestimate him. And remember, we have the element of surprise," I lectured the other people in the cab. "After all, he doesn't know where we're going. By the time he sees or hears us, it'll be too late. We'll already be on the bridge."

I convinced no one.

Nevertheless, Phillipe took off. He pulled onto the ramp, pointed the nose of the car down the center of the roadway, and smashed down on the accelerator. Gaining speed, we whizzed toward the bridge, alert for any sign of a lurking lizard. But it looked as if I had been right. Gojira didn't spring out at us. As we sped toward the shoreline and left the buildings behind, the East River came into view. Suddenly we were confronted with a new problem: Gojira *wasn't* chasing us. We were supposed to be luring him out into the open, but he was nowhere to be seen. Realizing this, Phillipe eased off the accelerator just a bit.

Nothing now stood between us and the bridge. We were fast approaching the huge sign we'd seen before and looking out the windows for any sign of him when the road in front of us cracked apart and lifted upward. The huge section of the ramp lifted into the air and broke apart. Gojira's enormous head erupted from below, using the flat, bony part of his skull to crash through the pavement. Where there had been three lanes of asphalt, there was suddenly nothing but quivering snout and jagged yellow teeth. The beast unhinged his great jaws and waited for us to drive inside.

Everybody screamed.

If Phillipe's reflexes hadn't been as sharp as they were, we would have given a new meaning to the phrase "drive-thru food." But he managed to lock up the brakes and whip us around into yet another perfect one-eighty. As we spun around to face the city the passenger-side door cracked hard against the concrete base of the road sign. We had come dangerously close this time. The rear end of the cab was only ten or twelve feet from the monster's hideous mouth. His misshapen teeth glistened like blood-red razor wire in the glow of our brake lights. The second we were pointing downhill again, Phillipe pounded the gas pedal, and the tires spun and squealed. And squealed, and squealed. We weren't moving. A cloud of choking smoke surrounded the rear of the vehicle: burning rubber. It took us a moment to realize he had taken a quick bite out of the ramp, chewing through the asphalt as if it were a slab of peanut brittle. His last bite punctured the taxi's trunk, pinning us to the roadway.

Everybody screamed again.

My life flashed before my eyes—especially the hideous way it was going to end. I was certain we were going to be swallowed, taxicab and all, into the body of the infuriated, gargantuan dragon, just as Jonah had been swallowed into the belly of the whale—and, the mind being the mysterious thing that it is, it occurred to me that Jonah hadn't had to deal with caustic reptilian digestive juices. The teeth lifted out of the trunk and the cab squirted free once more. Phillipe had never lifted his foot off the accelerator, so we whiplashed forward immediately. But we didn't get very far. And my nightmare vision became a horrible reality. The roof of the creature's mouth was suddenly above us and craggy yellow teeth bit down, lowering in front of us like the closing gates of hell.

"We're in his mouth!" Animal started yelling. "We're in his mouth!"

As I'm sure you can imagine, it was not only dark in there but appallingly malodorous. The mouth couldn't close completely because he'd also bitten down on the metal road sign. But as the powerful jaw muscles flexed, all the light bulbs on the sign exploded and the metal began to bend. The roof of the taxicab began collapsing on top of us. One of the windows shattered, and everybody was screaming at once. But no one was louder than Animal, who shouted over the top of everything, "We're in his mouth! We're in his mouth!"

The cab started shaking from side to side in a violent manner. The road beneath the car was still anchored to the ramp, which temporarily prevented his tongue from shoveling us backward into the gaping red hole of his throat. It was wide open and waiting for us, guarded by a huge set of tonsils that swung back and forth like wet medicine balls. We got a lucky break when the sturdy road sign next to us refused to collapse any further. It stabbed into the roof of his mouth, preventing him from flattening the car any more. The violent shaking continued. Gojira, we realized, had literally bit off more than he could chew. As the concrete and asphalt fell away, we saw there were hundreds of steel reinforcing rods laced through the structure. The reason we were shaking was that Gojira was trying to tear the entire section of roadway out of the ground. This he could have accomplished easily, except that he seemed unwilling to open his mouth even for a second. Now that he had us, he knew better than to let us go.

Smart lizard.

"We're in his mouth! Oh, crap, we're in his mouth!" Animal continued to shout. Finally Phillipe, who was trying to think of something to do, turned and yelled at him to shut up. But Animal couldn't stop. "Whaddaya mean, shut up? We're in his goddamn mouth!" The shaking continued, but instead of a side-to-side motion, we started rolling left and right. I crashed against Phillipe, then he tumbled against me. With patience and tenacity, Gojira was twisting the steel bars, weakening them further with every passing second.

"Gun it! Get us out of here!" Audrey screamed, freaking out.

"I'm trying!" Phillipe screamed back at her, his foot still jammed down on the gas pedal. It was sheer mayhem. With everyone sliding and crashing around the interior of the cab, it was impossible to think clearly. To brace myself, I wrapped one leg around the side of the seat, shoved the other against the dashboard, and used both arms to push against the ceiling. And then, as if matters weren't already bad enough, one of the electrical cables to the road sign tore loose and began swinging wildly around the inside of his mouth. Each time it brushed the hood of the taxi a buzzing shower of sparks erupted in the darkness.

The reinforcing rods anchoring us to the rest of the ramp began to snap one by one. Gojira had pulled them taut, and they twanged like guitar strings when they broke. I realized we were only seconds away from a slide down the wet hole of his esophagus. As a last resort, I began climbing out the window. When Audrey saw what I was doing, she hollered at me.

"Don't, Nick, it's too dangerous!" (I'm still rolling my eyes about that one.)

I slithered into a sitting position with my elbows

resting on the roof of the cab. My head banged against the rigid upper palate of Gojira's mouth. The inside of his cheek, a slab of wet flesh as thick as a wall, spanked hard against my back. I felt his warm saliva leaching through my T-shirt. As I struggled to maintain my balance, the loose cable swiped right past my nose and struck the metal sign, sending sparks everywhere. I lunged across the top of the cab and somehow managed to grab hold of the insulated part of the wire. I immediately jabbed the exposed tip of it into the rubbery pink flesh where tooth met gum.

The electrical surge shot through the lizard's body. Reflexively he jerked backward with enough force to snap all the remaining cables. As he threw his head to the side, we felt ourselves whip around 180 degrees at spine-snapping velocity. The huge mouth opened and was flooded with the lights coming off the bridge. Gojira had spun himself completely around and put his head close to the ground, trying to cough us up. The bridge was right in front of us. As soon as the wall of teeth lifted out of our way, the battered taxicab lurched forward with me still dangling halfway out of the window.

The thirty-foot section of pavement sat like a doctor's tongue depressor inside the big reptile's mouth and acted as a natural launch ramp. We shot out of Gojira's mouth like a dented yellow missile. We flew, but not far. We were at least fifteen feet off the ground when we left the mouth. The cab plummeted downward and hit the ground so hard I was sure the chassis had broken in half—to say nothing of our spinal columns. When at last I picked myself off the floorboards and looked outside, Phillipe was racing us across the bridge, speeding toward the first tower.

"Oh, my God, he ate it! He ate the whole thing! I can't believe this guy."

I turned around to see what Animal was talking about. "What? He ate what?"

"The whole damn on-ramp. He just swallowed it! He ate the whole thing!" And then, as if the idea were occurring to him for the first time, he added, "We're all gonna die."

It may help if I describe the bridge for those who haven't seen it. First, it's a suspension bridge, rather like the Golden Gate Bridge. From end to end it is just over a mile long, but the part overhanging the river is only half of that. Twin gothic towers, built of brick, rise 276 feet out of the water. On the night in question, their peaked archways, lit from below, looked as though they had been designed by the same architect who built Count Dracula's castle in Transylvania. The main suspension cables sagged in long graceful swoops between the towers and were connected to the roadway by means of many smaller cables—thousands of them—that crisscrossed to form giant, geometric spiderwebs. The whole structure was stout, spooky-looking, and built to withstand just about anything. Phillipe had us moving at well over a hundred miles per hour, so it didn't take long to reach the first tower. I looked behind and noticed the absence of two-hundred-foot-tall lizards. He hadn't followed us onto the bridge.

"Whoa, slow down a little bit. He's not back there."

Phillipe did more than slow down. He coasted to a complete stop and parked. We were just beyond the first tower. After studying the situation in his rearview mirror, he switched on his emergency blinkers to make sure we were easy to see. In the backseat Animal was still shaking his head and muttering, "He ate the damn on-ramp."   .

"He's still back there," eagle-eyed Audrey reported.

"I see him." Staring into his side mirror, Phillipe was as calm as a gunslinger. He reached into the pocket of his camo jacket, pulled out an unfiltered Gauloise, and lit it. He noticed the dirty look I was giving him and blew his smoke out the window.

I wagged a finger at him. "Those things are gonna kill you," I said.

He didn't smile.

Gojira was hunched over in the shadows, partially out in the open now, staring at us from near the foot of the bridge. He was only a few hundred feet from where he had first stepped out of the river and entered Manhattan less than forty-eight hours earlier, near Pier 17 and the Fulton Fish Market. Streetlamps cast a pallid glow across his left flank, and we could see his rib cage heave each time he took a breath. We waited tensely for him to make a move, and finally he did. With all the stealth of a hunting jaguar, he began slinking forward into the light. But something caught his attention and stopped him. A moment later our less-perceptive ears picked up the sound that had spooked him. Over the sound of the rain, we heard an angry rumble growing in the sky. The F-18s were back. They roared past, high above and hidden in the rain clouds.

"He knows it's a trap," I said. "He's not going to chase us out here."

"He has to!" Audrey declared as the sound of the jets began to recede. "We've got to get him out in the open."

"I am sure he will come." Phillipe flicked his ashes out the window. "We killed his babies." And almost as soon as these words had left his mouth, they came true. With the F-18s temporarily out of range, Gojira's desire for revenge overcame his instinct for self-preservation. I realize it's a strange thing to say about a reptile, but I suspect he was *calculating* he would be able to kill us before the planes returned. He erupted out of his hiding place and, with a shrill war cry, charged out onto the bridge.

Phillipe hit the gas and we peeled out again. Before we could get up to speed, the roadway beneath us began to jump and sway and twist—all at the same time. Gojira's great weight, over five hundred tons by most estimates, shook the bridge as though it were made out of paper and string. The shaking was even worse inside the moving taxicab. We advanced in bullfrog fashion: flying through the air one second and bottoming out hard the next. It was like driving during a massive earthquake, and we were moving far, far too slowly. Out the rear window I watched Gojira run down the bridge on his hind legs, quickly closing in on us. We had moved barely a hundred yards before he was approaching the first tower.

The main suspension cables were about eighty-five feet apart, barely enough room for the furious giant to slip between them. But the inner cables, the thinner strands that formed the spiderwebs, were only about thirty feet apart. As he thundered toward the tower, he lowered his head as if he would use it as a battering ram. There is no doubt in my mind that he could have broken through the massive brick tower. But the suspension cables slowed him down before he had the chance to try. Individually they were not strong enough to stop his progress—he barged through the first ten or twelve of them effortlessly. But the closer he came to the tower, the more of them he had to penetrate. They slowed and then stopped his progress. Biting and kicking, he raged against the insignificant little barriers, slashing at them with his fore claws until one of his arms became tangled up to the shoulder. For a moment he stopped moving and appeared to consider the predicament he was in. He cocked his head slightly to one side as a dog might do, staring down at the puzzle of wires.

With Gojira occupied, the swaying of the bridge eased up. We took advantage of the moment to shoot forward, getting most of the way to the second tower. The sight of us escaping brought his blood back to the boiling point. He screamed again and used his massive strength to shrug free of the wires, snapping them with a series of sharp cracks. For a moment he glanced behind him. Either he'd heard something back there or he was considering retreat. But the sight of us escaping proved too much. He coiled his hind legs, pounced astonishingly high into the air, and landed atop the tower itself! Even after all I had seen him do, this leap was utterly astonishing. With the languid, heavy grace of a big cat, he used his claws to climb over the top and leap down on the other side.

That leap was probably the only serious mistake he'd made since coming to Manhattan, but it was to be his last. The cables interrupted his fall, and he crashed headfirst onto the roadway, where he found himself caught again in the semitransparent cage of wires. The bridge shook furiously as he struggled to find his feet and continue the chase. The motion wave that came up behind us and snapped the bridge like a blanket tossed us high into the air. We landed precariously close to the edge, nearly spilling over the side and into the drink. But Phillipe took it all in stride; just another day at the office for a secret-service agent. He maintained a slow but steady pace over the undulating roadway. We drove under the second tower and were able to speed up again as we approached the far shore.

The cables were taking their toll on Gojira's

strength. The entire bridge vibrated as he screamed out in anger and frustration.

We reached the Brooklyn side of the bridge which was crowded with military personnel and civilians waiting to be let back into the city. We skidded to a stop and jumped out of the cab. We didn't dare go any farther and lead him into the crowds. If he could push through those last wires, he would have us. We had run out of real estate. When I looked back, the creature's head was twisted into a garrote of cables, hanging off the side of the bridge and over the river. But he still hadn't lost sight of his goal. He craned his neck in our direction and screamed.

I believe he took the sight of us standing audaciously out in the open as a taunt, one that stoked the fires of his hatred once more. With a surge of strength he ripped his head free. But in doing so he stumbled backward, entangling one of his hind legs.

The noose was tightening.

In the distance we heard the F-18s coming in for another pass. Phillipe was sitting half in and half out of the cab, listening to the military radio and the conversation of the fighter pilots.

"Target is locked in and stable."

"You are red and free. Stallion ten, Fox two, make your runs."

"Roger that."

"Stallion twelve, Fox three, you are also red and free, follow them in."

"Roger."

In the blink of an amber eye, a quartet of war-
planes dropped out of the clouds, ripping through
the sky like small darts thrown at a very large target.
They came in low, hugging the river, their engines
roaring. They looked almost comically puny,
dwarfed by the size of the colossal lizard struggling
midway across the span.

I felt another pang of empathy for Gojira. The
harder he thrashed against the cables, the more
entangled he became. As the jets swooped toward
him he turned his head to look at them. I may be
reading too much into his behavior, but it appeared
to me at the time that he seemed to know what was
coming. He filled his lungs with air, preparing to
lash out at the jets with his power breath. But the
first set of guided missiles was already deployed,
sailing toward the bridge. He jerked to one side,
dodging the first set of missiles, but the others connected. They slammed squarely into his chest and
abdomen. Huge bloody chunks of his body sprayed
into the air, and he shrieked in pain.

But he wasn't finished yet. Drenched in his own
blood and badly mauled, he tore free of the cables
and ducked under the second barrage of missiles.
They sailed past him and disappeared under the surface of the river without detonating.

For the last time he staggered to his feet and
focused his eyes on our tiny figures, standing below
him next to our cab. He stood up, stretching to his
full height, and tried to cry out in that distinctive,
screeching wail. But the only sound that came from

his throat was a rasping moan, a gurgling death rattle.

When he heard the jets coming in for their final run, he looked briefly in that direction. But a moment later he chose to ignore them and turned his attention back to us. I think he knew it was finished.

He had come all the way from his home in the South Pacific, obeying a biological impulse that told him to find a nesting place for his young. By chance, his migration brought him to Manhattan, which at first must have seemed like the ideal place to accomplish his simple goals. He went about his business without realizing how much hardship he was causing. In spite of his prodigious intelligence, he had simply been following the dictates of nature—he had been born into this world with no expectations beyond frolicking for food and perhaps leaving some offspring behind. But it was not to be.

The missiles fired away from the jets and streaked toward the bridge. Gojira took a final, unsteady step in our direction before they ripped into his neck and rib cage. In quick succession, a dozen explosions carved craters deep into his tough flesh. His massive body convulsed as he struggled to scream once more.

Like a felled redwood, he leaned toward us and toppled, all two hundred feet of him. The crowd of stunned New Yorkers at the foot of the bridge screamed in unison as the shape plunged toward us. Then I realized that, even in death, he might still get his revenge on us. I grabbed Audrey by the arm and pulled her along, retreating. Phillipe and Animal were right behind us.

We turned around just as Gojira's enormous head came crashing down onto the bridge. It landed directly on top of the taxicab, crushing it like a paper cup. The bridge swayed violently and the steel cables moaned, threatening to pull loose from their mighty anchors. But the bridge—or what was left of it—held, and the swaying slowly subsided.

I took a few steps back toward the creature's head, which towered above me. One of his hundred-pound eyeballs was pointed in my direction, but I don't think he saw me. The nictitating membrane was half closed and the iris had a glazed, weary look. He blinked slowly and exhaled, the breath of life slipping out of him.

I felt like rushing over to him and trying to offer him some comfort. I wanted to explain that we'd only done what we had to do. The earth just wasn't big enough for both our species. But in the end I just stood there. And then he was dead.

All of us had fallen into a stunned, reverent silence. It melted away as the mob of rain-soaked New Yorkers began to applaud, nervously at first, but then vigorously. In a moment I heard a great rousing cheer go up, and when I turned around, a couple of thousand people were streaming onto the bridge toward us. Soldiers and civilians alike, all of them cheering, came up and surrounded us with congratulations and thankful pats on the back. We were all crazy with joy and relief. Even Phillipe seemed elated. I noticed him duck into the backseat of the cab for a moment, but then he turned around and lifted Animal off the ground with a great bear hug. Although it was uncharacteristic, I thought nothing of it at the time. Later I would realize why he had joined the celebration with such enthusiasm.

I can't explain how relieved and glad I was that it was finally all over—especially since I was still in one piece. A big, silly, uncontrollable smile spread across my face as I pushed through the crowd exchanging hugs and handshakes with perfect strangers. For a moment I lost Audrey in the crowd, but I quickly made my way over to her. My grin must have been infectious, because we both stood there beaming at each other like a pair of dopey cartoon characters. News crews jostled their way through the crowd, clawing and scratching their way toward us. They had broadcast the entire confrontation live to TV sets around the world and now they wanted follow-up interviews.

As I would learn later, the whole city—the region, the nation, the planet!—was at that very moment bursting out into one giant victory party. In the command center Colonel Hicks threw his clenched fists into the air and laughed. Elsie was so overwhelmed by the moment, she threw her arms around the person closest to her and planted a big wet kiss on his lips. Since this person happened to be Mendel Craven, she met with a rather passionate response. At the Palotti apartment in New Jersey, Lucy and a roomful of refugees bounced and cheered and swapped high fives. Everywhere that people were following the story, they felt the exuberant rush of victory over an unbeatable foe.

Flashbulbs started popping like mad all around us. The news photographers and camera crews had muscled everyone else out of the way. Reporters crushed in around us, shoved microphones under our noses, and began shouting questions. I grabbed Audrey and we headed for shore.

"How did you discover the nest?"

"What was it like inside the Garden? Weren't you scared?"

"Are you angry the army booted you off the project?"

"Is it true the French created the monster?"

"How did you get Godzilla to follow you onto the bridge?"

I draped my arm over Audrey's shoulders and flashed them that same stonewall smile I'd learned from Colonel Hicks. "Sorry, guys," I yelled without breaking stride, "but I've already promised my story as an exclusive to another reporter."

"Watch out! Move it, pal! Out of my way!" A slender little man in a yellow rain slicker came elbowing his way viciously through the crowd until he stood directly in our path. He wasn't much taller than a dwarf and his expression changed radically the moment he saw us. A warm, sweet smile spread across his face and he extended his hands to us, as though he were welcoming good friends back home after a long absence. Audrey recognized him.

"What do you want, Caiman?"

"Audrey, baby, we did it! We got the exclusive!" He laughed and clapped and hopped up and down Rumplestiltskinesquely. "It's beautiful, you're beautiful, everything's beautiful. We got the story!"

She couldn't quite believe what she was hearing. "*We* got the story? *I* don't think so."

His smile evaporated into thin air. "Look, young lady, this Godzilla story could be your big break if you play your cards right. Just remember who you work for."

"Not anymore, *Chuck*." She leaned close and filled him in on a piece of late-breaking news. "I quit. And by the way," she added with a smirk, "it's Gojira, you moron."

Animal was yelling and waving his arms to get our attention as he zigged and zagged his way through the rain-drenched celebration. His expression told us something was horribly wrong.

"What is it? What's the matter?"

"Did either one of you take the tape out of the camera?" he was desperate to know. Audrey raised her hands in the air to show that she was clean, and I assured him I didn't know anything about it. But if the truth be told, I had a pretty fair idea of where the cassette might have disappeared to.

I glanced around the crowd and asked, "Where's Phillipe?" He'd been standing there a moment before but had somehow disappeared. Like a bloodhound on a cold trail, Animal wandered through the crowd scouring the deck of the battered and half-ruined bridge for any sign of his missing video. "Damn! I couldn't have just *lost* it. What'd I do with it?"

A phone rang. It took me a few moments to notice the ringing was coming from my pocket. I looked down and realized I still had the cell phone Phillipe had tossed me. I pressed the TALK button.

"Hello?"

"It's Phillipe."

"I thought it might be. Hi. Hey, where are you?" I used sign language to tell Audrey who it was. Together we scanned the area, wondering if he might be calling from a nearby pay phone.

"Tell your friends I will return the videotape after I have removed a few items from it. National security."

"I understand."

"Also, I wanted to say *au revoir,* and thank you for your help, my friend."

Before I could return the sentiment, the line clicked and went dead. "*Au revoir,*" I said into the dial tone. As I was putting the phone away, Audrey looked at me with a quizzical reporter's expression.

"Who was that French guy, anyway?"

"Who, Phillipe? Just some insurance guy." She looked up at me skeptically. I kissed her before she had a chance to ask any more questions. I'd intended for it to be a quick peck, a brief distraction.

But once my lips were touching hers, I think the both of us forgot what was happening around us. We wrapped our arms around each other and kissed and kissed and kissed, drinking in all the dizzying sweetness of the moment.

The night had come to a fairy-tale ending. We'd crept through dank underground tunnels where we were nearly squashed, survived our encounter with the horde of baby Gojiras, destroyed their nest, and barely eluded Gojira as he pursued us madly through the city. To recycle something Lucy Palotti said, we had come within a chihuahua's butt-hair of getting killed. We'd gone into the heart of radiation-mutated darkness and come out the other side to be greeted like heroes. Naturally, I was a little light-headed. And as I stood there locked in lip-to-lip delirium with the woman who had saved my life as many times as I'd saved hers, I had a mild out-of-body experience. It was not unpleasant. I imagined myself lifting into the air and looking down on Audrey and myself. I continued floating upward, lifting above the bridge, until I saw the bright lights of the command center far across the Hudson behind Manhattan's impossible crowd of skyscrapers. Below me, Gojira's vast body slumped peacefully on the half-ruined bridge. It was a perfect moment, a perfect evening, a perfect ending.

EPILOGUE

Well, that's my story. I hope you've enjoyed reading it, and that maybe you've learned a thing or two. One of the most difficult things about writing this book has been resisting the urge to speak more about environmental issues. I went back and cut out all the long speeches.

I would, however, like to say one brief thing in closing. In recent years we've discovered that the earth's ecosystems are deeply interconnected and surprisingly fragile. We know, for example, that chemicals dumped into a river in Mexico can hurt the wine crops in Italy, or that driving to work instead of using mass transit depletes the ozone layer, which leads to more cases of skin cancer as well as the phenomenon of global warming. There are hundreds of examples, but the point is that harming the environment in one part of the world can have indirect but powerful repercussions in another. That's why we all have to start taking personal responsibility for our environment. Of course, after my work near the Chernobyl power station, where I've seen up close what the disaster has done (and is still doing) to the area, I'm especially sensitive to the dangers posed by nuclear contamination. For example, we've witnessed a 2,500 percent increase in the number of cases of thyroid cancer since the accident. Unless we act to reverse the effects of our damaging actions, I wouldn't be surprised if we find other such anomalies in the not-too-distant future. Bumblebees the size of Apache helicopters? A real-life King Kong? Earthworms that collect samples of scientists and take them back to their labs for dissection and analysis? If we continue along the path we're on and don't clean up our act, the next mutant species we confront might even be ourselves.

Okay, end of sermon. I promise.

I couldn't be happier about how things turned out for Audrey. She's a big-time reporter now who's proving she's not a one-story wonder. WIDF offered her Caiman's job, and she was tempted to take it just so he'd be shipped off to a station in Poughkeepsie (not that there's anything wrong with Poughkeepsie). But he's still anchoring the ActionNews broadcast five nights a week. Audrey accepted a position with one of the major networks and is stationed in New York City, her new hometown.

Elsie Chapman is supervising the postmortem on Gojira and offered to take me on as part of the team. But I decided against it. Gathering and dissecting earthworms may not be as *sexy* as conducting the autopsy on Gojira, but ultimately it may be more important. I haven't lost my faith in those oversized worms. Many highly distinguished scientists from around the globe are volunteering to help solve the scientific riddles posed by Gojira's appearance, but only I can finish my work with the worms. By the way, one of the experts Dr. Chapman has brought in is Mendel Craven. Rumor has it that he is currently at work on a book in which he postulates that Gojira laid a second clutch of eggs on a small island somewhere in the Caribbean Sea before continuing his migration. From what I hear, the eggs hatch and the baby Gojiras grow to adulthood before they are discovered by a team of scientists. He's calling it *Cretaceous-period Park,* or something like that. I hate to say it, but the whole idea sounds rather ludicrous to me and I don't know if anyone will be interested in reading that sort of make-believe. As usual, Dr. Craven is mixing his science with large doses of fantasy.

It wasn't long after Phillipe disappeared that I saw the French agent again. His picture started showing up on the covers of magazines with captions like "Is this the man who created Godzilla?" A whole series of photographs began surfacing: Phillipe on the beach near Great Pedro Bluff in Jamaica, planting the listening device on Mayor Ebert's collar, and driving the Humvee through Manhattan dressed as an American soldier. No one knows who took the photos. Naturally, the ministers in the French government launched an investigation into the matter, and they learned everything. When

Phillipe's role was made public, he was instantly declared a hero. The next day he was fired. I got a post card from him not long ago. It said: *Nick, now it is safe to tell everything. See you soon, P.R.* Although he and his men broke quite a few international laws, we owe them a great debt. If they hadn't been willing to lay down their lives in order to destroy the nest, the rest of us would probably be spending our days scampering under rocks to avoid a growing population of gigantic reptiles.

As for me, now that I've completed this project, I'll be headed back to the Ukraine to finish up my worm research. It shouldn't take long. I feel I'm close to isolating the physiochemical process causing the abnormal growth and hope to publish a paper in one of the scientific journals sometime later this year. My working title is "Size-Indexed, Radiation-Correlative Mutations of Annelid Morphology in Ecologically Distressed Environments." Keep an eye out for it.

If you're like most of my friends, you're probably saying, *Nick's going back to being a worm guy? Could there be anything duller than that?* First of all, I don't think it's dull at all. I believe in the work. It may not be the latest hot topic in science, but even Darwin's work on evolution was considered tedious and uninteresting at one time. And do you know how he spent the last thirty years of his life? Studying worms. It was earthworms he was referring to—not Gojira—when he wrote the following: "It may be doubted whether there are many other animals in the world which have played so important a part in the history of the world." And I know of one other person who no longer considers worms and the guys who study them to be boring: Audrey Timmonds. She's actually the one who found that quote. She's been reading Darwin's 1881 *The Formation of Vegetable Mold*. And guess what? She likes it! So these days, being a worm guy ain't half bad. Knowing she'll be here when I get back should make those cold Ukrainian nights easier to bear.

THE END

P.S. I've been doing some more thinking about that book Dr. Craven is writing, the one about Gojira stopping off in the Caribbean to lay a few eggs before continuing his trek north. On the one hand, the whole idea strikes me as downright silly. I realize it's only science fiction, but who would believe that could really happen? It's preposterous.

And yet, during the long hours of sitting here writing this memoir, I've been having a recurring vision. I suppose you could even call it a waking nightmare. One moment I'm sitting here at my desk typing out the manuscript, and the next I'm floating through some dark place. I'm moving fast, flying down a narrow, underground passageway. It could be a twisting, turning tunnel. At the far end of it I see a shaft of light. And in the light sits a large brown oval shape. Zooming closer, I realize what it must be: one of Gojira's eggs, one that was laid away from the nest in a place no one would have thought to look. I am speeding closer, out of control, with no way of stopping my momentum, and just as I'm about to slam head first into the parasite-encrusted shell, it gurgles loudly and begins to crack open.